SUE CURRAN

Battle
of
Wills

I could not have completed this project without the help of the city of Prattville website, my son Jim, who read it and gave his seal of approval, and to my two dearest friends Robbie and Chris who also read each draft and gave me great suggestions for improvements. A special thanks goes to Helen Johnson for her never-ending support.

As always my works honor my father, Wiley, mother Robbie and my sister Diane, my muse.

Legitimate Decedents of John Royal Pennington I
b. 1818
m. Elizabeth Fielding 1822

John Royal II 1845
m. Daisy Wallace

Sarah 1847
m. Cecil Lloyd

John Royal III 1869
m. Mary Frances
Buchanan

William 1871
m. Delilah
Harrington no
children

Hannah 1875
d. in childbirth

John Royal IV 1894
m. Caroline Boyce

John Royal V 1919
m. Virginia
Covington

Liza
m. Sam Bean

Clayton
died WWII

John Royal VI
b. 1955

Timothy b. 1956

Illegitimate Descendants of John Royal Pennington I

Ruby May slave b. 1831 m. Cyrus Fielding b. 1829
bought from Elizabeth's family

Abraham Fielding
b. 1850

m. Nellie Barton
b. 1852

Eli Fielding b. 1860
mar. Esther Watson

Jacob b. 1893

& Annie 1893

Lucy b. 1928
m. Donald Lewton
Peabody

Sadie b. 1930
m. Conner Overton

Roland b. 1931
m. Emma

Lilly b. 1956
m.Charles Camden

Naomi b. 1958 m. Archie Claremont

Vernon b. 1955

Grace

Cami 1983 m. Sam
Littleton

SUE CURRAN

Battle

of

Wills

December 23, 1852

Flames from pecan logs stacked in a five-foot Italian marble fireplace warmed the front parlor at Twelve Oaks and reflected amber light on its occupants. Jon Royal Pennington scribbled numbers with a quill into a leather-bound book. His wife, Elizabeth Fielding Pennington, sat across the room near the fire working on a cross-stitch likeness of the Greek revival mansion in which she sat. The room smelled of wood smoke and freshly-cut fir from the Christmas tree, which stood next to Jon's desk.

In the drawer of the desk, Jon kept the letter written half a century earlier by his great-uncle Samuel Pennington, urging Jon's father Charles to move his family from South Carolina to the Alabama River bottomland where the Alabamians were growing cotton.

Over the desk hung a charcoal drawing of the cabin Samuel had lived in before Charles had it destroyed to build Twelve Oaks. Other drawings by Elizabeth and daughter, Hannah, hung on smoked-stained, paper-covered walls around the room.

A soft knock came at the pocket doors before they were slid open, and Penelope burst into the room wearing a wool skirt, cotton blouse, and ruffled apron. Her disheveled hair was wet. "Come quick, Mama, Ruby's having a lot a trouble. Grandma Cenee thinks the baby's breach."

Without a second thought, Elizabeth pushed the needle through the edge of the cloth. She shifted squinting eyes back at her husband still at the desk. "Well, aren't you coming too? After all, this one is yours." She reached for a pewter flask on a table at the entrance to the room. Her skirt rustled when she twirled and left the room slamming the pocket doors behind her.

Five women of various sizes and skin color moved aside, as though Elizabeth was the most important person in the room. The largest one, the one they called Grandma Cenee, stared at Elizabeth with pleading eyes, their sadness accentuated by the shadows of a single candle burning on a crude table next to the rope bed where Ruby lay screaming. "That girl gonna have a breach baby if she live."

Elizabeth scraped the chair the little one had vacated across the wood floor and set it at the end of the bed. It creaked with her weight, though she barely weighed one hundred, twenty pounds. She put one hand on Ruby's round belly. "Bring that candle down here," she said to Grandma Cenee.

The roly-poly woman squeezed between the closed door and followed Elizabeth's order. Cenee was the Pennington's cook and, judging by her hefty weight, she tasted equally large portions of what she prepared.

Elizabeth produced the flask and handed it to Cenee. "Now, I want you to give Ruby a generous sip of this. Then to Ruby, she said, "I've got to check on the position of the baby, Honey. Try not to move."

Cenee turned up the flask at Ruby's lips, and though the younger woman tried to refuse, Cenee forced her to drink. She screamed again, when Elizabeth flipped up the rough wool blanket and forced her hand fist deep.

"You're right, Cenee, I felt a foot."

Elizabeth swallowed her contempt for the young slave, who had given herself to Jon, and said, "Now, Ruby, I want you to relax. Your kind has been giving birth in primitive conditions for thousands of years." She shoved her hand into Ruby again. "You better be thankful I'm such a generous, God-fearing woman, or I'd just let you and this baby die." She yanked her hand out again.

"She doesn't need hand-holding now, Cenee." Elizabeth folded the blanket up over Ruby's belly and slipped her dress above her bare hips. "This is going to hurt more than any beating you've had. I want you to grab Cenee's arm, squeeze, and push when you feel a contraction." This time she gently reached inside. "I've got the baby's feet, but it's up to you to push it out."

Ruby's breathing was hard and fast just before she screamed, "Oh precious God, help me."

Warm liquid soaked Elizabeth's hands and arms, and she prayed it wasn't blood. She tugged gently and felt resistance. She tugged and lifted, making out the silhouette of a newborn. A quick slap on its bottom and it released a wail strong enough to make any mother proud.

The footsteps on the floor were too heavy for Sarah. Candlelight flooded the room once again.

"It's a boy, Jon." Elizabeth took one of the sheets from the tub of now warm water and rung it out. Then she wiped the baby down and wrapped it in a dry one.

3

She laid him in Ruby's outstretched arms. She touched the boy's brown cheek. "Do you have a name picked out?"

Ruby stared at the baby with wide adoring eyes. "He'll be called Abraham, after my Papa."

ONE

On that steamy July night, members the church gathered under the tent for its fiftieth anniversary. For three days, preachers quoted verses and presented lengthy sermons concerning the abomination of evil and baptism in faith. We came together to bask in God's word and to be "dunked" in the Holy Waters of Pennington Pond. More like a lake at a mile and a half long and a mile wide, the locals had always known it as "the pond."

My father, The Reverend Jedidiah Allgood had served as host minister at First Methodist Church revival for as long as I could remember. Held every third week in July, the men of the church have packed up that old circus tent left by a traveling troupe back in the 1950's and hauled it to Pennington Pond State Park.

My name is Sue Allgood Backman. I teach tenth grade science at a high school in the north-Atlanta suburb of Marietta. I've referred to my father as "The Reverend" since I was a teen. Now, in my later years, his title has become a sign of my fear and respect for his never-ending faith in God and me. He is a force powered by God.

I sat erect and rocked back and forth on the wood bench, trying to get a better view of the back of the tent, looking for Ruth Palmer, my very best childhood friend. We had a standing date at the First Methodist revival to get caught up, but so far, she hadn't shown. Her absence didn't surprise me. Ruthie'd never been what you'd call a dyed-in-the-wool church attendee.

Every five minutes, I glanced toward the back of the tent, knowing she'd appear at any minute. My gaze wandered out the side of the tent toward the pond. Past the tent lights, only blackness appeared below an embankment at the pond's edge.

He was there, peering from the dim light of the canopy of trees—Vernon Fielding, a man who had been given permission by the state to live in the park, and some say my cousin.

Those same folks consider him dangerous, because in 1970, he was accused of murder. The woman's body was never found, and Vernon had been acquitted. Yet, the legend—along with the town's fears and mine—remained.

I swallowed hard and turned back around. Perspiration beaded on my face and neck, and a drop slid between my breasts. Logic and a lifelong friendship with Vernon held my fears in check, but tonight, the way he stared in my direction, my fears were heightened by his presence and the perpetuation of the stories of his rape and torture of the woman, before he strangled her and tossed her lifeless body into the river. Of course, the perspiration could have simply been caused by a sweltering summer heat and the kind of humidity that made you sweat just breathing.

I glanced up at my father, standing at the temporary lectern at the front of the tent. His gaze followed mine past the members of the church and right onto Vernon, who sank farther into the shadows. The Reverend's words were meant for him, an attempt to save his soul from eternal damnation. He had called out to him several times over the years, knowing Vernon was not far from the tent or the dock during baptisms, trying to coax him into joining the group into the water with no success.

He remained at the edge of the sphere of light created by the tent lights, as he had been every night of the revival. My experience with him was that he was just shy and wary of strangers, but I squirmed in my seat, trying to stop my skin from crawling. Knowing what he'd been accused of doing to that woman before he killed her and dumped her body in the pond gave me the creeps. And he just kept watching.

Something tugged at my arm and, for the moment, I forgot about Vernon. My head whipped around only to find my seven-year-old, John Earl, giggling. When I bent down, he put both hands around my ear. "He reminds me of Uncle Fester from The Addams Family."

A smallish man with a wrinkled bald head, wearing what The Reverend always referred to as a Sunday meeting robe, stared down at the folks gathered under the revival tent and began his sermon on renewing one's spiritual life.

I sent John Earl my best impression of my mother, Gladys Mae, minus the glasses to glare over, and whispered for him to hush and listen. The Reverend leaned forward in his chair and squeezed bushy gray eyebrows together, sending us a look from the University of Evil Stares over his wire rims.

When it was The Reverend's turn to speak again, he quoted Chapter Three, Verse Three of the Gospel of

John. "Truly, truly, I say to you, unless one is born of water and the Spirit, he cannot enter the kingdom of God." He continued with Verse 6. "That which is born of flesh is flesh, and that which is born of Spirit is Spirit." He slammed his fist on the lectern. Everyone jumped including me. Even though I'm a thirty-four-year-old woman, he scares me sometimes the way he gets to ranting in the pulpit.

I leaned close to my mother, Gladys Mae Allgood, pointed toward The Reverend, and whispered, "He's is in fine voice tonight considering how hot it is. I just don't understand why in the name of goodness he always chooses July for the revival." My gaze never left my father, until it darted to my right toward my mother.

Over the course of my lifetime, we'd learned how to disguise conversation in church. She smiled, but gritted her teeth, hiding her displeasure with my questioning of The Reverend's judgment. Her gaze remained on him. Her lips barely moved.

"A little suffering is good for a soul, Sue. Reminds us why we're here. Besides, I doubt the Marietta School District would grant you time off to come home just for a revival during the school year. And if it were any cooler, those being baptized would catch cold."

My son, John Earl, sat between us, his head moving left and right, following the sounds of our voices like a spectator at a tennis match. He spoke with a stressed whisper. "Couldn't we suffer just as much in the air-conditioning at church, Grandmother? Then those getting baptized could just get sprinkled like they do in our church." She should be proud; at least I took him to church.

Several folks around us chuckled at John Earl's question, but soon quieted with his grandmother's glare. She had a way of intimidating even the biggest of men. "Enjoy it now. Soon this park may be gone."

Just then, The Reverend announced a short break, and we stood but didn't move away from the bench that substituted as a front pew. Gladys spoke again in a normal tone. "Rumor has it somebody's trying to buy up the park and sell it to folks looking for water-front property."

I pursed my lips together and frowned. "Mama, you know as well as I do that no one can buy this property. It was willed to the state over a hundred years ago." I kept a close watch on John Earl who was making faces at another youngster sitting a few rows back. "And the rest of the land by the river belongs to Naomi and Archie."

Gladys rolled her eyes at John Earl's shenanigans. "I'm just saying it may be easier than you think for someone to sell it. First we'd need copies of two wills, one from John Pennington and the second from his mistress and slave, Ruby's daughter, Sadie. Over the generations, records got lost and, with two fires, one at Twelve Oaks and one at the county courthouse, some believe that those wills never existed."

John Earl was spinning around, flailing his arms in the air, and I put my hand on his head to still him. "Even if the will never existed that gave that parcel of land to Ruby and Cyrus, it was passed down through the family, and Roy would never sell. Besides, where would Vernon go?"

I dropped my voice another level as though I was about to spill a national secret. "Remember, he already persuaded Virginia to let him sell that section to the east for that golf course." My disdain came as thick as the humidity. "If Cousin Roy was in control, Vernon would have been sent to a home years ago."

The Reverend glanced down over the top rim of his glasses right at me again. If I didn't know better, I'd swear both he and my mother had graduated from the School of Evil Looks. With only seconds to spare before the break was over, I asked John Earl if he needed to go to the restroom, and when he said no, I ran to the portable toilets before The Reverend announced the next preacher.

I took my time getting back to my seat. A sultry breeze from oaks, pecan, hickory, and pine cooled the perspiration on my cheeks. Shouts of "Amen" and "Hallelujah" combined with the humidity, capturing and mingling the sweetness of cologne, perfume, and honeysuckle with acrid body odor. Pine moths, cicadas, and saw flies drew circles around bare bulbs strung from the tent flaps, rolled and tied to the roof, to invite whatever cool air might mosey over from the pond. They jingled in the breeze, and crickets and frogs added joyous singing to the tune.

Ladies in stockings and low-heeled shoes, wearing skirts modestly covering their knees, flapped fans caned out of palm fronds by the summer Bible School classes. They helped move the air and kept the hungry mosquitoes at bay. Their husbands stood alongside, stifling in slacks, suit coats, and shirts with ties tight around their sweaty necks.

Not five minutes after I sat down again, John Earl squeezed my hand with all the strength he could muster.

His other hand pressed at the groin of his twill shorts. "I gotta go, Mama."

I knew it. I should have insisted he go at the break. I tilted my head toward his and, as low as possible, I whispered, "So go. Use one of the portables across the road. Just don't run over there, think you're out of sight, and drop your pants. Your granddaddy'd have a fit if someone told him they saw you watering the grass."

His bottom lip rolled out and tears formed in his huge brown eyes. "Don't make me go over there in the dark by myself. I'm ascared."

Still sitting erect on the bench, Gladys Mae leaned back, reached around John Earl, and tapped me on the shoulder. "What's his problem?" Her whisper held a twinge of irritation and her gemstone green eyes stared, telling me to tend to my son. They said, "You're The Reverend's daughter, Sue Allgood Backman, make him behave."

I heard them loud and clear. "He's got to go now," I whispered to her.

Mother's head turned so fast I thought she'd morphed into the little girl from The Exorcist. She sent us both another one of her notorious looks. I'd become familiar with this glare over the course of my childhood. She leaned close to John Earl and sternly whispered, "You'll have to wait until we're done, now. You should have gone while you had the chance."

I apologize if it seems I'm making Mother out to sound like a witch. She's not. But during church, you'd better behave or she would get mad, probably because she'd hear about it later from The Reverend.

John Earl got her message loud and clear, too. He curled into his comfort spot at my side, and I held him

11

close, feeling the need to protect my offspring from his grandmother's wrath. Hands folded in his lap; he peered up at The Reverend like the angel I knew he could be. Sometimes, I could swear I saw Gabriel on his left shoulder, Lucifer on the right, tugging at his young conscience. He knew right from wrong, but sometimes those boundaries needed testing.

Not five minutes passed before he tugged at my arm again. He pressed the front of his shorts hard with his other hand. A little too loud, he said, "Mama, I gotta go right now."

Some of the group around us responded to his loud voice with disapproving stares, while their husbands released muffled chuckles.

I twirled around in my seat just in time to hear Ruthie say loud enough for everyone to hear "Leave him alone. He's a little boy with a full bladder."

I couldn't help snickering. My friend and hero had arrived in the knick of time.

My grip on John Earl's hand tightened as we walked past Gladys. "Be careful," she called out in a strained whisper, "the sheriff warned of strangers roaming around in the park."

Safety in numbers, parents tell their children. I motioned for Ruth to lean toward me. "Want to go with us?"

She looked flushed, like she'd just run for miles, and I wanted to know where she'd been, but we'd made a big enough scene. I'd hear about that later. She nodded toward the back of the tent. "Okay, let's go." She sauntered up the center aisle between the rows of wooden benches to the back of the tent. John Earl and I followed. All the while, he squeezed his crotch.

Little girls his age, wearing frilly dresses and patent leather shoes, giggled behind their hands at his antics. Their mothers shushed them, trying to grab their hands and return them to their laps.

A few more heads turned at the commotion, but most of the congregation packed in the standing-room-only, makeshift church, concentrated on The Reverend.

A single security lamp bolted to a pole near the row of portable toilets helped light our way across the park road toward the pond. The second he crossed the threshold of the tent, John Earl disappeared down the path that led to an old wooden stairway to the old forested picnic area.

I ran after him, convinced Vernon was watching us. "You come back here, young man," I called. "The church is paying good money for those port-a-potties for you to use."

His little boy voice rang out in front of us, getting farther away. "Mama, I hate those things. They smell like pee and the air freshener Grandmother keeps in the bathroom for when somebody poops. I'm going down to the other ones, in the old part of the park near the pond." I had to admit he was right. They did stink.

Ruthie and I jogged, trying to catch up to him. We moved out of the light of the security lamp and a first quarter moon, hidden now and then by pearly clouds, shone down on the aging blacktop path in shadowed light. It wasn't wide enough for us to run beside each other, so I followed Ruthie. I had been following her most of my life, whether it got me in trouble or not.

She let out that childlike giggle. "Hey, at least John Earl didn't slide down that hill directly across from the

13

tent. Otherwise, we'd have to crab-crawl down it after him, and Gladys'd have a conniption if you ruined that fancy dress."

I heard footsteps on the wooden stairway leading to the old park and assumed John Earl was headed for the bathrooms there. We slowed to a walk, and I pointed to the frilled skirt of the spaghetti-strap summer dress I wore. "Don't you like it?"

"You always overdress for this thing." Ruthie tugged at her sleeveless shirt and spread her jean skirt. "Comfortable and washable."

Ruthie was always thinking ahead. She rarely did more than the absolute minimum in her personal life, but she gave everything she had to her job. Even her makeup was minimal. A dash of mascara and a little lip gloss added to her natural beauty.

Speckles of moonlight hit John Earl's profile off to our left. He'd only made it halfway to his destination before nature insisted he stop. To give him privacy, I tapped Ruthie on the shoulder and we turned away.

His voice squeaked. "Where were you?"

Before I could answer, crackling acorns under foot must have startled him, because his young voice creaked from the wilderness. "Mama, Aunt Ruthie, y'all stay right there, okay?"

I called out to John Earl. "Ruthie and I are just going over by the docks. It's only a few yards. You catch up when you're done."

A wide muddy area from which many would wade into the waist-deep channel to be dunked and baptized separated four piers, jutting out almost halfway between the shore and a tiny island about fifty yards out. Behind

14

us, the old restroom, five picnic tables, and several grills sat on an acre or two. We each stood on a pier, peering between the trunks of multi-story oaks, some dating back almost a century, dripping with moss that stifled the air. Specks of light twinkled from houses along the far shore of the river.

Ruthie wiped the perspiration off her brow with the back of her hand and hopped off the pier. She pulled a penlight out of her purse and pointed it at her face. That wicked grin appeared that I'd come to know oh so well, and I swear I smelled whiskey on her breath. "What say we sneak away and go see what's happening over there?" She pointed toward a local bar on an island near the far end of the pond.

Southern jazz floated on the warm breeze from The Boondocks, the only bar west of the city. An original butt and pass log cabin, it had once been slaves' quarters on Twelve Oaks, once the largest cotton plantation in Elmore County and owned by my great, plus four, grandfather. Flooding years ago on the Alabama River left the bar on an island about five hundred yards off the far shore and just outside the park.

"Ruth Ann Palmer, I need to wait for John Earl, and we need to get back to the revival." I looked around for John Earl. "Vernon's probably out here right now, watching us. Besides, smells to me like you've already been there throwing back a few."

Ruthie shined the light on her face again. Taut anger deepened to a frown and her bottom lip stuck out. Her soft brown eyes begged.

I shook my head. "The Reverend would disown me if I let John Earl see what goes on over there. They serve

15

what he calls Devil's spirits." I giggled. "Remember, I'm a grown woman with a child."

Ruthie motioned that John Earl was behind me. She clasped her hands behind her back at her waist and rocked on her heels still grinning. "I heard your daddy and mine talking about the sin and evil that goes on there. Daddy says women dance naked on the tables, while snakes crawl all over them."

Feigned disbelief shot from my mouth with a nasally whisper, audible only to her. "We were never naked."

Ruthie released her infectious laugh, and mimicking my whisper, said, "Oh yeah, what about your bachelorette party? I have trouble remembering that night."

I squinted with my right eye. "I vaguely recall Jell-o shots of tequila."

Leaves and acorns snapped behind us. "Mama? Whatcha'll talking about?"

Ruthie aimed her penlight at his face. His eyes were huge. "I got scared over there. I heard something in the woods."

She aimed the light toward the trees in a half circle at shoulder height, until she found what she sought. "Did you know that your Uncle Thomas carved this for me? Remember, Sue?"

She ran her finger over the initials R.P. and T.A. carved inside a heart.

Nodding, I said, "Your sixteenth birthday." I grinned, but my eyes blurred with the tears. "He loved you from the day your mama had us all over for dinner our first night in town. Maybe if you two had stayed together, he would've stuck around."

It hadn't been Ruthie's fault that Thomas had left. Faint images of an argument between The Reverend and Thomas floated along a stream of memory. I missed my brother. Years had passed since we'd spoken.

Ruthie moved her light to the next tree. The initials V.P. appeared about five feet from the base of its trunk. She leaned close to me to whisper. "That crazy loon marks his territory with his initials." Her voice had lost its joviality.

"Great, so now you're comparing Thomas to Vernon?" I no more than got the words out when something touched my arm, and I heard someone whisper my name. I turned, ready to scold John Earl for calling me Sue, but he was on the other side of me.

I couldn't scream. All I could think was Vernon creeping up, grabbing us, and dragging us all into the woods. I grabbed John Earl and took off, bouncing along back up the trail toward the tent, heavy with his weight. I stopped about a hundred yards up the path and set him down.

"John Earl, hold onto my hand and don't let go." My words came out in a terrified whisper.

His blue eyes glistened with tears. "Mama, what's wrong?"

I grabbed my son's hand so hard he yelped with pain. I couldn't let him know my momentary terror. "I just realized how long we've been gone."

Moonlight passing between two clouds illuminated a human form I assumed was Vernon's crouched in the underbrush.

John Earl's young legs couldn't keep up, so I swept him into my arms again. The two of us bounced along the path. Acorns cracked under our feet and another set of footsteps behind us. Reason said it was Ruthie, but my terror screamed Vernon, ready to kill us. I carried John Earl up the slope and called back for Ruthie to hurry.

When we reached the upper level, I put John Earl down and whipped around, looking back.

Ruthie wasn't behind us.

Then I heard the scream.

My voice strained. "Ruthie?"

"Where is she, Mama?" John Earl held tightly to my arm.

"I don't know, Sweetie, but I'm sure she'll be along shortly."

We stood very still for a few minutes. I scanned the forest, moving only my eyes so as not to terrify John Earl in the process. Acid rose into my throat. It burned it dry and, when I tried swallowing, I couldn't produce enough saliva to wash it back down.

There came another scream.

I scooped up John Earl around the waist and pressed him against my side. I didn't stop running until I was able to set him down at the back of the tent. I ran up the center aisle ignoring the stares from disapproving eyes. I didn't care. All I could think about was what Vernon was doing with Ruthie, or to her. Tears gathered in my eyes. "I believe Ruth Ann Palmer was just grabbed in the woods."

Ruthie's father, Lee Palmer, rose from his seat at the end of dais and started toward me, but The Reverend arose and stepped in his path. "Sue, tell us exactly what happened?"

I looked down at John Earl, now standing below the lectern, his eyes marble-size. I began my habitual nervous babble. "As most of you heard, John Earl needed to go to the bathroom. He took off for the old toilets down by the pond." I pointed in that direction and noticed a few nods. "Ruthie and I were chatting about old times when somebody whispered my name. I started running back, but Ruth never came out. We need to find her before he does something to her."

I stepped off the temporary dais, took John Earl's hand, and walked him to the bench next to Gladys. "You stay with your Grandmother. I'm going to find her." Ignoring The Reverend's commands for me to stay with my son and mother, I dashed out of the tent again.

My mind was racing a mile a minute. About a hundred yards away, a row of green portable toilets stood side-by-side. Vague thoughts reminded me that a crazed killer might have knifed her and left her in one of them as part of some disturbing ritual. All the slide locks were green, so I threw each door open with such force, the entire row swayed. I knew I wouldn't find Ruthie in any of them, but I had to make sure she wasn't just horsing around. She always had been one for a good practical joke.

Another mile for my brain. I was going back out in those woods, Vernon or no Vernon. He wouldn't be there. He'd dragged my friend off to one of the islands in the middle of the pond.

I threw out all notions of my own welfare and climbed down the slope across the road from the tent without thought of damage to my dress. The low-heeled slings hurt my feet after my escape, so I flung them off and left them by the path.

A clouded moon created lagoon monsters out of the moss-strung trees, adding to my terror. The slightest noise slowed me down. My faith pushed me forward.

19

Gladys referred to my belief as cookie-jar faith. I only opened the jar when I needed a helping hand from the Holy Spirit; otherwise, I kept the lid on for safekeeping. The Reverend preached all or nothing, but my background in science told me it was all just a nice story.

There, at pond's edge, the cookie jar opened, and I prayed that Vernon hadn't committed lewd acts on Ruthie and left her body mangled and floating in the water. Or, to be discovered later in the pitch-black woods having been assaulted and her throat cut.

I fought the urge to vomit.

Common sense reminded me of Ruthie's earlier interest in The Boondocks. She was probably there, having a beer and a good laugh. I wouldn't put it past her escape there. She'd always been a bit of a daredevil, pushing her father's buttons until they were all on alert.

When we were in high school, Thomas had dared her to dive off the highest point of Carson's Hole, a water-filled gravel pit on the other side of town. We'd all held our breath after she'd disappeared off the cliff, waiting for that sickening thud of her body shattering on the rocks below. Like a cat with nine lives, we'd heard her hollering for us to follow.

Most had. I hadn't. I'd been the chicken to friends and brother, the sensible one to my parents and hers. They used to tell me how thankful they were their daughter had a friend who would look after her. Now my chance had come to prove to Mr. Palmer I could live up to his expectations.

I swallowed my fear, shook out trembling hands, and walked back to the piers, calling Ruthie's name in a strained whisper. I almost turned and ran when I heard something off the shore.

Moonlight caught a rowboat in the middle of the pond. The captain pushed the oars through the water, until the boat hit the far shore of one of the small islands. I was sure it was Vernon, and I wished I had a boat so I could follow, because Ruthie was being held captive in that boat, crumpled body unconscious—or worse—laying in the bottom already dead.

Leaves and acorns popped like bubble wrap being flattened behind me. My heart moved one notch closer to bursting, but reason found me once again. It couldn't be Vernon if he were captaining the rowboat making its way between two far islands.

"Sue?"

Lee Palmer stood behind me. He carried a camper's lantern, which he shone in my face. Streaks of moonlight revealed a scarlet tinge and ugly shadows on his face. He gasped for breath and his brow dripped with sweat.

I held my hand to my chest. "Mr. Palmer, you 'bout did me in. What are you doing out here?"

"I came to help you look for Ruth Ann."

I had to admit, after the initial shock wore off, I was relieved to see him. "I've had some time to think about it, Sir, and I don't know if anything bad has happened." Though I'd moved away from my parents and most of the conventions of my Southern Methodist upbringing, old habits were hard to break. I still gave my elders the respect I was taught they deserved.

"Like I told you before, I felt someone touch me, then we saw him crouching in the underbrush. I picked up John Earl and ran. I thought she was right behind us." I patted his shoulder, realizing his need for reassurance.

21

"Anyway, it was probably just some kid out here partying, who didn't want to be seen. Probably the same kid who screamed to scare us off."

"You heard her scream?"

I nodded. Idiot, he didn't need to hear that. A split second before I opened my mouth to tell him about the rowboat I'd seen, my cell phone rang.

The voice was deep and barely audible, like the speaker had a hand over the phone. "Don't say anything except okay. And if you ever want to see Ruth alive again don't hang up. Tell her father that you're going to The Boondocks to look for her."

I said the required words and then heard silence.

I faked a smile at Mr. Palmer while trembling hands replaced my phone in my purse.

"Who was it?"

"Gladys. She said The Reverend was gathering a group of men to search. You want to get back so you can accompany him. I'm going to The Boondocks to look for her."

He ignored me. Instead, he checked his watch holding the stem so the face lit up. "It's been a good half an hour. You don't think she's back in one of the…" He pointed over his shoulder indicating the portable toilets I had ravaged moments before.

"No, Sir, I checked. They're all empty."

"I'll bet she was meeting someone to go over there." He indicated the lights of The Boondocks reflecting on the pond. Music and voices drifted on the hot night air from that direction. "I'm going to fetch her."

I almost screamed, "No, Sir, you can't." I knew I had to be the one to go there alone. "Mr. Palmer, please go back. Let me go over there. It'll be better for all concerned if I'm the one who finds her. Tell The Reverend, John Earl, and Mama I've gone to get Ruthie, and we'll be back directly."

"You can't just walk in that place alone, young lady. It isn't proper."

I almost laughed at his paternal instinct, and the number of times Ruthie and I had slipped away from college on any given weekend with mostly boys, to party until the owner showed us the door. Forget that; I needed to just prattle off something to make him go back to the revival. "Mr. Palmer, I don't want to soil your pristine opinion of Ruthie's reputation as a God-loving, sinless Methodist woman because, as far as I know she still is. But the truth of the matter is, she and I have been there before."

Funny, he didn't look as shocked as I would've expected. One thing I'd learned: we all have something in our past for which we are not proud. Why, I'd bet even my mother, the squeaky clean Gladys Mae Allgood, had a secret or two.

In spite of my arguments to the contrary, Mr. Palmer wouldn't hear of my going to The Boondocks without back up. "I will not allow you to wander through the park with Vernon Fielding skulking around. Why, for all we know, he already has Ruthie, though that's a thought I'll try not to allow. And I'm certainly not going to let you enter that den of iniquity alone. Come back to the revival with me and pray Ruth Ann is not there." His eyes saddened. "Like you said, your father is organizing a search party. You can be part of that."

"Fine." I followed him off the pier, but three strides before we reached the path, I snuck one last peek.

The bar had windows across each side wall, and on sweltering nights, the owners opened them to form overhangs, inviting in whatever breeze might come off the pond. I didn't spot Ruthie, but I thought I saw the profile of a man I hadn't seen for some time. He was standing on the deck, leaning against the railing.

I wasn't sure what to do. Suddenly, my heart was pounding at the back of my throat, and no amount of swallowing slowed it. I owed the person the chance to escape before all Hell broke loose and I lost Ruthie forever.

TWO

My chance to break free of him came when we reached the old picnic area. I ran back to the long flight of stairs that led to street level and on to the parking lot. I'd driven over in my own car, anticipating the need to escape the festivities in case John Earl grew restless.

"I'm going to get the flashlight from my car, Mr. Palmer. I'll be right along." Okay, so I lied to a man one-step down from a preacher, two steps down from God. If the Almighty really did exist, when my time came, he would lock the Pearly Gates when he saw me coming.

I knew The Reverend, John Earl, and Gladys were worried sick by now. And my son had probably already spilled all the beans about the man in the woods. Part of me said turn back and let The Reverend find out who was hanging out at The Boondocks. Let Lee Palmer discover his daughter with him. The other part told me I had to get over there before a posse stormed in, demanding answers to questions they had no business asking yet. Gladys Mae would understand, after I told her the whole story, if I ever did, but The Reverend? Never.

I didn't know if Ruthie was in trouble; after all, I could've mistaken the screams for squeals from kids partying in the park. I tried convincing myself she'd gone around the point on her own accord to bask in some sinful fun with regular folk who liked to throw back a few and have a good time.

Even as worried as I was, having a beer and shooting pool with those people sounded more appealing than listening to another preacher ranting about sin and baptism. I'll probably go to Hell for that, but sometimes I had trouble believing everything The Reverend preached. I sent up a quick, "Sorry, God," just in case.

Besides, reconnecting with the man I thought I saw at The Boondocks intrigued me.

I'd put my shoes back on, but gravel slipped under my arch in my slings, as I ran to the parking lot, so I removed them again. I often drove barefooted. Ever since I was little I've hated wearing shoes.

My car's tires sent clumps of red mud and gravel flying behind them. There'd been talk several years ago of having the lot blacktopped, but the city council, persuaded by a prominent member of the Historical Society, decided restoring some of the downtown buildings was more important to the area.

I kept the speed down, and when I checked in the rearview mirror, I saw Mr. Palmer, The Reverend, and a group of men gathered just off the dais under the tent. A prayer of thanks went up for giving me time to get over to The Boondocks to warn Ruthie and the man I knew wasn't ready for a confrontation with The Reverend.

One side of the Y in Pennington Pond Road was a two-mile stretch of pot-holed pavement that dead-ended at a park ranger's station. The other led to the campgrounds. Halfway there and across the rutted road was the gravel parking lot for The Boondocks. A blue neon sign at the peak of the tin roof drew folks from either end of the pond.

When the tires hit gravel, I threw the Taurus into park, ran across the road, and down a slight embankment to the pier. Nothing about the place had changed since we'd visited for my Bachelorette party. The building sat at the far end of the island down a hundred-yard path from the nearest point to the pond's shore. Dirt clung to my damp feet.

Frogs serenaded anyone who would listen. When I drew close to the water, a couple of them plunked in. Without moving my head, my eyes darted left, then right, anticipating someone grabbing me. Nothing happened. No one appeared.

I chose a small aluminum rowboat, flipped it over onto its bottom, and pushed it into the water. My biceps and pectorals strained, reminding me I hadn't rowed in years. I promised my body I'd exercise more as soon as I found Ruthie.

The boat hit sandy shallows at the north end of the island. I sank my sore feet in the cool water. In one hand, I held the hem of my dress and, with the other, yanked the boat ashore.

The whole way over I tried to decide whether, if I found Ruthie, I was going to squeal for joy and hug her, or ring her cotton-picking neck. I decided on the latter first, followed by the former. Then I'd drag her out, with force, if necessary.

The path across the island was straight and lit by battery-powered, multi-colored lanterns hanging from low branches of trees so close they stopped the breeze. Lights near the building illuminated the area, giving me a better assessment of the immediate area. The building was set on stilts to prevent flooding as many in this part of the country do.

To the right, a new padlock hung on double doors of a dilapidated, un-painted boathouse. Several row-boats like the one I'd used lay near a mesh steel stair-case, which led to the front door on the second level. Beer signs hung from chains in two front windows, on both sides of a covered front entrance.

I replaced my shoes a third time and climbed the stairs on my toes so as not to catch my heels in the holes of the steps. The original screen door, older than Gladys, hung loose on rusty hinges. They screamed as though I'd caused them horrific pain when I opened the door. A lack of air movement pushed acrid cigarette smoke at me with the music. I might as well have been walking into a burning building. It burned my eyes, forcing them to tear for a moment, but they soon cleared enough, and I could see my way through the crowd packed at the bar.

He was sitting halfway down a wood bar with a warped laminate top.

I pushed my way through, excusing myself, enduring stares from the women and lingering, lustful leers from bleary-eyed men, until I reached my target. "Thought that was you I saw a little while ago out on the deck."

Thomas pushed up from his position, leaning on his elbows, caressing a tumbler half-filled with amber liquid and whispering to Naomi. He spun, surprised to hear my voice. Bloodshot eyes glared from deep sockets and, at first, I wasn't sure he recognized me. He stared at my feet. "Well, well, Suz, you get stuck in the mud?"

I made a feeble attempt to wipe the dried mud from one foot with the other.

"I suppose you're in town for the big meeting. Come to save our souls or join in our debauchery?" His tone held its usual snide condescension. So maybe I didn't miss him so much.

I wanted to strangle the truth from him, but I forced myself to remain calm. I gathered a strong voice. "Ruthie Palmer disappeared from the revival tonight. I came here to find her and to warn you that The Reverend and a posse of Bible Thumpers are on their way here. I wanted to give you the opportunity to escape, if you wished, but I'm kind of sorry I did now."

His mouth held its droop and, with no change in his eyes, I wondered if Thomas' foggy mind refused to register what I'd said, so I turned to go.

He grabbed my arm. Those eyes, so much like Gladys Mae's, peered through his squint. He raised his glass and downed its contents. Maker's Mark, his favorite I recalled. "And why would the high and mighty Reverend Jedidiah want to soil his soul in a dump like this?"

Even the smallest noise heightened my senses. My stare never left Thomas, but my peripheral vision caught Naomi taking the tumbler and refilling it with what appeared to be a double shot and a few ice cubes thrown in for good measure. They sounded like bullets exploding, settling in the glass.

I got the distinct impression whoever she was, she didn't want me there. What was happening to me? Why should I care what anyone in that Hell hole thought of me?

I ignored her and spoke to Thomas. "I told you he's coming looking for Ruthie. She disappeared from lower part of the park about an hour ago." I waited for his reaction.

Thomas' hand shook, taking the glass to his mouth, as I recounted the evening's events. Time had not been nice to him. Gray thinning hair had replaced the thick auburn of his youth. Brown eyes, once deep topaz, had lost their luster.

I stared into them trying to convince myself they weren't the menacing ones belonging to the crouching man, but I couldn't be sure. Even standing straight, Thomas' shoulders hunched, probably a result of much time spent leaning over bars.

"Why would you come looking for Ruthie Palmer here? She'd never be caught dead unescorted down at The Boondocks."

Thomas' melodious laugh sprinkled the area around us, fairy dust lighting the deadpan faces.

While Billie Joe crooned in my head, I leaned on my elbows with my face in my hands. "Don't say dead, Thomas. I have no idea where she is." Though tears began to well, I refused to cry in front of him. "I think maybe Vernon took her."

I'd promised myself never again, after he'd made me cry on my wedding day. He'd shown up drunk, as usual. After the best man made his traditional speech, Thomas somehow made it to his feet and proceeded to extol upon our guests the sexual encounter he'd witnessed between Paul and me the day Paul proposed.

I'd run crying from the hall, swearing I'd kill the asshole if I ever saw him again.

His habit of getting drunk, and then apologizing the next day after sobering up, lost him friends and his parents' respect, even a job. But he was my brother. Despite my threat, I would never give up on the dream that someday he would pull himself from the alcoholic stupor ruining his life.

At that moment, Ruthie concerned me more than Thomas' bad habits. "You haven't seen her in here have you?"

"She wasn't out on the deck, and she hasn't passed by my spot here at the bar, because I'm sure I would have recognized that cute little—" He didn't finish his lurid thought. "Hey, but I did see her in here a couple of weeks ago with that ex-husband of yours." He chugged the whiskey. "Anyway, Ruthie might talk big, but she wouldn't risk getting caught in here during the All Mighty Revival."

I grabbed empty glass and slammed it on the bar. "Look, Thomas, I know you asked her to marry you on more than one occasion, only to have her reject you." Ruthie could be downright cruel to him at times. "But if you're drinking to forget, it won't work. Seems like you want to forget a lot."

"Don't you worry about me, Little Sis. I got another woman in my life now."

I kissed his cheek and his scraggly beard scratched my lips. I wiggled them to dispel the tickling sensation. "That's great, Thomas."

I hadn't had time to put my head around Paul and Ruthie's presence in town when the screen door opened and flapped shut again.

31

The posse had arrived. They stalked across the floor on a mission from God, scanning the crowd.

"Quick duck out on the deck," I told Thomas. "I'll detain them long enough for you to get back there, and I'll tell them I've already looked out there for Ruthie." The crowd prevented them from moving too fast across the wood floor. "Hopefully they'll take my word for it and I can convince them to go."

Thomas stood tall with indignation. "I'm not afraid of him." When he caught sight of The Reverend, I think all his teenage angst returned. He kissed my cheek. "I'll keep an eye out for Ruthie. If I see her, I'll send up a flare."

He whispered something to the bartender and disappeared into the crowd.

My heart sank with my shoulders.

I wanted to know more about Thomas' new woman, but years had passed since we were close, and he'd just tell me it was none of my business. Fair trade, since I'd told him the same when he said my marrying Paul was a bad idea. He'd been correct on that one.

I missed having an older brother to confide in, gripe at, and take care of. He needed of a younger sister's care. The long-sleeved rain jacket he was wearing despite the heat led me to wonder if he wasn't hiding something—track marks, perhaps—but I couldn't think about that now.

Judge and jury were waiting.

THREE

The Reverend's arrival caused such a commotion, everyone near us stopped their conversations, curious to see what man stood in their midst. His words came like an exploding bomb. "Susan Marie Allgood." Anger forced him into such a state, he'd forgotten I still carried Paul's name, even though we'd divorced two years ago.

His chin came close to touching his chest giving him the ability to glare at me over his glasses. "Do you know the whole camp is in an uproar? Your mother is worried sick, and your son has asked several times where you disappeared to."

I tried to stand up to him, show him my strength. My explanation sped up with each word. "Yes, Sir, I'm sure she is, but when Ruthie disappeared, I panicked. I went back to where we'd taken John Earl to make sure she wasn't there, injured. Then I thought maybe she'd come here to escape the revival."

The tears I had been holding finally fell, but I refused to give him the satisfaction of watching me wipe them away, an act tantamount to confessing some crime I hadn't committed. I know I'd already asked a lot of God that night, but I asked him to guide The Reverend. Would it have hurt him to admit he was worried about me, too?

No one around us said a word, waiting for the next twist in the plot.

Mr. Palmer stepped around The Reverend. He gave me a sorrowful expression, as though he commiserated with my suffering from The Reverend's wrath. Even as long-time friends, many an argument had taken place between them around our dinner table.

Lee Palmer's hazel eyes appeared to droop in their sockets, a sign of his embarrassment, and I wagered his dread for the answer to his question. "So you haven't seen Ruthie in here?" His face strained with anxiety of all aspects of Ruthie's absence.

Even the noise of the crowd, now bored with the drama, couldn't hide the rasp of his haggard breath. "Then he's got her." He wobbled on his feet as if he might faint.

The Reverend took charge, not letting his friend fall apart before we knew all the facts. "We need to go to the ranger's station. He will get in contact with the local authorities. Chances are, Ruth simply wandered down the wrong path and is lost in the woods."

Highly unlikely, considering all the time we spent in those woods with Thomas and his best friend, Charlie, but I couldn't tell The Reverend what we'd been doing now. "Ruthie knows these woods better than anyone I know, except Vernon."

He dismissed my words and spun on his heel with the presence we had all grown accustomed to. He drew his lanky frame back through the short doorway and into the moonlit night. "I'll catch up," I called on the way to the ladies room. "I drank a lot of water tonight." I pointed toward the restrooms sign.

Once in the stall, I let out a giant sigh. No sign of anyone wanting to speak to me. The thought of never speaking to Ruth again sent me reeling.

"You Sue Backman?" A voice came from outside the stall door.

I froze.

"Yes, who wants to know?"

"Guy out there told me to tell you that your friend is safe and to meet him on John's Island tomorrow at ten a.m."

I flung open the stall door, but the messenger was gone.

The Reverend was waiting, tapping his foot with the patience of...well, John Earl. We all followed, ever his flock, even outside the confines of a sanctuary.

Before I took my first step on the iron mesh stairway, I looked back through the screen door. Thomas had resumed his place at the bar. He raised his glass in a salute—a thank you—for staving off a full-out attack from the Bible Thumpers.

A most horrid thought crept in. What if he was the one holding Ruth? But why? What could possibly be his reason for kidnapping a woman he'd once loved? I wanted to rush over, grab him by the collar, and scream those questions in his face, but The Reverend waited.

He preceded the posse and me down the path. At the pier, he climbed into one of the rowboats and then helped me in. My anger lingered, first for his calling me out in the bar and, second, his assumption that I couldn't crawl into a boat without help from a man.

Mr. Palmer and the others piled into the other boats hanging over the pilings. Soon, oars hit the muddy water in cadence with one another. Their long strokes proved these men grew up rowing the waters of Pennington Pond. The Reverend surprised me, matching the strength of the much younger men.

We walked in silence together until we reached the cars. The Reverend held the rear passenger door open of Mr. Palmer's car.

"I drove over," I said, heading to my car.

"You're coming with us, Sue." He remained, holding the back door open.

"I don't want to leave my car here all night, and besides, Mama might call saying John Earl needs me."

I put one foot in the Taurus proud of my minor victory. Anytime Thomas or I stood independent from The Reverend, we'd felt great strides in our maturation. He would say something to me later about my obstinacy to him in front of Mr. Palmer, but I didn't care. My years away from home, married to Paul, allowed me to see The Reverend as a part-time, demanding, self-righteous hypocrite.

John Earl and I had made this trip, not only to please Gladys Mae, but also to allow him the opportunity to see The Reverend as others did, a formidable force in the Central Alabama Methodist conference. At least his admiration could survive a while longer.

The Reverend called out to me again. "Sue, don't make this about you and me. It doesn't make any more sense to have two cars at the ranger station than it does here. We'll have one of the men drive your car to Lee's."

Fine. I was too tired of acting the part of the perfect daughter and mother for a week, and too frightened for Ruthie to argue anymore. I lowered my chin in servitude and returned to the Bonneville, where I climbed in the back seat, as commanded.

God forgive me, but I would never again allow him that kind of power over me.

Mr. Palmer was in too bad a state to drive, so The Reverend did. He reminded me of the time Thomas wandered away from the revival when he was twelve. He was terrified when they found him, cowering in the woods. Later, he tried to convince me he'd done it on purpose just to scare the bejabbers out of our parents because he was bored.

Once a black sheep, always a black sheep.

Too many questions leaped into my brain. Why Ruthie? Why now? Thomas? Vernon? If this was about a ransom, why hadn't he contacted Mr. Palmer?

We needed to find her before that butcher slaughtered her. "I think we should go see the sheriff."

"Before we go getting the law involved," The Reverend announced, "I think we should check in at the ranger's station. I don't want a lot of folks panicked, seeing police and state troopers on an all-out manhunt when Ruthie could simply have wandered too far and gotten lost. And with what happened in previous years, I'll postpone getting the sheriff's department involved as long as possible."

It was a well-known fact that one of the former County Sheriffs hadn't taken too kindly to "a bunch of backwoods preachers" holding a revival meeting in a state park. I believed it revolved around separation of church and state nonsense. The Reverend was certain the same bad blood flowed into the next generation of the law, and no argument to the contrary would convince him the new sheriff thought any differently than his predecessor.

He patted Mr. Palmer's arm. "God will not let anything happen to one of his children." The words he uttered came with equal parts determination and fear. "In fact, Ruthie's probably back at the camp right now, embarrassed and wondering what all the fuss is about."

Mr. Palmer tried Ruthie's cell phone, but got only her voicemail. For a while, he stared at his phone, anticipating her call. It refused to come. The air in the Bonneville, though cooled by the air conditioner, hung heavy with our fear.

I admit my participation in religious activities of any kind had come to a standstill of late, with the exception of making certain John Earl got to Sunday school at least once every other week. With Ruthie's disappearance, my faith spun in disbelief with a healthy undertone of better-keep-my-options open.

I knew Ruth wasn't back in the fold, unharmed, but I couldn't speak. Even a hint of my call might mean her life. To make them believe I knew nothing, I tried her cell myself. Mr. Palmer watched in the rearview mirror. I got her voice mail, too. At least we knew her phone still worked. I just didn't know where she, or it, was. Or who had her, or what they were doing to her. Don't think about that.

"Ruthie, call me as soon as you get this message," I pleaded. "Everybody's worried sick about you."

The headlights lit a sign pointing down a gravel road, with the promise of a ranger's station at the end. Only trees and underbrush stood beyond the scope of golden illumination. Gravel spilled behind the tires as a doe crossed the road, forcing The Reverend to slam on the brakes.

Motion-sensor lights splayed the area in front of a cabin with yellow rays of eeriness. I could see little of the building, except for its log construction and expansive porch along the front. Wood blinds covered the windows, allowing only horizontal strips of interior light to escape.

Park Ranger Jack Carmichael greeted us at the door with friendly professionalism and ushered us into his office. "Thought I heard a car. What are you doing out here this time of night?"

He offered me the only other chair in the room besides his, a black vinyl one with a tiny rip at the front. The Reverend stood behind me, resting his hands on my shoulders. I reached back and patted one in a silent effort to apologize for my obstinacy earlier.

Mr. Palmer stood beside and slightly behind The Reverend. He wasn't always timid, but he acquiesced to The Reverend whenever they were together. I don't think Mr. Palmer believed The Reverend was right more; instead, he allowed him authority out of respect for the collar.

Carmichael walked around the metal desk with wood veneer covering the front and sides. Files and papers from other cases smothered its surface. I would've never known a park ranger in central Alabama could have so much work to do.

He was medium height, medium build; his brown and tan uniform fit his body well. Gray hair at his temples transitioned into dark blonde hair, cut short.

He had no telltale drawl; this man was not Alabama born, or bred.

I guessed him to be Midwestern.

Mr. Palmer cleared his throat. "My daughter went missing from the revival more than an hour ago. Sue, here, was the last to see her."

He grabbed a pencil and cleared a stack of papers off the desk until he found a legal pad. "Tell me everything you can about her and what you remember about tonight. Was your friend acting nervous or uninterested?"

"Ruth Palmer, age thirty-seven, five-foot-six, ash blond. The last time Ruth acted nervous was her first date with my brother." I turned to look to The Reverend and smiled.

He scowled and shook his head.

I turned back and stared at my hands. "I didn't see her until my son, John Earl, had to go to the bathroom."

The Reverend cleared his throat, and Carmichael's expression curled into a question.

"Let's just say, he wasn't too quiet about it. I heard whispers coming from behind us, complaining about John Earl's lack of discipline on such a reverent occasion. That's when I heard Ruth turn around and tell them all to be quiet."

That said, I continued. "Everything got back to normal, until John Earl insisted he had to use the bathroom." I held tight to the chair arms while I recounted, for a second time, the story of the man in the woods and Ruthie not coming back to the tent with us. "Some think Vernon Fielding might have her."

"It's possible." The ranger's crisp uniform crinkled when he arose behind the standard metal desk. A grin stretched his lips and forced me to question whether he even believed me, or if he found me attractive.

The Reverend stepped forward, ready to bring the fires of Hell down upon the man. "Are you laughing at the plight of one of our congregation?"

Carmichael put up a hand and took his seat again. "No, Sir. I take every story of missing persons seriously." The swivel mechanism on his wooden chair creaked when he leaned back in it. "Tell me more about…Ruth, is it? Is she known for outbursts or irrational acts?"

Her father stepped forward, and I think, if The Reverend hadn't intervened, Lee Palmer would have slugged the man.

I stood between them, protesting the suggestion. "Ruthie has been known to do a foolish thing or two, but she'd never just wander off knowing we'd all be worried sick." Okay so maybe that was a bit dramatic.

Carmichael eyed me, and I wished I could have read his mind. "We'll try to find him and go speak to Vernon. He's got a place out on one of the islands in one of the old slave cabins that survived the flood. He's crazy as a wily old coot, but we haven't been able to arrest him for anything since that Camden woman disappeared."

An intense gaze from his bright blue eyes met mine, as I sized up the man's words and demeanor. For a nanosecond, he seemed worlds away. "I'll be glad when they find that will so he can stay on the land. Otherwise, they'll send poor Vernon away for good." He seemed so certain of Vernon's innocence, I almost felt sorry for the man I'd grown up believing was family even if it wasn't registered.

"Anyway, I'll go talk to him. He probably saw something, the way he wanders the park."

My lips rolled under the way they did when I was mad or frustrated. "I should go with you. I might be able to identify him."

"No, Ma'am. Vernon doesn't like strangers. It'll be better for all if I go out there alone."

"I'm not a stranger," I started. "If family lore is correct, Vernon and I are distant cousins."

The Reverend groaned and rolled his eyes. He didn't believe a word of Pennington history.

I'd almost forgotten he was in the room, until Mr. Palmer took one of his customary ragged breaths. He pressed his palms against the desk. "Sue, Vernon was accused of kidnapping that woman a few years back. He's just the kind of man who'd do something crazy." He turned toward Carmichael. "Now, what are you waiting for? My daughter's life could be at stake." He glanced at his watch. "I've seen those detective shows on TV. The quicker we get out there with a search party, the quicker we might pick up a trail."

"If you don't mind, Mr....?"

"Palmer. I'm sorry; I guess we were in such a rush to tell you about Ruthie, we forgot introductions." He pointed at me, then at The Reverend. "This is Sue Backman, Ruthie's best friend. And this is her father, The Reverend Jedidiah Allgood." He paused for a moment, while Carmichael stood and shook The Reverend's hand. "I'm Ruth's father, Lee Palmer." The two men shook hands.

42

Carmichael remained standing in a slightly defensive stance, protecting some imaginary territory. "Hold on there, Mr. Palmer; we can't go off half-cocked. A bunch of people traipsing through the woods will only drive Vernon in farther." He turned to me. "Now, can you show me on the map the last place you saw her?"

I peeked over The Reverend's shoulder at a map of the park. Pennington Pond looked like an aneurism of the Alabama River dotted with tiny islands. I pointed to the picnic area where I'd last seen Ruthie.

Carmichael turned to Mr. Palmer. "Do you have a recent photo of your daughter?"

Mr. Palmer pulled his wallet from his black trousers and removed Ruthie's senior portrait from its frayed plastic sleeve and apologized for its age. Then he gave a detailed description.

Carmichael picked up the phone and pushed one button. "Martha, is he in? Okay, I'll try his cell." He pushed the disconnect button and then another. "Bill, Jack here. Sorry to call so late, but we've got a missing woman out here at the park. Just a little over hour now." He grinned at me again. "Yeah, I'll call John and Tuck, and we'll meet you at the revival tent."

He disconnected again and laid the receiver on the cradle. "That was Bill Halvorson, the Elmore County Sheriff."

The name stirred the waters of my memory pool and brought to the surface a skinny kid with acne and wire-rimmed glasses.

"We'll find your daughter, Sir." Warm, almost gold eyes gazed at me with a sort of fatherly reassurance. "Lots of woods around the pond to get lost in. Could be she wandered too far, took a wrong path, and circled back. For all we know, she's already back at camp, embarrassed as hell for getting lost."

Before I could argue that Ruthie wouldn't get lost at the pond, Carmichael realized his faux pas, and offered an apology to The Reverend. With his next breath, he said, "Any chance she wandered over to The Boondocks?"

I glanced over my shoulder, and The Reverend shot a quick glare back in my direction. "We've already been there. No one there has seen her." Why had it sounded like an apology? Because being in the presence of The Reverend makes me forget I'm thirty-seven and can go wherever I darn well please.

"Well, I've known Bill for years. You can rest assured he'll put all his available deputies on it. If she's not safely back by dawn, he'll call in the FBI." Carmichael's words appeased Mr. Palmer and me. "Like I said, a bunch of us racing out there on the pond might scare Vernon. He's never hurt anyone as far as I'm concerned, but I don't know his mental state right now."

The Reverend took the opportunity to voice his opinion of the current sheriff. "If this sheriff is anything like his predecessor, he'll take us all as snake-charming imbeciles who've allowed one from our flock to slip away and do little or nothing about it."

The ranger stood and moved around the desk again toward the open door to his office. "Reverend, Bill Halvorson is nothing like the former sheriff. We're going to do everything in our power to lead an extensive search."

He turned to me and smiled with sugar-coated, over-confidence, a habit I would soon grow to hate. "Now, Sue, if you'd like to ride back over to the revival with me, you can fill me in on a few more details about this evening's activities, and give a description of the man you saw."

FOUR

At first, I liked Ranger Carmichael. He was a take-charge, level-headed sort, like the Reverend, but I sensed a hint of irreverence when it came to organized religion. I didn't want to get personal, but I couldn't help speculating about the reason.

I found myself nervous being alone with him, after The Reverend and Mr. Palmer left. My habit when in such a state was to start talking up a blue streak. "So have you received many calls about the revival?"

"We always get a few every year. Those anti-religion folks, or religion-state separatists, claiming it's against the law to hold religious ceremonies on state-owned grounds. Funny thing, they always seem to come in from other states." His laugh was kind of cute. "I guess if they want to take it up with the judge, they can find him sitting on a bench under the tent singing those hymns a bit off key."

Was that sarcasm I heard? "So, I take it you're not a religious man?"

The lines at his temples deepened, but he smiled. He twisted his mouth back and forth the way I did when I was considering something mindful. "Wouldn't say that. I was raised in a good Baptist home, but after I finished with college, I moved around with the Forest Service. I guess you could say I just got out of the practice of attending services." He shrugged but kept his sight locked on the curvy road leading up to the pond.

He didn't seem to be in any hurry to ask me more about Ruthie, so I continued my verbal rambling. "Funny, riding in a car with a man I just met puts butterflies in my gut. Even if he is a park ranger." Great, you just admitted you don't trust him. Shut up, Sue.

Carmichael wasn't the true cause of the nervousness. It was my own silly fear about riding in a car with a man in uniform. The black Jeep reminded me of ones I'd seen on the police forensics shows I was addicted to watching. Equipped with all the bells and whistles, the vehicle included a navigational system. Necessary for the job I presumed. And it was too clean. Gray cloth upholstery carried nary a speck of dust, and even the floorboards were immaculate.

The quiet brought on an overwhelming sense of self-consciousness. The dam on my mouth burst again, and I started blubbering like a convict confessing to a crime. "I was in a police car once, all a terrible mistake." I leaned onto my right side and propped against the door of the SUV as though getting as far away from him as possible delivered me from any guilt.

"See, Ruthie and I went out to celebrate my thirtieth birthday at this place in Birmingham. We were both sitting at the bar drinking piña coladas, when the vice squad raided the bar. Seems all the time we'd been sitting there, we'd been talking to two ladies of the evening. The cops hauled Ruthie and me off and stuck us in the back seat of a cruiser. Of course, yours is much nicer." I grimaced, realizing once again how my last statement must have sounded like a silly schoolgirl. I was making a complete ass out of myself. I told myself to shut up again, but mind and mouth were not communicating.

He let out a light airy chuckle, instead of one of those annoying deep belly laughs, which shake a man's entire body. His well-defined pectorals bounce just a little under his crisply pressed shirt. The temperature in my cheeks and neck climbed a degree or two at the thought of seeing them outside the confines of the cloth. The man was in excellent shape.

"So they arrested you two?"

The question tossed my way drew me back to reality and set my thoughts back on finding Ruthie. "They were going to until we called Ruthie's mother. She explained who we were. Combined with the other women's promise they'd never seen us before, the officers let us go." A smile came, but it was bittersweet. I wanted to laugh with Ruthie about the story. The truth slammed me in the heart. I might never see her again. No, I would not allow such a thought.

"Why Mrs. Palmer instead of your mother?"

I stared straight ahead into the beams of the headlights and snickered. "Caroline Palmer was not the typical church mother. She never pretended to be holier-than-thou, never tried concealing the facts of her imperfect past before she met Lee Palmer and became a member of First United. I guess Ruthie and I share some leftover anger from stories Mama told me. Seems some of the congregation refused to accept Caroline into the fold. She died of lymphoma three years ago, but until then, she was the one I went to when talking to Mama was impossible. Caroline never judged."

His gaze never wavered from the road. "So what happened to her?"

I prayed to her to keep Ruthie safe for us until we found her. For somebody who had rejected church and God of late, I sure was doing a lot of praying that night.

"She died of cancer when Ruthie and I were in college."

He fell into a few moments of silence, then broke it. "Well, you don't have to worry. I'm not going to arrest you, unless you've done something illegal." That chuckle again, half snicker, half guffaw.

I cringed when I heard it that time. He was making fun.

The Jeep spewed red mud and gravel behind us when he stopped it across the road from the tent. Carmichael jumped out before the engine stopped purring, came around like a true Southern gentleman, opened the door, and offered his hand to help me step down off the running board.

Three strides took him across the road to the tent to join The Reverend, Mama, Mr. Palmer, and three wearing county uniforms, and two others dressed in uniforms similar to Carmichael's. "Any word?"

They all shook their heads in rhythm. Folks were gathered in small groups whispering about Ruthie I was certain. None of it good, either; she had a bit of a reputation for being a rebel rouser.

I mousy voice came from behind me. "Mama?" John Earl's face was smudged from wiping tears with dirty hands. I squatted and John Earl ran from behind Mama's legs into my awaiting arms. His exuberance almost knocked me flat on my backside.

His expression exploded into a bright smile, and he stood shoulders wide, back straight. "I saved a bat.

Some of the ladies tried to kill him with their fans, but I told 'em that he was the one keeping the skeeters off. But mostly I was worried, Mama." Tears, the size of peas, made clean tracks down his dirty cheeks. "We didn't know where you were at first. Then Grandmother and The Reverend kept whispering with those men. I knew they were talking about where you'd gone, but they wouldn't tell me. They just kept saying you were all right."

I hugged him tighter, and then, with a mother's gentleness, pushed him far enough away to speak to him face to face. I blinked away a few tears of my own. "I'm fine, Sweetie. I just went out to look for Aunt Ruthie." Great, I had just lied to my son for the first time.

Giving him the once over I asked, "How'd you get so dirty?"

"When you didn't come back, I told Grandmother I knew where you might be. I heard you tell Aunt Ruthie 'bout hating them outdoor potties, so I thought you might've gone in the woods like I did. I took her out looking to the place where we saw the man, but I fell down running out of there, when I heard something rustling up ahead, and I thought it was him again."

He'd exhausted his breath and sucked in another. Then John Earl Backman did something he had not done in years. He fell into my arms, shaking and weeping with fright. Since my divorce from Paul two years ago, John Earl had become my strength, taking to heart The Reverend's instructions to take care of me. Once again, he was just my little boy, needing nothing more than the comfort of his mother's embrace.

I would've joined him in a good cry, if it had not been for an interruption by a lanky, but well-built man, sporting a county uniform and a badge. His stature paled in comparison to The Reverend, but few men reached daddy's height. "Mrs. Backman, Sheriff Bill Halvorson." He extended a strong hand and held mine a little longer than etiquette required. He stared at my face with his head tilted to one side. "Sue? Sue Allgood?"

I released John Earl and stood. "Bill Halvorson. The last time I saw you, you were a scrawny kid with thick glasses, and a crush on Ruthie." I held my hand out at arm's length, chest high.

He reached out, ready to hug me. Throat-clearing from The Reverend halted his move toward me.

Carmichael laughed. "I can't imagine Bill was ever scrawny."

Bill balled his fist, but smiled. "Watch it, Ranger-Boy."

I looked to Gladys and The Reverend, who were both looking confused. "Don't you remember Bill? He was in youth fellowship with Ruthie and me. We graduated together." I turned to Bill. "What happened? You're buff, as my students would say."

"I got sick of being beat up, so after high school, I joined the navy and when I got out, I studied law enforcement." Bill transformed into his official capacity. "If you could show me where you and your son were when someone grabbed your arm, and the last place you saw Ruth. It'll make the best starting point for our search for Vernon."

"Bill, you and I both know it was probably just some kid who touched Mrs. Backman's arm and not Vernon.

And for all we know Ms. Palmer wasn't kidnapped. Why are you always accusing him?"

"I'm not accusing him yet, Jack, but remember what happened to that Camden woman." Bill extended his arm and allowed me to step in front of him.

Carmichael followed us. "He was acquitted for the Camden woman's disappearance. I still say that woman got drunk and lost her way in the woods, then fell off the docks. Or she accepted a ride from some fool who left the area with her."

Carmichael continued his argument against Vernon. "Doesn't it seem just a bit suspicious to you the woman was the wife of one of the golf course architects? Vernon would have never wanted that thing on what he considered his territory."

Bill pointed his finger at Carmichael and half-closed his right eye. "And I'm telling you, Jack, you can't say with absolute certainty that it wasn't him."

I got between them and interrupted their tête-à-tête. "Who cares what he did ten years ago. All I care about is getting Ruthie back."

One of Bill's eyebrows rose at the end. "I know, Sue, and you're right. We need to concentrate on the problem at hand."

"There is that rumor about someone wanting to buy up all this land so they can sell to some land developer who wants to build houses around the pond." Carmichael's eyebrow's rose in speculation. "That would have Vernon mad as hell or scared, just like he was ten years ago. It might be possible he thought Ms Palmer knew something about that."

Bill took a few steps toward the woods. "After you show me the spot where you felt something, I think we should check with Naomi over at The Boondocks. He's always hanging around his cousin's place, even though Archie doesn't like it."

My head tilted to one side and I stared up at Bill. "Doesn't make sense. Ruthie doesn't have anything to do with any land deal. And neither would Vernon, so why would he take her."

Before either man could comment, John Earl came up beside me and asked if I'd go with him to get a drink from the fountain by the bathrooms. We walked hand in hand across the park road, both tentative and searching the tree line. "Mama, I've heard people whispering about a man named Vernon who did bad things to a woman before I was born. Is he really your cousin, and do you think he has Aunt Ruthie?"

Something snapped acorns behind us, and I grabbed his hand. "I don't know, but we need to get back."

Under the tent lights, The Reverend, Bill, Carmichael, and Mr. Palmer, along with the two deputies, had pushed several benches together and spread out the park map. Bill called out, inviting any able-bodied man to join in the search.

I sent John Earl to join Gladys, who was chatting with some ladies. Then I moved next to The Reverend and listened.

Carmichael slid his finger along the map. "There are three possible directions she could have taken. Easiest and quickest out of the park would've been for her to head west for a while and circle back around for her car and simply drive out of the park by way of the park road."

Mr. Palmer cleared his throat. "Her car is still at home. She rode over with me. Then she stopped to answer her cell phone."

"Does she know anyone in the area who she could have called for a ride?"

"Look Carmichael, my daughter has plenty of friends in the area," Mr. Palmer said, his indignation raised another notch toward fury. "But she had no reason to disappear from the revival in the dark."

"Sorry, Mr. Palmer, but we still need to explore every possibility."

Bill stepped in. He suggested to Mr. Palmer he try his home number on his cell phone. "Your daughter may be safe there, and all this worry's for naught. After all, she's been in town for a while."

Mr. Palmer glared at Bill. "What are you talking about? Ruthie lives in Nashville. She teaches English at a small college there."

"That may well be true, Mr. Palmer, but I've seen Ruthie around town a couple of times in the last month or so."

After Lee Palmer stopped staring at Bill with utter disbelief, he pulled out his phone and said, "Ruth" into it. No answer prompted him to try his home number. There was no answer there either, so he left a message for her to call him right away.

Several men and women gathered nearby and Bill pointed at Carmichael. "Jack knows this park better than anybody except Vernon. He'll coordinate the search parties."

"Bill, if he sees folks coming, he's going to disappear so far into these woods," Carmichael said angrily, "we'll never find him. Let me go out alone in the morning."

"Jack, you know as well as I do, that if we don't start now, it could be too late. If Vernon's heard about this land being sold no telling what kind of state he's worked himself into. For now, we'll only cover the perimeter of the pond."

"I'm going too," I chimed in.

Carmichael relented and pointed in three different directions. "One path heads around the point southwest toward The Boondocks and the Alabama River with little side paths to picnic points. A second leads east, straight toward the golf course and up top on the cliff overlooking the pond. The terrain along the shore is treacherous, but the draught has created a place to walk. A third leads behind the meadow, through the woods to the north, and circles back down to the new boat ramp."

He shouted over the din growing at the back of the tent. Children ran and played, and their mothers chattered away. "We're going to divide into three groups. I'll lead one west around the point. Bill will lead another east, along the shore to the creek, dividing the park from the golf course. Reverend, if you wouldn't mind taking a few men and searching the upper level of the park to the new boat launch."

The Reverend nodded.

Bill sent one deputy back to question the owners of the gas station/bait shop at the highway. "Also, approach with caution if you encounter Vernon. He may be armed and dangerous."

"I thought you were going to speak to him?" I whispered.

Carmichael frowned and spoke in a most condescending voice. "He could be on any of those islands out there."

I almost let him have it, when I saw Bill getting ready to leave. "I told you, I'm going along."

The Reverend pointed his finger at me. "You need to stay with Mother and John Earl."

"No, Reverend, I'm going with Bill. Like I said, I know these woods too. I grew up here, remember?"

John Earl sat up out of a sound sleep. "What's going on?"

I knelt in front of him. "I'm going with the sheriff to help look for Ruthie."

He threw himself at me, and I swallowed him into my arms. "Don't go Mama. I don't want Vernon to get you, too."

"He won't, Sweetie. The Sheriff will protect me." I looked up at Bill. Though he wasn't more than six feet tall, he must have seemed a giant to John Earl. "Besides, Vernon won't hurt me. We're family."

He cried to come with me, but Bill dropped to his haunches and spoke to John Earl at his level. "I promise I'll keep her safe if you promise to stay with your grandmother. She'll need a strong man to protect her." Then Bill stood and saluted.

John Earl pushed his shoulder blades together and returned the salute. "Yes, Sir."

Just before I headed out of the tent, I looked back over my shoulder and blew John Earl a kiss.

He stood next to Gladys, holding her hand and sniffling, swiping his runny nose with his free hand. He was giving all he had to be brave, but with all the speculation about Ruthie's disappearance spreading like wildfire through the crowd, the poor thing had to be confused and scared. *Ascared*, he would say.

Bill stopped and looked back at me over his shoulder. "Maybe your father's right. Maybe you should stay here with your son."

At first I thought I saw fear in his eyes and, for that moment, I was touched.

When he added, "Let the men folk do what we're trained to do," I saw his good-old boy chauvinism was shining through. He'd just lumped himself in that group—along with my ex—of men who think women are too fragile for anything but childcare and housework. I wondered if it was regional or if rednecks existed throughout the country.

I wasn't about to back down now. "Ruthie needs me now more than ever. She's my best friend. She's out there somewhere, maybe injured or captured, and I'm going to do everything in my power to find her, even if that means following a narrow-minded sheriff into the woods."

His sideways grin was different than I remember from school. It carried strength and confidence with a hint of suggestiveness. "Fine, then stay with me and do not wander out of sight at any time. We don't need two pretty young women running 'round out there in the backwoods getting lost."

"I won't get lost, Bill, and for your information, Ruthie isn't lost either. Vernon has her on one of his islands out there. Doesn't it make sense to get a few men in boats and go search them?"

Bill sucked in a breath and I could see by his expression that he was tiring of my presence. "No, it makes more sense to search the park around the pond first. I you disagree, stay behind."

I was going, and swore with the Girl Scout pledge I would stay close. Ruthie and I attended scout meetings, but we were never textbook Girl Scouts.

Then all of the sudden, the idea of tagging along didn't seem like a good one. Tromping along behind Bill, and possibly finding Ruthie's mutilated corpse could prove as difficult as forcing a bunch of rowdy teenagers to dissect an eyeball.

FIVE

While the search party waited for two members of the K-9 Search and Rescue Team, Carmichael's insistence that Vernon wouldn't harm Ruthie reigned in my thoughts, a beacon of hope she was still alive. My stomach rumbled with anger, frustration, and the fear of never seeing her again.

Tears blossomed. I squeezed my eyes shut tight to halt them from multiplying. I wouldn't allow myself to collapse into a wailing, doomsday female.

I was carrying an emergency lantern with a beam the size of a tractor-trailer headlight, which allowed me to see what the darkness had hidden before. Spanish moss hung in strands from the branches of aged pin oaks like tentacles ready to grab me.

Something stirred behind me and excitement about being involved in the hunt for Ruthie began to wane. I wanted to return to Gladys' comforting arms, aware of how little I wanted to be present if we came upon Ruthie's lifeless, mutilated body.

Bill's voice caused me to jump. "Everybody in town knows the Allgoods to be a notoriously stubborn bunch, but Sue, please rethink this. I don't need to deal with a hysterical woman if we find Ruth's body."

I took a deep breath, set my shoulders straight, and sent Bill a determined stare. "I'm going."

A voice came from behind me. "Bill, you'd think you'd have learned by now that once a woman makes up her mind, neither tides nor twisters are going to change it."

I spun, hiding a grin.

"Sue, this is, for now, Deputy Cody Duffy and this beauty is Quixote." Bill puffed out his chest with pride. "Quixote is our best tracker. She and Duffy here make up the best team in three counties. Took second place in the state K-9 competition last year. They'll be on point, we'll follow." He pointed an index finger at my nose. "And I do mean follow."

I shook Deputy Duffy's hand and scratched the full-grown German Shepard behind her ears.

Deputy Duffy was having a little trouble restraining the bright-eyed dog, her mouth open, tongue wagging, waiting for instruction. He petted and spoke quietly to the dog, then to us, he said, "If we have anything of Ms. Palmer's for Quixote to get the scent from, she'll find her if she's in these woods."

I didn't have anything.

Mr. Palmer headed back up the trail. "I'll be right back. There might be something in the car."

I stared at the edges of the light sphere, while Bill and Duffy discussed strategy. I understood the need for a personal article, but Bill could have saved us precious time by asking Mr. Palmer to fetch something earlier.

In the amount of time it took for me to complete the thought, he had returned. He stepped into the conjunction of the light beams. He seemed to be wandering in a fog, lost without his daughter. "I searched the car. Found this." Pure sadness resonated from his voice as if resigned to Ruthie's death.

His outstretched hand opened to reveal a silk scarf. I recognized it as the one Ruthie had inherited from her mother and the one she carried everywhere to honor her mother's memory.

The deputy thanked Mr. Palmer and stuck the scarf at Quixote's muzzle. In one movement, the dog's head dropped, nose to the ground, quivering with the prospect of picking up the scent, his ears standing high, aware of every sound in the area. Quixote bounded off with Duffy in tow on the trail, and they become only a spot of light ahead.

We waited a few minutes to let them get a head start.

A breeze off the lake brought the scent of Bill's cologne to my nostrils. Not overpowering, but masculine without pretense. While being the source of ridicule as a kid spurred him to bulk up, he seemed to lack the ego some men in a position of authority possess. Watching him, enjoying his scent, I lost my fear.

Other men and a few women trudged along in the distance swinging lanterns and spraying light on the woodland floor. They called Ruthie's name, but each time, the sound died without response.

The farther we trekked into the woods and with every passing sweep, I noticed Bill glancing back with concern, and I couldn't help wonder what he was thinking. Was he simply making sure I was close by? Was he convinced Vernon was following? Or had a madman already killed Ruthie, dumped her body, and Bill was making sure he came upon it first. Then a truly far-fetched notion twisted in my head. What if Bill was the crazy guy we'd seen? I'd seen plenty of police shows about cops gone bad, and nobody in the town knew, until he made a mistake.

A barn owl screeched in the distance, probably signaling a furry beast's demise and dinner for the fowl. Chester Farley's two old hunting dogs barked at nothing in particular, apart from the fact that they could, and most likely complaining about the noise from the jukebox barring their sleep.

Quixote answered with a series of barks. Perhaps Farley and his dogs had joined the search and the responsive barking was a signal.

I hoped it meant, "Nothing here."

Bill's light caught the yellowed, fiberglass piers, and I recognized the spot where John Earl, Ruthie, and I had encountered Vernon or whomever. "Stop, this is it."

Bill came to such a quick halt, I almost stepped on him. "Careful there, Sue." He angled his lantern so I could see his face. The glow deepened the appearance of crow's feet as his eyes twinkled.

His gaze forced my eyes away, and I stared down at my clumsy feet. "Sorry, guess I wasn't watching where I was going."

He gave me a paternal pat on the arm. "No harm, no foul." It was dorky, yet kinda cute.

"Ruthie and I walked this way while we were waiting for John Earl to pee." I continued up the path away from the pond. "Ruthie wandered closer to The Boondocks, but I told her we needed to get back before they missed us."

Duffy yelled back for us to stop, and Bill stepped out of the reach of my lantern beam. The iota of time they spent out of sight seemed like a lifetime. Had they found Ruthie's body? Had she been injured or simply wandered off the path and fallen in the water?

Bill called out a warning to the group. "There's a washout area ahead. Move around it to the right. Watch your step." To me, he whispered, "You can relax. I checked and she isn't down there. Just chunks of good ol' Bama red clay and a bunch of trash. Looks like kids used it as a party spot."

He aimed his flashlight, I think to prove Ruthie's body wasn't crumpled at the base, but also so I could see what to avoid. "Looks like a giant pond monster rose out of the water and took a chunk of the shore right off, doesn't it?"

The closest tree stood erect, but its trunk and roots were exposed, dangling precariously near the edge and in danger of toppling in. Bill's warning disturbed a flock of birds sleeping above in the tree. They flapped wings and chattered before settling down again. Quiet crept back into our circle of light.

Lee Palmer's sigh of relief echoed through the trees.

The leaf-carpeted path narrowed ten yards ahead, and I was forced to follow Bill again. I heard him chuckle, and I found his attitude disrespectful to Ruthie. "You find this whole thing funny?"

He stopped, spun, and glared at me. I think he spit saliva with each word but I couldn't see in such little light. "Look, Sue, I take every missing person case seriously, but let's face facts. We don't know anything unlawful or evil has happened to Ruth."

His eyes twinkled in the dim light, and the right side of his mouth rose in a cocky smile. "For all I know, she got tired of the revival, walked home, and could be in any of the nightclubs in Montgomery right now, dancing the night away. You know how she is…or was. That's all I was chuckling about."

My fists pressed against my hips. "Don't you understand? She wouldn't have left on her own without telling me where she was going. She would've told me to meet her later, after I dropped off John Earl with my mother at her father's house."

He started walking again, speaking over his shoulder. "And did it ever occur to you that maybe she wanted to go alone. Maybe she was meeting someone."

"No." I shook my head. "She would have just said so."

His attitude rekindled my need to search. I was sure we would find Ruthie. That is until Bill squashed it. "You need to return to the tent, and your son. We need calm thinking, not emotion."

He gave me his extra walkie-talkie and said I would act as base to relay to in the event Ruthie showed up. Then, as if I needed more guilt on top of letting Ruthie wander off alone, he reiterated how much I needed to be with John Earl.

"Look Sheriff, Bill, I need to look for Ruthie. I saw the man, I can identify him." I hoped my squint added enough intensity to my words. "I can assure you I'm not an emotional female who flies off the handle at every little thing." I took my stance again, the one Paul always hated, with my fist pushing against my hips. "Did it ever occur to you I just might be able to help?"

He put a hand on each of my shoulders and tried to turn me back toward camp, but I squirmed away to the

66

edge of the path. Surprised by my reaction to his touch, he linked his hands behind his back. "Sue, I understand all that, but the best thing you can do for us now is go back and wait. You have to understand. This is no place for a woman at night. Like I said, we don't need to be out looking for the two of you."

I looked to Mr. Palmer for aid. "Tell him. Tell him I know these woods probably better than he does. After all, I've been tromping around in them every year since I was five."

Mr. Palmer stood mute despite my hurtful stare. I should have known he was not going to stand up for me. Ruthie'd been right. He was a wimp.

"Vernon believes we don't know where he lives," Bill yammered on, "but Carmichael can find him just about anytime. First thing in the morning, Jack is going out to the all the islands, find him, and to talk to him. As much as I'd like to, I can't arrest the man on innuendo."

Before I could even suggest I go see the man, to identify him as the crouching man or clear him, Bill vetoed the idea. "I know what you're thinking, Sue. You know Vernon. He's a funny sort. Like Jack said, if he thinks too many people can find him, he'll vamoose. If he knows anything, he'll be more likely to share the info with just Jack."

As long as he put it that way, I couldn't argue.

Since The Reverend and his group had the smallest area to search, they finished and caught up to us. They'd found no evidence of Ruthie, no hacked remains. The Reverend volunteered to see me safely back to camp and tell Gladys he would be returning to the search with Bill.

I felt like I was seven again, unable to go to the bathroom without being accompanied by a parent. Some things never changed. When we came close to the washout, he put his arm around my shoulder and drew me close, in an annoying paternal manner.

I wriggled away and kept walking.

"Now you listen up, Susan," his booming voice shot out, "we're going to come to an understanding right now. Despite your thoughts to the contrary, I know you're a grown woman. You're panicked over Ruthie's disappearance, but John Earl needs to see and feel your strength." He caught up and turned me to face him. "Honey, they're gonna find her. God will lead them."

"You really think God's going to help you find her?" I couldn't look him in the eye. "He's the one who allowed the maniac to take her in the first place."

I reached the tent with The Reverend only a few steps behind me, spouting scripture about doubting Thomas. I couldn't help but laugh.

He shushed the crowd. A few stragglers still awake, who had stuck around for word on Ruthie, fell silent as he made his way to the lectern. Several women had pulled benches close to the tent poles, using them as backrests and had dropped off to the sleep, but they stirred to follow The Reverend's voice. It was closing in on midnight and most of these women and children should have been home, safe in their bed.

"Ladies, it looks like it could be a long night, so if those who live close could return to your homes and brew up as much coffee as possible, we would appreciate it. Perhaps make sandwiches or bring the makings. In addition, anyone with extra flashlights or battery-powered lanterns, bring them. It's up to us to find her. But first, let's offer up silent prayers for Ruthie Ann Palmer's return, unharmed, and comfort for her father until that time."

Pride swelled in my thoughts and squelched the anger. My father had transformed into a calm, authoritative organizer and a comfort to his congregation. Sure, he could be a Bible-beating, hardheaded bully when it came to his beliefs. He'd led hundreds to Christ, baptizing them in the Lord's name, praying over their ill and dying bodies, and those of their children, but in an emergency he revealed a helpful, practical side.

Gladys rocked John Earl. I reached for him. "Let me take him for a while. You can stretch your legs."

"I'm fine. Why don't you lean back, close your eyes and rest?"

I had to admit I was close to exhaustion. My legs ached, though I hadn't walked the four miles I walked at the gym back home. Amazing, isn't it, how the mind can wreak havoc on the body? I sank onto the hard bench next to the two of them. I kicked off shoes and dozed for a few minutes.

A full bladder awakened me. Cool grass feathered between my bare toes, until my feet hit the ruts and dust of the road, then the aged concrete path. Occupied stalls in the bathroom forced me out to the port-a-potties. I headed for the one farthest away from the tent, paranoid about someone else hearing me.

The door slammed shut. I sat in the dark, until my eyes adjusted. The thin ray of light coming through slats at the back threw a ghastly shadow at the ceiling. Sure enough, there in the back corner right above my head hung granddaddy long-legs. I shuddered aloud. My inane fear of spiders began with Thomas throwing them on me when I was a kid.

Reason and science proved the creature too small to be dangerous, but I didn't care. One wrong move and Charlotte's brother was going to slide down a string of spider spit and sink his venomous teeth into my neck. I would be dead in seconds.

Two explosions ricocheted from the direction of the pond and shattered my thoughts of Granddaddy Bite-cha.

Women from the tent screamed.

Someone shouted, "What was that?"

Another said, "Sounded like shots."

I stared at my hand void of the walkie-talkie. I'd either left it on the bench or dropped it on the way back to camp. "Please don't let anything happen to The Reverend or Bill."

Women continued to scream. Staying put in the box with Octolegs would be the safest place for me. If Vernon was determined to kill us all, he had plenty of targets. Seeing me dash back toward the tent might draw his fire toward the innocent women and children there.

Think, I told myself. No more shots came. I dropped to my hands and knees and crawled back under the tent. On the way, I think I palmed and kneed every rock and pothole on the road. Some folks were on their knees, leaning on the benches, moaning prayers to the same god who had allowed some maniac to drag my best friend off into the night. My anger hit the boiling point. I stepped just inside the tent.

"Is this it?" They stared up from their prayers aghast as I screamed at them. "A woman has been kidnapped in the dead of night, someone's out there possibly shooting at the rescue teams, and all ya'll are going to do is pray, make coffee and sandwiches?"

John Earl awoke with the sound of my voice and lurched up from leaning against Mother. "What you so mad about, Mama?"

Gladys whispered to him, probably telling him I was just upset about Ruthie. If not for my son occupying her lap, I think she would have dragged me away to the woods for a good tongue whipping.

A teenage boy, face covered with acne, stopped at the entrance to the tent just a few feet away. An audible breath exited his lungs with each word. "Deputy's been shot. Ambulance should be on its way." Spinning, he looked in every direction. "Which one of you is Mrs. Backman?" He turned to face the back of the tent again.

I tapped him on the shoulder. "Right here, what do you need?"

He turned so fast, his feet tangled with each other and he almost fell. "Lord Almighty Ma'am. You 'bout scared me shi...my socks off. Sheriff sent me back here to find you. Wants you to lead the EMTs out to where you were before he made you come back. He'll meet you there."

A woman, carrying a few extra pounds, ran to him, sobbing with joy her son was not carrying the bullet in him. She fired question after question at him, and after answering a few, he told her he had to get back to the search. Her cigar-shaped fingers squeezed his arm and led him back into the tent, telling him there was no way

71

he was going back out into the darkness with a lunatic out there shooting at anything that moved.

"Come on, Mama, I don't want to stay here with the women and the babies." A few women joined me in a chuckle at his response. However, after the stare his mother sent him, he sank onto a bench, with elbows on his bony thighs and fists pushing up his cheeks. Some young men just know not to push their mother's buttons.

An ambulance from a local hospital pulled over the curb and right up to the tent. Emergency lights spread an eerie glow over and through the canvas tent, creating an alien-like aura over the women and children inside.

The petite, but sturdy, woman who jumped from the vehicle wore the uniform of the Prattville Station 2 Response Team. When the ambulance came to rest, she reached back and grabbed an orange plastic carryall out of the bay door. Her blonde hair was pulled back and tucked under a baseball cap carrying the PS2RT logo. Her partner followed, a man a few inches shorter than The Reverend, but wide enough to have played defensive end for the Atlanta Falcons.

I met them halfway between the tent and the back of the ambulance.

Fear captured the woman's eyes. "Name's Marie Warren. This is Ron." She didn't waste time shaking hands. "From my information, Deputy Cody Duffy was shot while searching for a lost woman. Can you lead us to him?"

At first I couldn't find my voice and could only nod. I swallowed and, for the moment, the fear went with it.

I led them to the edge of the forest. "I'm Sue Backman. The search party is this way. The sheriff is with him."

We walked single file, with Ron, the defensive end EMT, holding up the rear. Bill's voice resonated over Marie's radio with an exact location, and she answered with professionalism. "Ten-four that."

Holding the lantern shoulder high, the arc of light before me allowed a search for nocturnal predators. I caught sight of eyes reflecting the light. Vernon was watching.

Another beam from a lantern waved across the trail ahead of us, and for the moment I forgot Ruthie and Vernon. I responded in kind, signifying an approaching friend to those traveling in darkness.

A deputy with a lantern waved us on. "Cody's this way, took one in the gut. Marie, he's lost a lot of blood."

As we wound our way along a path that ended close to the drop, the group of men stood over the fallen man holding their lanterns close. Bill looked up from kneeling next to his deputy.

Even in the dim light, I could see the worry digging lines on his face. I leaned over him, wishing I could do or say something to assure him his deputy would live.

Deputy Duffy was lying in a puddle of blood, moaning with pain, while Bill pressed what appeared to be his undershirt to his deputy's wound. He spoke to the female EMT with a father's calm. "Now, Marie, it looks a lot worse than it really is."

She stood with palms pressed into her hips. "Bill, let me be the judge of that." She replaced him at Duffy's side and began to dress his wounds. She worked and didn't look Duffy in the eye.

Her voice cracked. "What'd you go and get yourself shot for?" She and Deputy Cody knew each other well. She spoke softly, while she inserted a needle for an IV. Every time Duffy attempted to speak, she shushed him, calling him by name with an intimacy shared only by good friends or lovers.

Bill and his other deputy helped Ron load Duffy onto the gurney, pausing just long enough for Marie to check the intravenous drip. He would be transported via AirEvac to the hospital in Montgomery, only a few minutes travel time by helicopter, but each one crucial.

Ron and Bill pushed the gurney up the path, and each time they jostled him, he groaned and Marie complained. Twice the path narrowed, and Marie was forced to follow, but the second it widened again, she returned to his side. Gusts of swirling wind drowned her words.

Ladies held their skirts down against the wind created by the helicopter waiting in the parking lot. The head of the crew jumped from open doors and grabbed the gurney getting Duffy's status from Marie.

Bill stood beside Duffy. "I'll be along as soon as I can. Now you do everything those doctors and nurses say, or I'm gonna kick your butt when I get there.

Duffy, in turn, even wracked with pain, nodded in Marie's direction. "I'm sure this one's not going to let anything happen to me. At least not until after the wedding."

Bill grinned with a glimmer of tears in his eyes. "Better watch what you say or Marie here's gonna shoot you, and she might not aim so high."

We stood in silence while the helicopter crew loaded Duffy on and closed the door. Bill hung his head. "Damn shame. Cody's the best deputy I've ever had."

I wanted to embrace him and whisper comforting words, but I couldn't. Such an act would spark an explosive trail of gossip that would not soon be extinguished. I was The Reverend's daughter. I must remain righteous. I just stood next to him and prayed.

Bill called to the other deputy. "Get everybody here now. I want a manhunt for the shooter." He pressed the button on the radio attached to his collar. "Carmichael, I want to see Vernon ASAP. Cody's been shot. Probably a rifle and I know Vernon's got his daddy's old Remington. Check out the shack on John's Island."

He got no reply.

SIX

The light of a full moon reflected in the pond as the helicopter's red flashing lights disappeared over the canopy of trees and into the partly cloudy sky.

I touched Bill's hand. "Can you tell us what happened?"

His shoulders sank with his body onto a bench. "Cody and Quixote took point again," he said, his voice wavering. I held the rear. We split at the Y in the path. You know, where the one goes along the pond and the other heads up toward the ranger station?" He pulled a handkerchief from his front pocket and wiped his eyes.

"Quixote lost the scent at the pond. The shot came out of nowhere." He put one hand on each of my shoulders and I thought he was going to collapse into my arms.

Carmichael came down the road on a dead run and ducked under the tent flap and sat next to me. "Jeez, Bill, I can't believe it." He fell silent, dropped his head and closed his eyes. His chin doubled. A second later, his chin was parallel, and his flirtatious gaze fell on me. "Anyway, I've got news. I couldn't find Vernon, but I spoke to Naomi at The Boondocks. She says she saw him out in a boat, fishing. Said the first time she saw him was about nine, and he was still out there when she checked a couple of hours later. Proves he doesn't have the woman." He glanced at me. "I think she walked out on her own. The woman you described seemed independent enough to do such a thing."

"Oh, she's that all right," Bill agreed. He must have seen the disbelief on my face, because he offered up another theory in the next breath. "So maybe it's not Vernon although Naomi seeing him fishing doesn't prove doodly. With the revival and all, this town's swarming with strangers. Someone might have grabbed her, gagged her so she couldn't scream, and hauled her away in a boat. Nobody would've heard it, since outboards aren't allowed in the park." He leaned his head toward Carmichael. "Or Naomi lied to you, Jack, and Vernon's up to his old tricks."

"I don't think so, but just in case, I'll head a search team to the islands first thing in the morning and find him."

"Make sure you ask him to let you have a look at his rifle. See if it's been fired recently." Bill twitched his nose, impatience rising. "Could rule him out as the shooter."

My body trembled, though everyone around me wore perspiration-soaked clothing. "I don't even want to think about what terror he might be inflicting on her." Every effort to stop my tears failed.

Carmichael must have thought I was going to faint, because he grabbed me and helped me back onto the bench. Growing up accustomed to The Reverend's conservative, non-demonstrative ways, I tended to shy away from a stranger's touch, and I cringed with his.

He sat down beside me, too close for my comfort. "Don't you fall apart on us now, Sue. We're going to need your help. Bill's got books of mug shots he'll want you to go through. Maybe you can identify the man you saw sneaking 'round out there." He looked up at Bill. "And I'm sure it's was not Vernon."

At last, something constructive to keep my mind occupied and off whatever was happening to Ruthie. Maternal instincts returned when I heard John Earl calling.

He ran to me and put his arm as far around me as he could "I was worried, Mama."

I hugged him as tight as I could, without squeezing the breath out of him. "I'm all right."

"Is that deputy going to die, Mama?

I couldn't lie. I was tired of sugarcoating life to him. Besides, John Earl knew better than to believe everything was rainbows and cotton candy. After all, he'd survived the divorce better than I. "I don't know. I know the doctors are going to do everything they can to save him."

"Did the man who took Ruthie into the woods shoot him?"

I didn't want to answer his questions, but I couldn't squelch his curiosity. "I'm afraid that man we saw before is very sick."

"You mean he's crazy? I heard some people talking about a crazy man who lives out there." He pointed toward the pond. "They're all scared of him."

Tears collected in my eyes. He appeared to be underwater and created a fear I wouldn't shake for days. I put my head in my hands but, no matter how hard I tried, the tears wouldn't blink away.

Carmichael tried to console John Earl. "I spoke to a woman who knows Vernon Fielding. He was out in a boat fishing tonight and didn't have anything to do with Ms. Palmer's disappearance."

I stared up at him. The gleam in his eye and the tone in his voice left me tingling with suspicion. He was so cocky.

John Earl twisted his mouth and bit on his lip. He swung his leg and the toe of his sandal dug in the grass. "Mama, I heard another lady say she thought Aunt Ruthie didn't love Mr. Palmer anymore and might have wandered off on purpose 'cause she didn't want to see her daddy anymore." He bit his lip again. "Like when you and Daddy stopped living together."

How could somebody that small break a person's heart without even knowing it? I patted my leg and John Earl climbed in my lap. "That lady was just gossiping. Ruthie still loves her daddy, but she's a grown woman and sometimes Mr. Palmer forgets that. But it's not the same as your daddy and me."

I could have recounted plenty of Paul's sins, but John earl didn't need to hear it and neither did Carmichael. His mentioning Paul reminded me of my need to call him and ask what he was doing in Prattville two weeks prior, but Ruthie took priority.

Gladys interrupted. "John Earl is exhausted. Why don't I see if Lee will take us home and we can put this little one to bed?"

John Earl stared at her through half-closed lids. "I'm not a little one, Grandmother, and I want to wait with Mama until they find Aunt Ruthie."

Under different circumstances, I would have taken him to Palmer's myself and put him to bed, but I couldn't leave the park, knowing Ruthie was still out there.

Her whereabouts and what the lunatic was doing to her made me sick. "John Earl, you go with Grandmother. I just need to talk to the sheriff a while."

He stomped one foot and started to complain, when The Reverend approached. "Bill's sending searchers home for now. Says there's too many ways others could get hurt in the dark." He swept John Earl into his arms, promising him a story after a snack and a bath.

I watched them walk toward the car, and then I went to find Bill.

He was standing near his car with Carmichael and the other deputy. The authorities around these parts each had unique rugged good looks. Both had well-worn faces. Carmichael was a few inches shorter and stockier. Bill had a few more gray hairs scattered on his skull.

Bill had nothing new about Ruthie but assured me no news could be good. "There's a better than fifty-fifty chance she's still alive, since we haven't found her body yet."

"What if Vernon wasn't the sweet innocent I'd always thought him to be. And what if he has her out on one of those islands torturing her, or raping her as we speak?" I spat the word and then admonished myself for even entertaining the thought.

Carmichael scoffed and moved an inch closer. "He doesn't. Sue, you've got to stop this. You're gonna drive yourself crazy." His words tickled my ear. "I know this is hard right now, but I guarantee you at least ninety per-cent of folks who want to be found in my park are found within twenty-four hours. And Vernon doesn't have it in him to torture anyone or anything."

His tone smacked of condescension. He threw his arm around my shoulder and pulled me to his chest. He seemed so at ease with the move, as if he knew I wouldn't bolt.

Had my attention to him earlier sent a signal? "Woman on the lookout for a good man," flashing in neon. Followed by, "Try a hug on for size."

I jerked away from him. "Don't ever do that again. With my eyes squinted, my gaze darted from Bill to Carmichael. "Now, are you two supposedly respected members of the community going to do something about Ruthie's safety?"

Carmichael stepped back and Bill took his place. "We're following protocol and we haven't lost anyone out here who didn't want to get lost."

My gaze fell to the grass. "I'm sorry. My emotions are fried. Maybe Ruthie wanted to leave and found her opportunity. I know she wasn't thrilled about coming back for the revival." Strength returned and I looked at both men.

I nodded at Bill. "You remember how it was for Ruthie and me. Being children of church officials, pastor or council members, we were expected to be perfect. Attend every service. Come when called like well-trained animals. Ruthie hated it."

The sigh I released expelled a gaggle of feelings— exhaustion, fear, guilt, and jealousy. I shook my head. "Nope, if Ruthie didn't want to be here, she just wouldn't have shown up. She wouldn't have publicly embarrassed her father. Some lunatic snatched her and has dragged her into the woods. I heard the scream."

Members of the revival congregation huddled around Bill, Carmichael, and me. They fired questions at Bill.

He rapped on the lectern.

"Sheriff, if you think Ruth walked out of here, then what about the scream I heard?"

His patience was low. "I'm figuring it was an animal."

He had an answer for everything, but I was certain what heard was human.

"Ladies and gentlemen, I want to thank you for all your help this evening with our search. Unfortunately, Ms. Palmer has not been located. We are not stopping our efforts for the night. One of my deputies was shot, and I feel continuing the search in the dark would put others in danger." He scanned the crowd. "My advice is to go home and rest for now. The sheriff's department is available to answer any questions. If Ruth Palmer contacts you, tell her to contact us right away."

I couldn't believe how different Bill was from the boy in high school. Pennington Pond was a small state park near a small town in Alabama, but he was no Andy Taylor with that "Aw shucks" attitude. He was all business.

He looked straight at me, and I thought I detected suspicion in his expression. What did he think I was hiding? Did he think I was part of some big conspiracy to help her escape?

Mr. Palmer was suddenly beside me and said something, which, if we'd been playing tennis would have had me point, set, match. "She was seeing someone."

I was flabbergasted. First because I thought he'd gone home with The Reverend, and second because of his bombshell. "She never mentioned anything to me." Why hadn't she said something? I was her best friend. "Who is he?"

Mr. Palmer let out a sigh. "Don't know. The night she arrived in town, she said she was meeting him in Montgomery."

I wanted to discuss this with him longer, but Bill interrupted. "Sue, we need to get going if you're going to try and the guy in the woods by his photo." He took my arm and tugged me away from the dwindling crowd.

"I need to call Gladys and tell her I'll be a while longer."

Bill strolled back toward a gathering of officers while I dialed.

"You on your way?" Gladys asked on the phone.

"No Ma'am. The sheriff has asked me to go back to his office with him to look at photos. He thinks I might be able to identify the man we saw in the woods."

John Earl grabbed the phone from her and came on, asking me when I coming home. I explained where I was going, and how I needed him to be a good boy for his grandmother and go to bed. He agreed with a yawn. "Okay, Mama, and don't worry about Grandmother. I'll take good care of her."

I snapped my fingers when I realized the Taurus was still parked at The Boondocks. I'd just have to retrieve it in the morning.

Bill led me to his vehicle, a metallic red Chevy Tahoe, parked along the road across from the tent. He opened the passenger door and waited for me to swing my legs in before shutting it. Chivalry was alive and kicking in Alabama. I never expected it from little Billy Halvorson.

His head faced forward, eyes on the road, lit by only the headlights. "Let's go over again what happened before you realized Ruth was missing."

I settled into the charcoal leather interior, and stared at the gray hairs on his temples and sideburns. "We left the revival because John Earl needed to pee. He hates those port-a-potties so he started running for the facilities in the old picnic area down by the old piers. We were in the woods maybe two hundred yards past the old boat launch and those piers, when someone touched my arm, and I could swear I heard him whisper my name. Then Ruthie pointed to a pair of eyes watching us. All I saw was a moving shadow. Come to think if it, I'm not even sure it was a man, Bill."

A quick glance and a smile came in my direction. "I sure am glad someone calls me by my name. Every time I hear the word *sheriff,* I look behind me to see if old Ron Cornutt is strolling in, spitting tobacco in the soda can he always carried as a spittoon." He snorted a laugh, but this one was a nervous one, and I was sure he was worried about Deputy Cody. And I hoped for her sake, Ruthie.

He turned the vehicle north onto US 31, to locals known as McQueen Smith. Three miles east, Cobbs Ford Road became Alabama River Parkway, where the Coosa and Tallapoosa rivers joined to form the Alabama. Though blocked by rows of pines and oaks, the muddy river lay just to the south. The headlights showered the dark roadside with dim light and I searched, half hoping to find Ruthie walking there, but also praying not to see her corpse.

A tense silence filled the car while we circled the city of Wetumpka. My window was down and, in the distance, bells from the county courthouse announced the hour. Eleven o'clock. The trip to the Sheriff's office wasted half an hour when I could have been out looking for Ruthie. I didn't care that it was almost the middle of the night.

I wasn't convinced Vernon had her, but someone did. Otherwise, she would've returned my call long ago. I called Lee Palmer's.

Gladys answered.

"Any word?"

"Nothing." Her voice trembled and she was whispering.

"Why are you whispering?"

"Folks showed up at the door saying they needed guidance, so Jedidiah asked them in for an impromptu prayer meeting."

"What about John Earl?"

"Upstairs sound asleep."

"Great. I'll let you know if I here anything. You do the same, okay?"

Gladys agreed and was ready to hang up when I asked, "Mother, is Ruthie's car there?"

"Yes. Why?"

"It means Ranger Carmichael is wrong. She may have left the park, but she hasn't left town. At least not on her own." I said goodbye and promised to be home as soon as I could.

As long as John Earl was safe and not caught up in all the hoopla surrounding Ruthie's kidnapping, I could concentrate on helping Bill find her.

"Bill, Gladys says Ruthie's car is still in the driveway." I waited for a response. "Don't you see? That confirms our theory that she was kidnapped."

We arrived at the Sheriff's station. It claimed its own block on the east end of town and was more modern than those surrounding it. Bill pulled the SUV into a parking space with a metallic sign bearing his title and name. He climbed out and rounded the front end of the car to open the door, again offering his hand to help land me lady-like onto my feet. His hand was warm, but calloused. "All her car in the drive proves is she hasn't left town in it."

A keychain dangled from his belt with what seemed to be fifty keys. He didn't need any of them. The office door opened, and a woman sitting behind a glass wall leaned toward the silver grate in the center and greeted us.

I guessed her to be in her fifties, and a surplus from the previous sheriff's regime. "Before ya'll ask," she said, her voice dripping Deep South but with a modern snip, "I got no update on Cody. Marie's got her cell turned off. Any word on the missing girl?"

"Nothing yet." He patted me on the back, pushing me closer to the grate. "Martha, this is Sue Backman. She's the missing woman's best friend, and we graduated from high school together back in the dark ages. Seems the two women were attending the Methodist revival out at Pennington Pond over by McQueen. Sue and the missing woman took Sue's son out to use the bathroom, and wandered over to the old boat landing and picnic area. Vernon startled them. Ms. Palmer wasn't behind Sue when she returned to the tent and no one's seen her since."

"Pleased to meet you, Sue." She picked up the receiver when the telephone rang, but still spoke to Bill. "What does Jack say to you accusing Vernon?"

Battle of Wills

Bill opened the door to the back offices, and a hall came alive with a flood of blinking fluorescent lights. He called back an answer. "He says he spoke to Naomi over at The Boondocks who claims she saw him fishing on the pond from nine until Jack spoke to her around ten thirty. I'm going to give it another couple of hours, and if Ms. Palmer hasn't reappeared, I'm gonna go out at first light and have a chat with him myself."

Industrial carpet muted our footsteps. A sign straight ahead with arrows pointing in both directions told me Halvorson's office was to the right and the others to the left. We went left.

He pointed toward a standard metal office desk in the first room and cleared the top of manila folders. "This is Cody's office. You can settle in, but despite Jack's belief to the contrary, I see no reason for you to scour over those photos. It's got to be Vernon."

He started out the door, then stopped. "I'll get you some coffee and see if Martha's still hoarding some of Cami's famous sweet rolls." He grinned and patted the front of his shirt. His uniform shirt covered a slight bulge. "Just about fits the bill for late-night snacking. They may not be good for the belly, but they're sure good for what ails you."

He continued down the hall but returned seconds later. "Sorry, they're gone, but I promise you some the minute Cami opens the doors. Now, give me a minute, while I rustle up that article about Vernon's trial. There was an accompanying photo. It'll be a couple of years old, but you should be able to recognize him."

"Bill, I know what Vernon looks like." With a ragged breath, I rolled my shoulders and ran my finger along

88

the injured deputy's desk, absorbing the events of the evening. I didn't know him or his fiancée, but I couldn't help crying over their situation. Marie had made a stalwart attempt at bravery when she first saw Cody lying in a pool of his own blood, but the fear was undeniable. She'd dealt with emergencies; she knew the risks.

I was half listening to Bill ramble on about the trial when I heard the distinct noise of someone rattling file drawers. "Worst crime in the history of county. He was accused of kidnapping a woman as she left The Boondocks and taking her out to one of the islands. Body was never found and he was acquitted. I just know he's guilty."

Another drawer slammed. "Second worse was a domestic dispute between a couple out on County C."

His voice became louder and, when I looked up, he was right behind me. "A guy came home a little late from The Boondocks one night, and his wife was waiting for him with the shotgun. She didn't shoot him, or she'd have been charged with at the least assault with a deadly weapon. She waited in the dark until he got all the way in the house. He must have thought he was home free, sneaking through the door in his sock feet. According to the doc, she knocked him upside the head with the butt of the dang thing."

I started laughing, visualizing this tiny woman I didn't know, striking out with a double-barrel shotgun like it was a baseball bat and hitting a homerun on her husband's skull.

The laugh turned hysterical, until my tears became those of sorrow. He laid a yellowed, news article on the desk in front of me. Vernon was standing next to Bill, wearing what looked like it had been a new suit, shirt, and tie. He stood half a head taller than Bill and he was thinner.

I touched the paper. "I do know I saw him tonight standing across the road from the tent, but I can't swear it was him in the woods."

"You just proved he was in the area though. That makes him a person of interest."

"I don't want to get an innocent man in trouble, Bill."

His voice boomed with irritation. "Don't you see? He's not innocent, just devious."

Vernon and Ruthie remained in my thoughts despite my exhaustion. I pressed eyelids together trying to squelch any horrific ideas about what she might be suffering from her captor. My feet ached as much as my back, and I sneaked off my shoes, figuring I could sneak them back on in a moment's notice without Bill ever knowing.

He set a mug of coffee on the desk with a sad note, though his words were happy. "You're lucky, you know. Martha made this. Otherwise, you'd be subjected to mine, and that stuff is one level higher than Valvoline."

"Thanks, Bill." I gave a smile the old college try, but to no avail. Nothing to smile about. Ruthie was gone and our one possible kidnapper—if there indeed was one—wasn't the man I'd seen.

The cowbell on the glass front door to the Sheriff's Department tinkled. "Sheriff Bill, you 'round?" The bartender from The Boondocks appeared at the office door and, upon seeing me, she said, "Sorry, didn't know ya'll had visitors."

"Guess I got two now. What can I do ya for, Naomi?" Halvorson sipped his coffee, eyeing the buxom woman over the upper rim of the mug. By the expression in his eyes, he liked what he saw.

"Archie disappeared tonight." She pressed her fists into her hips like I did when exasperated or mad. "And before ya'll go saying anything bad about my Archie, I know he's not the most faithful dog in the kennel."

I tucked my head and snickered under my breath. This woman, Naomi, watched and then joined me. "But even if he goes off with another woman, he's always home before midnight. I just know something's happened to him."

Bill glanced at his watch, then ran four fingers through the crop of thick salt and pepper hair on top of his head, pondering the dilemma. "Great. Now I got two folks missing in a matter of two hours." His finger flung out at me, then Naomi. "Your friend and your husband are making me and this department look bad. On top of that, I got a wounded deputy in the hospital."

He moved back into his office. I slipped on my shoes and followed them into his office. He stared out the one-foot-by-one-foot barred window. Clouds now covered the moon, and I was certain he took note of the starless sky. "Have a seat, Naomi, and I'll be right with you."

He moved to the door and motioned for me to accompany him. "I'll be back in a flash, as soon as I get her statement." He pointed me back in the direction of Duffy's office.

He closed his office door, and I was left to search through a hundred photos of known sex offenders to find a man I'd seen in the dark for no more than a second or two. My stomach growled, and I remembered the sheriff's promise of sweet rolls. I sat back, my eyes closed, weeping and waiting for his return.

I opened my eyes and pulled a wad of partially used tissues from my purse. I dabbed my eyes dry.

Stop sniveling. I reprimanded myself. *Remember what Carmichael said? You don't have time to fall apart.*

I had to keep busy, and searching hundreds of photos for a face I didn't see was futile. So I explored Duffy's office. Shelves lined the walls filled with awards and medals of commendation. I read each one, but the silence begot questions swirling between my ears, starting with Ruthie's disappearance and ending with Paul's appearance in town.

Had she left of her own accord, or not? Did Gladys know that Thomas was in town? Why had Paul been here? Perhaps he'd come to make trouble about custody. If not for Ditzy Debbie, I'd suspect Paul of being the man Ruthie'd come to meet. After all, she'd been one of the few of my friends and family who liked him. But it still didn't make any sense. Why now, and why in a town where people would recognize her?

I lay my head on my arms just to rest. We all know how well that works and, sure as Carter made liver pills, I fell asleep. I saw Ruthie running through the woods, and at first, I thought she was screaming. Then I realized she was laughing. The dream stunned me awake.

SEVEN

A thin wall between the two offices did little to muffle the sound of Bill and Naomi's voices. Naomi was reaming Bill a new one for not jumping out of his chair and beginning an immediate search for Archie. He listened, and then, as he escorted her out, he explained the situation with Ruthie and promised Naomi that Archie's disappearance would be given equal effort.

His chair groaned and Martha knocked. "Bill?" She stepped in, leaving the door open. She whispered something, and then from him came a quiet. "Damn."

Martha walked past the opened door to Duffy's office and gave me the evil eye. I got the message. "What happened to Cody was your friend's fault."

Bill's steps beat out a slow, heavy rhythm against the floor. His breathing was ragged when he came in the room and leaned against the desk. "Cody passed away. Marie's taken the news so badly the doctor had to sedate her."

The desk released his weight with a metallic groan. He made a quick phone call, then turned to me and said, "We have a murder case on top of your friend's possible kidnapping and Archie's disappearance. Let's go."

I slipped back into my shoes and caught up to him. "Where are we going?"

"Back out to Pennington Pond. You could stare at these books 'til next year, and it won't do a bit of good. You said it yourself; you just didn't get a good enough look at the guy. We need to be out at the murder scene collecting evidence. I just called the forensics team. They're going to meet us there."

He said nothing during the ride, but the expression on his face said everything necessary. Concern drew vertical lines deep in his forehead. Another ran perpendicular between his eyebrows. The vehicle came to a stop at the first traffic light, and he squeezed the bridge of his nose. When he closed his eyes, the lids fluttered. These weren't just a deceased deputy and two missing persons to him. They were a friend, a coworker, and someone he'd cared about long ago.

Acid filled my stomach when Bill didn't retrace the same roads to the park, and I wished he'd made it to Sadie's for those doughnuts. "Where are we going now?"

No answer.

"Bill, I demand to know where you're taking me." My voice was steady, but I was trembling. For all I knew, he could be the loon. Hey, I read the newspapers. I watched all those suspense movies in which a seemingly sane cop is really a psychopath. After all, I hadn't seen the man in nineteen years.

He slowed the SUV at the curve, and I recognized the road. We'd entered the park from the south and turned onto the road to the ranger's station. He turned and looked me in the eye. "I want Jack on board with this investigation. He knows the lay of the land. He knows Vernon better than anybody. We also have to consider Jack's theory that Ruth probably walked to the road, got a ride back to Palmer's, and is probably home in Nashville by now, or in Montgomery having a good laugh."

I wanted to scream, 'You could have just said that. You could have called him.' Nevertheless, I didn't. I simply said, "She did not. Her car is still in the driveway at her father's."

"Did it ever occur to you that someone may have picked her up?"

I was too mad to answer. I considered for a fleeting moment making a run for it, when his SUV came to a stop, but I didn't do that either. I'm a mother, a teacher, not a hero. Living in a metropolitan area can alter a person's opinion on the manner in which tasks are completed. I was stuck in no-man's land with a bunch of rednecks in charge.

"Why am I here, Bill?" I didn't wait while he came around the front of the car. I opened the door and stormed toward the Carmichael's door, then waited impatiently for Bill to catch up. In the meantime, I got a better glimpse of the ranger station. It looked to be newly constructed, one and a half stories of hewn pine. Bill opened the door, called the ranger's name, and Carmichael hollered a friendly invitation to come on in.

"Sue, if you'll wait here in the outer office, I need to confer with Jack." Bill met Carmichael in the doorway to the ranger's private office and the two men began whispering. Twice during their brief conversation, both men looked back at me, grinning like two Cheshire cats.

Then Bill pronounced my sentence. "We've agreed that allowing you to go back out in the woods is a bad idea. This is a homicide investigation, as well as a kidnapping, and Lord only knows what's happened to Archie Claremont. Now, since you may be our only eye witness, you may be in danger, so I'm placing you under protective custody. I'm going to call your parents, Sue. Let them know you'll be staying here."

"Bill, I know you mean well, and maybe that's the way you do things here, but I'm a big girl." I stopped myself from pressing the middle of my face together like I was ready to hold my breath until I turned blue. Saying I was a big girl sounded so *little girl.*

He puffed out his chest like some species do when they are showing superiority. "Listen, missy, I could just arrest you."

My tongue clicked a guffaw on the roof of my mouth. "Go ahead, put me in a cell." I was serious, but a smidgen of worry leaked through.

The man's belly jiggled with his laughter. "I will if you don't cooperate." He looked over the top rim of his glasses, just like The Reverend.

"I'm appointing Carmichael here as your guardian. People trust him 'cause he's not the law, but close to it."

Spending extra time with the ranger didn't exactly float my boat. When he grinned, his lips thinned into a flattened 'u' that irritated me for some reason. The man was at least ten years older than I was and acted like he was superior or something.

"I am not leaving the area until we find Ruthie. She's been my best friend all my life." Last year's Christmas card, had arrived, personalized by the printer, and no personal note. "Okay, so Ruthie hid a few details of her life from me. I won't abandon her now, and I don't need a body guard." All the muscles in my body tensed, and

96

as I had several hundred times as a kid in front of my parents, I stood before these men in childish defiance.

Bill stood his ground as well. "I beg to differ."

"You are a condescending…" The memory returned of The Reverend shoving a bar of Ivory Soap in my mouth whenever I spouted out a naughty word so I shut up.

"Now, you listen here, Sue Backman. I am the County Sheriff, and I will not be spoken to in that manner."

My hackles stood erect and I went on the defensive. "Like I said Sheriff"—I spat the word—" I am a grown woman, a mother, a teacher, and I will not be treated like some little girl incapable of knowing how to stay out of danger."

Carmichael stood back, watching our sparring match, pleased with his assignment. "Sue, give it up. Bill thinks everyone is capable of becoming a problem." He looked over at Bill, his grin twisting into a smirk. "Maybe it's 'cause his own kids are a bunch of rapscallions."

Bill leered at Carmichael before he picked up the phone and tried the Palmer residence. I heard The Reverend's voice, groggy from being awakened. The call didn't go well. Bill made attempts at several sentences before The Reverend's anger and frustration came through with thunderous clarity.

I held out my hand. "May I?" Before The Reverend got a second wind, I started. "Sir, for once listen to someone else. The Sheriff thinks I might be in danger too. He thinks I need to be in protective custody. I'm going to cooperate, if only for Ruthie."

The Reverend threw a verbal sucker punch, asking if I had ulterior motives for wanting to spend time with the ranger, noting the looks we'd been sending each other during our earlier meeting. What looks? Was he referring to the ones I sent Carmichael out of pure disbelief?

I wanted to tell him exactly what I thought of my jailer, but unfortunately, the man was standing right beside me. My anger aimed at Bill earlier didn't compare to what I released on my father. "How dare you? I don't know what you think you saw, but you're way off base. I'm doing this for Ruthie. Vernon took her and I'm going to do everything I can to help the sheriff and the ranger find her. As always, you accuse me of some wrong doing without knowing the facts." I snapped the phone on its cradle before the Reverend had a chance to respond.

"Guess you're stuck with me for the rest of the night, Ranger, Sir. If I go back to the Palmer's house now, I risk the verbal thrashing of a lifetime for speaking to him that way."

That easy laugh Carmichael possessed echoed throughout the station. "What wrong-doing are you accused of?"

My face turned fifty shades of red before I answered. The words erupted from my mouth with disgust. "Flirting with you."

Bill chuckled. "Good, I'm glad to know I haven't gotten too old to recognize the signs when I see them."

I stared in disbelief and laughed. "You're just as cocky and mistaken as he is," I said wagging my finger at Bill. Then I heard Gladys whispering from somewhere in my brain, quoting Shakespeare incorrectly. "Methinks the lady doth protest too much."

Who was protesting? I planned to escape this custody as soon as the man turned his back.

EIGHT

Carmichael and I walked Bill to the Tahoe. I dragged the toe of my filthy sling in soft mud. "You really think the forensics guys can find anything tonight?"

"Sure, they'll set up a tent with lights over the area where Cody was shot and go over with every available piece of equipment they have. At sun-up, I'll call Cal over in Autauga County and Bryce in Montgomery to send their K-9 units." He shook his head. "'Course by then, Ruth could be in Florida."

Carmichael snapped his fingers. "Think its time to call in the FBI, Bill?"

Bill nodded. "And, Jack, I'm sticking both disappearances in the same file. Just too coincidental for me that they happened the same night."

I hadn't mentioned seeing Thomas and had no intention of doing such. Just because he was cozying up to Naomi at the bar earlier didn't mean he'd had a hand in Archie's being out of reach. Naomi had said he could have been with another woman.

Bill shook Carmichael's hand and patted me on the shoulder. "If she's still in Elmore County, Sue, we're gonna find her."

All I could do was stand there, watching him with tears streaming down my cheeks.

"Well, now," Carmichael said behind me, "we're not just going to sit on our fannies while Bill has all the fun.

What say we go have another chat with Naomi, while Bill checks on the crime scene guys?"

Bill winked. "Don't have too much fun." Had he mistaken my distain for Carmichael as attraction, too? Maybe I needed to practice both expressions in front of a mirror.

"Just find Ruthie," I told him.

The headlights on the Tahoe spiraled beams of blu-ish light on trees and the underbrush we used to claim was home to the boogie man, then disappeared around the curve. I jumped when Carmichael tried to put a hand on my back and lead me back toward the cabin. I made certain several feet remained between us. My eyelids came together in a determined squint. "Look, let's get one thing straight. Just because we're going to be spending time alone together, doesn't mean I enjoy your company."

He smirked again. "First, I want you to relax. Second, I apologize for that crack about you flirting with me. Just thought a little humor might help the situation and, frankly, the idea does this old man good."

"Just remember, Ranger Carmichael. I'm out here to cooperate with Bill while he finds Ruthie. Period."

His gaze crowded me, as if he could see right through my effort to uphold a tough exterior. "I don't want to brag, but I know this park better than any of those forensic specialists or any deputy in three coun-ties. I know of paths out here known only to the other person who made them."

"Yeah, well there's a good chance Ruthie, my brother, and I made them." My watch read one thirty a.m.

100

Ruthie'd been missing for more three hours. Bill was right. If she'd wanted to escape the revival, her father, even me, she could've walked back down the path, out of the park, and met he new beau out at the park entrance. But that didn't explain why she'd come back to the revival in the first place.

Carmichael and I began our trek north toward The Boondocks. He carried a battery-powered Coleman lantern shoulder high in front of us. It lit a fifty-foot radius in varying light density. The path along the shore was narrow and muddy so we walked single-file. Birds squawked at the intrusion, and furry creatures scurried away from the illumination.

He led. It's a man thing. He walked a slow, steady pace, scanning the underbrush on either side of the rutted path. "So tell me about Ruthie."

The request came as a welcome relief to the tense silence between us. I gave him information about her. "She's an English Lit professor at Emory University. Last time we talked, she was working on the umpteenth edit of her novel, but that was last summer."

Then I started telling the tale of our history as friends. "I've known her since we were five. Mr. Palmer was on the call committee, which hired The Reverend at the church. We became best friends right away." I let out a gloomy chuckle. "She was always cutting up, getting into trouble. I was the shy, goody-two-shoes. The Reverend had me convinced that if I did anything wrong, I'd go straight to Hell."

Carmichael stopped and aimed the lantern toward me. "I find it hard to believe you ever even thought of doing anything wrong, anyway."

I exhaled disgust at his lascivious humor. "In high school, we'd skip church or youth fellowship to go driving and smoking." I laughed, but only to hide my fear. "We used to sneak her daddy's cigarettes, come here to the pond, and smoke until we were almost sick. I know Mrs. Palmer must have smelled it when we got back to her house, but she never said a word."

He stopped, once again holding the lantern over his head to shine more light on the path ahead.

I stopped behind him, praying he hadn't discovered Ruthie's mutilated body. I tried swallowing the bile taking up residence in my throat. Throwing up now would be so unladylike.

He lowered the lantern but made no move in the direction he'd shined it. If not for the cover of the trees, he wouldn't have needed it at all. The clouds had vacated the sky, and beyond the moon, it was black as onyx. "Sorry. Thought I saw something in the water. Just a branch washed ashore."

I swallowed again and this time the nausea went with it.

"Keep talking."

I'm sure somewhere back in ranger training, he'd learned the art of keeping a person's mind off the reason for traipsing around in the predawn hours, and I appreciated his effort.

"For her eighteenth birthday, our families drove to Montgomery and celebrated at this fancy Italian restaurant. I remember she went to the ladies' room and, seconds later, my brother, Thomas, said he had to go, too. They were gone for a good while, when Mrs. Palmer asked if I would go check on Ruthie." Then

I remembered the outcome. "Maybe I'd better not go on."

"Now, wait a minute, you've got my interest piqued. I'm assuming Thomas didn't really need to go."

What the heck, he'd never meet Thomas, right? I hoped by the time he met Ruthie, he'd have forgotten the story.

"Nope. When I walked into the ladies' room, Ruthie was sitting in the sink, her blouse open and her skirt hiked up to her butt. Thomas' slacks were at his ankles. I'm sure you get the picture." My cheeks grew even hotter than they had been from the night heat.

He laughed aloud. "So what did you do?"

The motor on my mouth revved to Autobahn speed. "The only thing I could think of at the time. I closed the door as quietly as I could, walked right up to Mrs. Palmer, and lied. I told her Ruthie'd started her period and was having trouble with the tampon dispenser. She was about to go help, but I stopped her and explained that she'd borrowed one from me. Thank God she didn't see I hadn't brought a purse along."

Jack stopped when he realized the release of a new fact. "So you have a brother?"

The words slowed to in-town speed. "Thomas James, forty, considered the black sheep of the family. He and my father had a big blowout a few years back, and they haven't spoken more than a few words since."

"So what was it like having your best friend dating your brother?"

My mind warped back. Something about seeing Thomas suddenly didn't sit right. Had he come home to spite our parents or initiate a reunion? Then

103

I remembered Carmichael was waiting for an answer to his question.

I watched his form ahead of me. "Their dating was okay, but when they broke up, all Hell broke loose. Ruthie could be kind of mean-spirited. She knew Thomas loved her; he'd even proposed, but each time, she flattened his heart like the tire on my old bike."

"Oh, she's one of those." He didn't turn around or look back. Maybe he was afraid I'd slug him. He'd already been threatened once.

I wouldn't have anyway; his assessment was correct. "She could be, but Thomas wasn't the easiest person to get along with, either. He hasn't had the easiest life. The Reverend doesn't show emotions well. He didn't hug us a lot as kids, especially Thomas. He never said anything to us, but I think his father may have abused him and his brothers."

An image appeared so clearly, I reached out thinking I could touch it. My skin crawled. "Once, when I walked in on my father as he was shaving, I saw scars on his back. They looked like ones left from a belt or a switch. It explained a lot about the way he treated us."

I saw his shoulders drop and wondered if he was recalling a similar fate. I got my answer. "My grandparents lived with us when I was growing up. Granddaddy was a mean old bastard. I saw plenty of switches." He offered the description without apology. "Did you ever ask your mother about your grandfather?"

"Sure, plenty of times, but she always told me that when and if The Reverend ever wanted me to know, he'd tell me."

Talking about family kept me busy. Ruthie's disappearance got pushed to the back of my mind. "I don't know if it's true or not, but Thomas told me The Reverend's daddy showed up at church one day while he was preaching. Stood at the back of the chapel for the sermon, then turned around and left. I think I remember turning around and seeing an old man, but I'm not sure if I really saw him or if I'm just picturing the story."

Our voices and the light must have alerted Naomi Claremont to our approach. She stood at the railing on the deck at The Boondocks waving with a frantic friendliness. "Ranger Jack, is that you? Can I speak to you for a minute?" She wore the same dress she had worn to the sheriff's office, and the light behind her outlined long, bare, brown legs. She waved a handkerchief a couple of times and then pressed it against her neck.

Carmichael put his hands to his mouth forming a kind of loudspeaker. "Coming, Naomi. I have Sue Backman with me. We'll be over shortly."

The path at this point was little more than a deer run. Carmichael pushed through the underbrush, stopping once in while to hold a limb or bush back to allow me access to the next section of the ever-thinning path. Single rays from the lantern filtered between the upper branches, leaving most of our walkway in shadow. Rusted nails held "No Trespassing" signs to a few of the trees. On a couple, the person who had hung them had added, "Violators will be shot."

My mind raced. Is that what had happened to Ruthie? Had she wandered onto Vernon's territory and gotten herself shot? Couldn't be, Quixote would have found her body, unless Deputy Duffy's shooting precluded the dog picking up her scent. What would happen to Quixote now that her partner was dead? I pictured her lying on the deputy's grave, mourning her loss until she died.

"Vernon has a cabin over there on one of those islands, but he's hardly ever there. He camps on a different island just so no one can find him." Carmichael pointed toward the group of what amounted to dry humps covered with trees and undergrowth rising out of the river, but I didn't see a house.

"Then how did you?"

"What?"

"Where to find him."

A rustling behind us startled us both. Carmichael reached for his side arm, but his hand rested there.

I heard water over rocks. "I don't remember a creek on this side of the pond."

He hopped the rivulet. "Probably just runoff. We got a lot of water with the storms last week. Ground's too saturated to absorb it."

He reached for my hand to help me, but I refused it and slipped, sitting down hard in the center of the temporary creek. I let out a curse when cold water ran over my sore butt, and apologized with my next breath.

Carmichael yanked me up. His index finger touched his lips.

As if I could make a sound. Breathing eluded me. Then he grabbed my arm and pulled me into a squat on the path.

"Don't move."

Yeah. What did he think I was going to do? Jump up and down hollering? "Hey, Mr. Kidnapper, we're over here. Aim that shotgun in this direction." I pulled soaked cotton away from my butt.

A darkened figure of a man climbed out of the bushes and stood over us. The little breath I took caught with an almost silent gasp. I ducked lower behind Carmichael.

NINE

I was ready to bolt away from Ranger Carmichael when the huge man emitted a meek voice. "Ranger Jack, that you?"

The man moved into the ray of light coming from Carmichael's lantern.

Carmichael spoke to the man with a serious gentleness, a side of him I found surprising. "Vernon, you know better than to scare a body like that. Now, come over here and apologize to Mrs. Backman."

An intense glare came from his blue eyes. He didn't want me there. Or he was more scared than I.

"Hi, Sue. Sorry 'bout scaring you." I couldn't remember whether that was the voice I heard or not. All I remembered was being seconds away from having an embarrassingly mistimed bodily function. Maybe I hadn't heard him say my name. Maybe he'd said, "Shoo," instead.

I'm five-six, but I felt dwarfed, sandwiched between the six-foot-four Vernon and Carmichael, a few inches shorter.

Vernon's head was covered in only a few sprigs of brown hair and was as round as the ball atop the newel posts on any number of sweeping staircases in antebellum homes of the Old South. The skin on his bare arms and neck carried a ruddy tan from constant exposure to the intense Alabama sun. He wore a camouflage tee shirt and jeans. His feet were covered with muddy hunting boots. He and I were about the same age.

Acting afraid might give him the upper hand, and I wasn't about to allow that. "Vernon did you see anybody sneaking around the revival camp last night?"

"I was fishing near shore 'bout nine. I saw a man rowing 'cross the pond."

Soft eyes told me he wasn't anyone to arouse fear. I stepped around Carmichael. "Did you see Ruth Palmer with anyone?"

"Nope, not that I recall."

"Well the guy in the boat must have been the same one I saw."

"Why didn't you tell me this earlier?" Carmichael barked.

My heels dug into the muddy path, and I reverted to Defiant Sue. "Because I just remembered it."

Carmichael scowled at Vernon again. "Tell me exactly what you did see, everything you remember, or I'll make you go see Sheriff Halvorson."

Since he was leading, Vernon's attempted escape through the underbrush almost worked, but Carmichael grabbed his arm and spun him. "I'm not kidding, now, Vernon. I've got to go see Naomi Claremont. On the way, you tell me everything you remember about last night." He started toward The Boondocks pushing the man and forcing him to walk.

The woodsman stopped, forcing Carmichael to come to a halt, leaving me wedged between them. Would he strike Carmichael? I ducked to the side and got a strong whiff of Vernon's earthy scent. I suspected he had not bathed in a coon's age.

He touched his chin to his chest. "I don't go near that place. Mr. Archie and his high-faluting friends don't like me hanging 'round."

My interest piqued. "What high-faluting friends, Vernon?"

His shoulders tried to reach his ears. "I don't know; Mr. Roy, two other guys, and Ms. Ruth."

That was the second time someone claimed they'd seen Ruthie in town in the last few months, but I couldn't fathom that she'd be seen with Roy. I thought she hated him.

Carmichael discarded Vernon's claim and made reassurances. "Don't worry, seems Naomi hasn't seen Archie since last night. Betcha she'd fix you some breakfast if you carried the trash out for her."

Vernon glanced back and so did I.

Carmichael flashed a pleased grin at the two of us, knowing he had Vernon hooked.

I wouldn't have missed this for anything. I wanted to hear Vernon's version of the last five hours as much as Carmichael.

When he smiled, years of neglect and abuse from the chewing tobacco, which he stopped every step or two to spit into the underbrush, showed on his teeth. Still, it was an endearing one, but I didn't understand why a man like Carmichael allowed him the freedom to roam the park without restraint.

He began his story again, as we marched up the path winding deeper into the trees. "Well, like I said, I was fishing in my boat out by Royal's Island, taking advantage of the moonlight. Pretty soon I heard somebody row past me toward The Boondocks. Didn't think much

Battle of Wills

of it, since a bunch of us like to fish at night. They bite better then. Anyway, a while later, when I was pulling ashore, somebody came running along. I hunkered down and waited; didn't see or hear nothing else, so I just skedaddled outta there."

He pointed in the direction we were walking. "I was headed home when I seen somebody running this way too, but I'm always seeing them kids out here smoking and drinking and such, so I didn't think much of it." He giggled and I wondered if he meant having sex, or if he knew what that meant.

Carmichael started into him.

Vernon argued it wasn't his job to be on the look out for lost women and pushed his way a few yards off the path.

Carmichael waved his arm. "Vern, calm down." He went to him and patted the man on the back twice. "Just next time, tell me everything up front. Now, come on with us. I know you're hungry."

Vernon shrugged and fell in behind me.

When we reached the shoreline nearest to the island holding The Boondocks, Vernon looked tentative, as if he was waiting for Archie to yell from the opposite shore. Again, Carmichael promised that no harm would come to him if he would just get in the boat and row us over.

With one arm, Vernon flipped one of the boats upright and offered his hand to me. The weathered old boat looked unsafe and I hesitated. "It's okay, Sue. I know 'cause I come around once in a while, and if Archie and those others ain't here, I help Naomi out, fixin' up the boats over in an old shed over on the island."

Carmichael stepped in and sat on the seat at the far end of the boat from me, leaving the middle seat open for Vernon. "Can you describe these other men?"

He climbed in the boat. "I don't know. Two men and Ms. Ruth. I've seen her around lots of times."

Ruthie, what were you up to, I wondered, *and is it what got you into trouble?* Mr. Palmer said she was seeing someone. "You wouldn't happen to remember if Ruth mentioned to anyone that one of them was her boyfriend, would you?"

"No ma'am. I don't get close enough to hear what they're saying.

Carmichael growled, "What about the men?"

Vernon shrank away a few inches. "One's got gray hair, real short. You know, like a soldier. The other's just a regular looking guy, but he's always wearing a suit. Roy's always there with 'em too."

We reached the islet. Vernon climbed out of the boat first and lifted me out as if I were an empty flour sack, and set me on the landing. After Carmichael exited, he raised the boat out of the water and hung it by its end over a piling.

The lights along the path were out so Carmichael led the way, holding the lantern over his head to provide enough light to see.

Vernon pointed through the trees to the boathouse. "Wouldn't suggest going near there, Ma'am. The wood's rotting."

A security lamp provided enough light. Eyeing it, I saw it was just big enough for two rowboats, a medium height person, and whatever supplies they stored there. Waves lapped at its foundation.

We reached the bottom of the stairs at the bar and heard singing. Carmichael stopped. "That woman's got an angel's voice."

Her soprano lilted through the stale night air. It seemed the bar owner/seductress had attended church some time in her past. Naomi was doing a mighty fine rendition of a gospel hymn I hadn't heard in years. The stairs fussed under our weight, and she must have heard us coming because she stopped singing.

The screen door equaled the noise when Carmichael opened it, then it smacked shut.

Void of customers, The Boondocks appeared larger than I remembered from hours ago. The interior was dark and musty from years of cigar and cigarette smoke. Light came from dated copper chandeliers. They threw diagonal shadows across the floor.

Cases of beer and sodas stacked on the top of the bar meant Naomi was stocking up for the next night. She'd swept faded plank flooring, leaving a path of ashes and red dust for us to follow. She was standing around the corner of the bar at the back of the room. "Ranger Carmichael, y'all come on down here. I just put on a fresh pot of coffee.

"Vernon tagged along and wondered if you would exchange chores for one of your famous breakfasts."

Vernon bowed his head in respect, but I caught him sneaking lustful looks of approval at Naomi's lithe movements. I'd seen that same expression on the faces of my male students when one of the girls flaunted her endowments in a tight sweater or jeans.

Naomi was enjoying the attention. She slunk up next to Vernon, hugged him and held both his hands in hers. "I'll fix you a plate of bacon, eggs, grits, and biscuits just the way you like it if you'll put away the beer and soda. You can have seconds, if you haul the trash across the inlet and toss it in the dumpster."

"Be glad to Naomi." The courteous answer came as a surprise. After he pretended to tip a hat, Vernon almost ran through the opening on the bar. The speed with which he stocked the coolers proved this was not the first time he'd taken on the task.

She asked if Carmichael and I wanted the same, and before I could place an order for just one egg, a slice of bacon, and some grits, he burst out with a mighty, "Yes," for the both of us.

While Naomi donned a greasy apron and tended the grill, I wandered around the place giving Carmichael a chance to speak to her in private. Aged wooden chairs with the finish worn off sat upside down on the tables. A plastic bucket and mop waited in the corner, but from the looks of the floor, any attempt to clean it would have been a waste of time.

A hot breeze came off the water and set the hairs on my arms straight up. I'd almost forgotten. Ruthie had been missing for going on four hours. She could have been anywhere. Just not dead, I prayed.

When we were younger, folks had said we shared a spiritual connection similar to twins. Once, I could tell when she was in trouble, but our distance, physical and emotional, left the signal cold. I had hoped spending time with her during the week would prompt a renewal of that connection, but she'd only shown up at the last. I stood at the bank of windows at the back of the bar, closed my eyes, and willed Ruthie to send me one of our signals.

Nothing came, except images of the crouching man and those eyes staring back from the dark. The person I'd seen was smaller, I thought, but I hadn't stuck around long enough to tell for sure.

The sound of coffee dripping into a glass carafe drew me into the present. More than a pound of bacon, separated into thick strips, sizzled, and beside them, a dozen and a half eggs popped. The aroma almost replaced the ubiquitous stench of stale cigarette smoke and booze.

I walked back to the counter, excited to tell Carmichael my latest revelation, but waited so I wouldn't interrupt their conversation.

"Jack, can you speak to Sheriff Bill about Archie being gone?" Every few seconds, the sizzling sound increased, and grease popped when she smashed the bacon into the griddle with a metal spatula. "I mean, what's he planning to do about it? I realize that young woman's missing and all, but isn't Archie just as important?"

He walked behind the counter and helped himself to coffee, then poured a cup for me. Out of the last cooler nearest where he stood, he fetched a pint of half-and-half, and set a wire basket of sugar and its substitutes in front of me. I could see he spent a lot of time here because he knew where things were, but he wasn't Naomi's new boyfriend because Vernon wasn't at all scared of him.

"Bill's made Archie top priority along with Ms. Palmer. He thinks their disappearances might be related." His cheerfulness annoyed me. "I guess my question, Naomi, is what are you going to do?"

Naomi kept to the task at hand, but glanced in his direction. Was it anger or fear? "I already called his sister in Mississippi. She hasn't heard from him for months. Neither has his mama over in Sumter County. Either something terrible's happened to him, or he's run off with another woman and, if that's the case, I'll hunt him down myself." Her expression became stern, and then she looked back at me and giggled with a hint of evil sparkling in her slightly-squinted brown eyes.

Boy, I knew what she meant. When I discovered Paul's affair, I wanted to cut off his…never mind. Mother and all my friends kept insisting I needed to get on with my life without the…I promised myself I wouldn't call Paul that for John Earl's sake.

"Well, unless there's been some shady dealings going on around here like there used to be, I doubt anybody's kidnapped Archie." The ranger interlaced his fingers around the coffee cup and sent Naomi a knowing stare. Then he sent the glare my way. "Or your friend, for that matter. My guess is she decided she wanted to see her friend from Montgomery more that she wanted to stay at the revival."

"Ruthie isn't that deceptive," I retorted. "If she hadn't wanted to come, she'd have just 'fessed up. By the way, Carmichael, you were wrong. Vernon was not the man we encountered in the woods."

He gave me a sort of glare that said, 'you don't know what you're talking about,' similar to the one Paul used when I accused him of the affair with Ditzy Debbie, his bottle-blonde secretary.

Naomi turned and leered. I presumed she was upset about Bill refusing to hurry along the investigation in Archie's departure. Or maybe, she was mad because I had, for a while, thought her cousin, my distant cousin, and her part-time help had kidnapped Ruthie. Truth was, I liked Vernon, and I just didn't want him to be the one. He was such a gentle soul.

Vernon finished the first chore and came around to sit on the stool next to me. The stench of sweat burned my nose and left me with little appetite. His bottom overflowed the stool, but not because of excess fat. Living the way he did, off the land, supplemented by the occasional meal from Naomi, made him lean and muscular.

Naomi served up three plates piled with three eggs on Carmichael's and mine, five on Vernon's. "There isn't any of that funny business going on around here anymore, Jack. Archie quit after Sheriff Bill hauled his butt to jail the last time."

Carmichael shoved a forkful of egg and bacon into his mouth and followed it with a slurp of coffee. "So Vernon's been telling us about some men been meeting here with Roy and Ruth?"

I could swear I caught Naomi scowling at poor Vernon. "They're interested in buying the place, that's all. Roy's threatening that if we don't give it up, he'll go to court and prove there was never a will."

Vernon almost came off the stool. "You won't let him do that, will you, Naomi?"

"Don't know if I can stop him, Vernon. If the will Mama told me about never existed, we're living on this land illegally and so are you." Her sad smile gave away her thoughts. She was as afraid as I was about what would happen to Vernon. "Now, how about finding Archie, Ranger Jack?"

Both men shoveled forks full into their mouths, as though it was the first they had tasted food in months.

Between bites, Carmichael said, "And I'm sure Bill told you, there's nothing we can do if the man's gone off with another woman. You'd have to hire private for that. All he can do is put out a missing person's report. Maybe you should get in touch with Roy."

I picked at my food, half-listening to their conversation. I just kept thinking two people were missing and another dead, yet everyday activities around Pennington Pond continued. Anger rolled in my stomach. I was ready to demand action, when Carmichael's radio buzzed and Bill's voice crackled through.

"We've finished a second search of the area around the pond. I've sent three teams to expand to the rest of the park. I'm going to contact the sheriffs in Autauga County and Montgomery County since The Boondocks actually butts up to both."

A few seconds of static persisted, while Carmichael finished the bite of food in his mouth. Then he pushed a button on his walkie-talkie. "Affirmative. I'm at The Boondocks now. Will meet you at the station in half an hour."

He encompassed his mouth with the paper napkin and pushed the ends together with one hand, wiping toast crumbs from the corners. "Naomi, I'm going to leave Vernon here in your capable hands. Maybe he could shore up the left post on the railing out front. It's leaning a bit. Sue and I have to return to the ranger station to see Bill about the missing woman."

He pushed himself off the stool. "Can you tell me the last time you saw Ruth Palmer?"

She leaned over the bar and allowed Carmichael a glimpse down her blouse. "She came in with two

119

gentlemen just the other night. Comes in here whenever she's in town."

In a wink's time, her demeanor flipped from seductress to one similar to a whiny brat. "Now, you gonna find my Archie?"

Carmichael took a slug of coffee. "I promise."

A second wink and she reverted to a woman with a mile of wiles. She leaned in and kissed him on the cheek and whispered, "Thank you. You've always been good to me."

Watching the exchange, I wondered how well they knew each other. The man had confessed to suffering loneliness.

He stood and slapped Vernon on the back. "You stay here and help Naomi. If you think of anything else that might help us, just come on up to the station. If I'm not there, wait for me."

Vernon nodded. Then he tipped his coffee cup and held it out for Naomi to fill it again. "Don't you worry, Ranger Jack, I'll take good care of her."

Carmichael's long stride took him toward the door, but I hung back. Despite the stench, I leaned close to Vernon. "I saw those 'keep out' signs out there of yours. I don't think they're working."

"Oh, they aren't mine, Ms. Sue. I can't read nor write. Daddy said teaching me anything was a waste, being as I'm so dumb." He hung his head.

The schoolteacher in me wouldn't let the comment pass without encouragement. I took his chin in my hand and forced him to look me in the eye. "I don't think you're dumb, and I think your father was wrong not to teach you. There's a big difference between uneducated and stupid."

A toothy grin spread his mouth across his face, and his green eyes lit up. "You're just saying that to be nice."

Carmichael was waiting at the door. "Sue, we need to get going. Bill's waiting."

He took the stairs two at a time, then lifted the boat off the rail post and plopped it in the water. He held out a hand and helped steady me while I stepped down into the twelve-foot craft. "Thought we'd take the boat across the lake; it's quicker than walking around the point."

He set the oars in the supports and began strong, even strokes.

I almost began barking out words like a coxswain, but I refrained.

He reminded me of those fitness gurus, the ones who can bench-press twice their own weight. Even in the minimal light, I could see he was buff and he knew it. His biceps bulged, straining against his short-sleeved shirt. Good thing he was looking over my shoulder at the far shore and didn't catch me checking him out. Or maybe he had.

"I'd offer you a dollar for your thoughts, but park rangers just don't make that kind of money. The big boys in the national parks make the big bucks." He snickered, but the intensity in his eyes sold him out. He was as worried about Ruthie's safety as I was.

"A while ago Vernon mentioned somebody rowing across the pond. Why didn't you dig for more details? He could know who it was and be covering up for that person, you know."

"Sue, Vernon heard us talking about someone grabbing Ruth. He doesn't know what he's saying half the time. Mostly, he just wants to be left alone. And he isn't in cahoots with anyone on the wrong side of the law."

He was wrong. Vernon Fielding was not a mentally-handicapped man. Carmichael was hiding something, so I took a deep breath and formulated a plan of escape. After all, here we were in the middle of Pennington Pond and this ranger could've been the one who kidnapped Ruthie and had me pegged as his next victim.

If he made a move, I'd jump and swim for it. Of course it was the middle of the night, and I couldn't see a thing. In the end, all I could do was close my eyes, listen to my heart pound against my ribs, and pray.

TEN

Relief came in deep breaths as we rowed to a curve in the pond's west shore. We were only a short trek from the ranger's station. And if Carmichael was Ruthie's kidnapper, he hadn't brought her here. It was too small to hide a live person without The Reverend, Mr. Palmer, or me hearing her before, and surely he wasn't stupid enough to bury her corpse in the immediate area. After all, he couldn't shoot every human half of every K-9 unit.

The boat scraped against the shallow, sandy bottom. Carmichael stepped out and reached for my hand. I refused it. I held the side of the boat, stepped over a seat to the bow, and out onto a dirt landing, worn smooth by years of use. Weak waves lapped at my feet. Frogs croaked before they jumped in a few yards away.

Lights from the station hidden by trees illuminated the two-hundred-yard path. Crickets serenaded, masking the sound of tiny, furry beasts scurrying through the underbrush. The light grew brighter between the trees. We walked around to the only entrance at the front.

"You like living here alone?" I asked, trudging along behind him.

Carmichael didn't miss the sarcasm in my question. I detected pride in his answer. "Suits my needs just fine. Used to be a telegraph relay station." He stopped to open the door and turned to look me in the eye. "Those guys didn't have families either."

His squint and the tone made me queasy. I swallowed a bite of fear hard. *Sue, this is ridiculous. He's a park ranger, trained to prevent forest fires and help in searches of lost people in his park. He is not some crazed killer. Or is he?*

I wasn't about to stay and find out. I spun and ran around the building. I almost reached the road when he grabbed me. I struggled to escape, but he was stronger and dug fingers into my bicep. "Let me go."

He spun me back around and grabbed both arms. "Where the hell do you think you're going?"

"As far away from you as possible." I kept squirming to no avail.

He shook me, and I stood still. We were both breathing hard.

"Listen to me, Ms. Backman, I could possibly be the only person standing between you and Ms. Palmer's kidnapper, so I suggest you march back to the station and sit tight."

"And how do I know you're not the kidnapper?"

He drew close, only inches away. "Are these the eyes you saw?"

"I don't know," I cried. "It was dark and I got scared."

"Then you're just going to have to trust me."

He was right. Begrudgingly, I preceded him back to the station. I stepped through the threshold and took off my shoes again, holding one in each hand, ready to use them as weapons if necessary.

He made no move toward me, except to push me into his office. "Sit. I'll make a fresh pot of coffee while we wait for word from Bill." Intense green eyes glared at me. "Believe me, I don't like babysitting you any more than you like being sat."

He left me alone while he went to the kitchen.

I could have tried another escape but decided he'd just catch up and probably tie me to a chair, or kill me. *That's just silly, Sue. He'd have to explain my death to Bill.*

Instead, I explored the place. I crept out of the office into the living room. An old television sat on built-in shelves, over stuffed with paperbacks by Clancy to Steinbeck, and professional journals dealing with locating missing persons and life-saving techniques.

I chose one written by a former FBI agent and fell into a comfortable leather chair with a rip on the arm. A good whiff told me that something reeked, and I was that something. I was not only wearing the same clothes, I hadn't showered in almost twenty-four hours. I smelled of creek water, The Boondocks, and good old sweat. The soles of my pantyhose were shredded. The hem of my dress, tattered and drenched in mud from falling in the creek, added to my bedraggled appearance. Damp underwear clung to my skin and held the back of my dress in place.

How could I have been so uppity about Vernon? Boy, did I feel like the hypocrite.

Gladys would shake her head in disgust at my bedraggled appearance. I couldn't worry about that now, however. We had a murder, an assumed kidnapping, and a missing person in the span of eight hours. I wasn't about to be pushed into a backseat when it came to finding Ruthie, but I wouldn't be much help in my state of dress, and I needed to get back to John Earl.

"When can I go back to Mr. Palmer's and be with my family?" I called, tucking one leg under the other in an attempt to hide my holy hose and protect his chair from creek water.

"Couldn't say. Bill will make that decision. I would assume not until the danger of your kidnapping is past and we get to the bottom of this." The aroma of fresh coffee filled the cramped space. He returned, carrying a carafe of coffee and two mugs full. He set it on the rough-hewn coffee table, which separated us. Then he sat on the green plaid-upholstered chair with wooden arms.

He became nervous, checking his watch every few seconds. "Bill should've called by now. Could be your friend's turned up." He arose, saying he'd be right back. He went to his office and I heard his machine say he had no messages. He made two calls, but without sneaking over near the door, I couldn't make out his words.

When he returned, he said, "Just talked to Bill. Nothing yet, but they're still searching." He sat back down. "Oh, and he said to tell you he's checking out a lead at The Boondocks. Didn't say if it was Vernon or not." Sarcasm dripped in his voice like sorghum.

I studied his face while I presented a new theory. "So since everyone tells me Ruth has been back in town several times in the past few weeks, what if she and her new fella discovered one of Vernon's stills? Or don't you think Vernon's still making moonshine like his daddy did? I mean after all, not only is it illegal, but after government agents found the still out on one of the islands and shot Roland when he tried to escape, you'd hope Vernon would have learned."

126

He took a sip of coffee and set the mug on the coffee table. "I doubt it. Vernon doesn't have it up here to remember the recipe." He pointed to his temple. Gold flakes in his eyes reflected the incandescent bulb in the desk lamp like amber gems. I almost found it attractive, until I realized those eyes were laughing at me for being such a city slicker. "Too bad too, that kinda stuff goes on all over these forested areas. Sometimes, the recipe for moonshine is a most prized possession a family owns and selling it is the only thing keeping that family from starving to death. If Vernon does the mental capability, then he's got us all fooled."

His last words got me. What if Vernon was smarter than anyone gave him credit for and he was in on Ruth's kidnapping and Cody's murder. I drank my coffee, though it produced enough acid in my empty stomach to fill a car battery. I needed the caffeine to keep me awake. I didn't want to fall asleep in Carmichael's presence. I wasn't sure whom I could trust. Moonlight slinked in through the window. I shifted my weight onto my other leg, and I found my host eyeing my movements with interest. I held the cup in the air. "Good coffee."

His gaze jumped back to my face. "Thanks. It's the one luxury I allow myself." A steady hand lifted the brown ceramic mug to his lips.

I found myself making comparisons between Bill and Carmichael. Bill's mouth fascinated me the way one corner rose when he grinned, like he knew something the rest of us weren't privy to. He'd always been like that: secretive and a little peculiar. Guess that's one of the reasons we always got along. I wished he'd call or come and get me.

Funny what a mind thinks of when its person is exhausted, scared, and hungry. One of the most embarrassing moments in my life withdrew from my memory bank. I let out a sly chuckle I hadn't been able to twenty years ago.

"Are you going to share?"

"It's nothing really. Just remembering times with Ruthie, Bill, and our friends. We spent so many hours of childhood together."

He grinned, waiting for me to reveal my intimate thoughts.

My mind went blank, searching for a different memory, so I was forced to tell him the story. "I was a freshman in high school; the council at our church had put out a call to the conference for an associate pastor. Jim Davis answered, and with him came wife Francis and sons Mike and Mark. Mike was a scoundrel to beat the band, but he had all the charisma to charm fleas off a dog. Back then, the girls had to wear those awful one-pieced P.E. uniforms. Well, one day, when I was walking to the locker room from gym class, Mike ran by and unsnapped my P.E. uniform all the way down, exposing bra, belly, and panties."

I realized what I'd just said, and the way he grinned and nodded told me he was picturing me in my undies. I needed to supplant that image with another quickly.

"See, Bill had been the unspoken leader of the church fellowship group. That is until Mike moved in. Every week he persuaded several of the other guys to participate in some unholy prank."

With each new bit of the tale, I sipped on the coffee. "One time they poured liquid dish soap in each of the church's organ pipes. Well, you can imagine the choir director's surprise when bubbles began emerging as he played 'What a Friend We Have in Jesus.' I'm not sure even Jesus could've saved Mike from the whooping he got for that one."

Carmichael set his cup down, put his head back and released his genuine, easy laugh. "I'll bet you two went head-to-head a few times as strong willed as you are."

Warm embarrassment filled my cheeks again, after what I assumed was a compliment. "Actually, I fell butt over brains for him almost the minute he walked through the gate into our backyard. The Reverend and Gladys had invited his family, the Palmers, and the Halvorsons for a picnic their first night."

I leaned forward, stretched out the tucked leg, now tingling, and set the empty coffee mug on the table next to his.

His eyes locked on my every movement.

"When they arrived, I was practicing handstands, a requirement for gym class that semester. My first couple of attempts landed me flat on my backside. They warranted only mild chuckles from the boys, but during the last, I passed gas in mid air."

"No kidding." He bit his lower lip trying to stifle a torrent of guffaws I knew were waiting to escape.

"Go ahead and laugh. Mike, Bill, and Thomas sure did. They fell to the ground, laughing their heads off. I was mortified. I ran through the house wailing, claiming I was never coming out of my room again. Ruthie followed, swearing she'd get even with them. We were plotting when…"

"Let me guess, hunger got the best of you?"

129

"No, actually, Mike came up to my room and apologized for not only laughing, but at what became the gym uniform incident. Told me it could've happened to anyone, and if I didn't come back down and eat with him, he was going to fill two plates and bring them back up to my room." My eyebrows danced.

Bill walked in, shaking his head and making that same noise Mama made whenever she got angry or disappointed in Tom or me, his tongue ticking against the roof of his mouth. He helped himself to coffee. "Thought I told you two not to have too much fun."

He was right. Ruthie was missing; possibly...I couldn't bear to even think about the alternative. A deputy sheriff was dead, and here I was joking around with a park ranger—a man just half an hour earlier, I'd suspected of being Ruthie's captor. Had to be stress-induced energy.

Bill tossed a bag in my lap. "Jack mentioned your accident, so I stopped by the Palmer's a while ago. Gladys sent you some clean clothes. I'm sure he won't mind if you use the facilities here."

Relieved I didn't have to stay in wet clothes any longer, I opened the bag and found jeans a tee shirt and clean underwear. At least she hadn't sent another dress and a new pair of pantyhose.

Bill handed me my sneakers too. "She said you'd want these, too, since you've been wearing your dress shoes all night." The knife dipped in maternal guilt cranked once more to the left in my heart. "By the way, next time you talk to her apologize for me for scaring her half to death, waking her up like I did.

Carmichael pointed toward the bathroom to the back of the building, and Bill pointed to my damp behind. "So what exactly happened? Did Jack drop you on your butt in the creek?" Carmichael's laugh was just plain annoying; Bill's was almost cute. Reminded me of Eddie Murphy's.

I took what The Reverend referred to as my Peter Pan stance, fists on hips. "For your information, I slipped on a rock trying to jump it. I'd like to see you jump the creek in three-inch heels. Kind of like trying to do handstands."

Bill sent me an apologetic smile. Before I turned and walked into the bathroom, he warned me about hot water being a rare commodity in the Ranger Station, and Carmichael heartily agreed. Sure enough it ran out, and I found myself standing under an ice cold shower. The clean towel I found under the sink was small and scratchy from numerous washings in hard water.

I returned to Carmichael's office, towel in hand, drying my hair.

"That's a first." Bill stared with approval as I entered the room. "I think it's not only the first time a woman's ever used Jack's shower, I'm certain it's the first time one's ever come out of there drying her hair with one of his towels." He twisted his mouth and twitched his eyebrows. "Kinda nice isn't it, Jack? Maybe you ought to think about settling down and getting married."

Yep, that belly laugh was starting to get to me.

"Maybe you ought to, too, Sheriff Single-too-long." Carmichael sneered at him.

He spread a map of the park over the desktop and, after we refilled our coffee cups, we each took a side of the desk and perused it. Carmichael and Bill denoted areas already searched by deputies and police using pushpins for reference points. Bill relayed his theory of Ruthie's departure.

"The way I got it figured, the man you saw probably thought you'd seen some illegal activity over at The Boondocks and wanted to get to the two of you before you could get here or my office. I put in a call to the state police reporting Ruthie and Archie Claremont missing." He went to the kitchen to refill his cup. From there, he called, "I plan to drag the pond and the section of river just downstream, but collecting the equipment to do so could take a couple of days at least."

"Think that's really necessary, Bill?" Carmichael's retort came quickly. I mean, for all we know, the woman walked away from the tent, hiked back into town, got in her car and drove off."

I squinted, then closed my eyes, trying to imagine Ruthie just sneaking off like that. "Have you forgotten? Her car's still at her father's house. Have you spoken to Roy? Maybe the man we saw was one of the two he and Ruth have been hanging around with at The Boondocks. Let's face it, if the rumor is true, the person wanting to by Pennington land or Fielding land is going to have to speak to him or Naomi.

Hazy amebic notions, trying to surface in my frontal lobe threw my stomach for a loop, and I returned to the bathroom. It all happened so fast, I didn't have time to shut the door before I threw up the coffee I'd consumed. Let's face it, the acid in coffee added to my worry? Not a good combination.

Bill followed me asking the usual stupid question.

I was kneeling in front of the stool. "Sure, I'm fine. You think Ruthie's dead at the bottom of the pond, but she isn't. I think Ruthie's only involvement in this land thing is that the guy she's been seeing is part of it." Another bout of nausea brought dry heaves. "Go ahead, drag the damned thing, but you won't find my friend at the bottom. She's too tough to let someone murder her and toss her aside like an old shoe."

He spun.

"Oh, and Bill, I saw Vernon. He was standing across the road while The Reverend was preaching, but he was not the man in the woods. Vernon is huge, couldn't crouch as low as the person who touched my arm. I think. But I only saw him for a nanosecond. Now, I'd sure like to go see my son soon. Hanging out with Ranger Jack isn't my cup of tea." I closed the door after him, washed my face. I searched Carmichael's medicine cabinet for toothpaste and brushed my teeth with my finger. When I walked back into the other room, Bill was gone.

"He didn't mean to upset you, Sue. He's just doing his job."

I'd had it with placations from these two men. "And as for you? You don't have a fricking clue what you're talking about, if you think Ruthie'd just wander off in the night like that. She'd have just not shown up."

Once again, Carmichael attempted to pull me into a safe embrace.

This time, I not only pushed him away, I slapped him. "Don't you get it? I'm not some weak, needy woman who needs a man consoling her every second."

His hands pushed the air toward me as he backed up. "Sorry. I was just trying to tell you I know how you feel."

"How could you? Has your best friend ever been kidnapped?" I waited for him to shake his head. "Then how the hell could you possibly know how I feel?" I screamed, fingers digging into my palms. "Just because I couldn't identify the man we saw from the mug shots doesn't mean he's not still around. He could be anybody. And he could come after me or John Earl at any time. Hell, for all I know, it's you." My eyelids narrowed.

A frown of disappointment at my accusation quickly turned to a quirky smile. "Atta girl—woman—I mean. Get mad, fight with everything you got. That determination will see you through this."

I was not about to get sucked in by his words of encouragement. I wanted to get out of there and away from him. I requested he return me to the Palmer's house, but Carmichael denied my request. "We're going into town, but not to the Palmer's. Too early for that."

Anger swelled. I was not about to be commanded by this ranger who'd just tried to suck me into his embrace, trying to charm me with that smile of his. I started for the door, informing him that I would walk.

"Wait, Sue, hear me out." The keys jangled as he reached for them in his pocket. "We'll go to Sadie's downtown. Cami opens at three a.m. It's the place to go if you want to find out what's happening in these parts. Gossip should be a menu item. It's served all day, every day, along with the best pies in the state. The regulars who gather for breakfast linger on Saturday to discuss town news in great detail."

Carmichael wanted folks to see me in town doing everyday activities with a person of some authority in the area. That way, if I did see the man, or he saw me, he would see I was not hiding.

On the winding roads between the station and town, he pushed the oversized SUV to a comfortable speed just over the limit. Each curve he maneuvered with knowing care, using the few straight-aways to speed up and gain time.

The ranger station sat in a section of the park I had not visited by road for a while. It curved away from the pond and came to a tee at the park's main entrance. The headlights of the Jeep hit a wooden sign in a margin between the lanes for entering and exiting the park.

I listened to his plan as me made our way into town. It reminded me of the line from Shakespeare about method in the madness. I love The Bard's works. Sometimes, I think I should have been the English teacher.

He grew giddy as a school kid with the news. "The retired police chief is always at Sadie's first thing Saturday morning. He'll be able to tell us what's going on with any local police investigation, since he still visits the station every day before he meets his cronies for coffee at the café."

Bill was right. Living in constant solitude left Carmichael in need of a companion. He got so excited about the littlest details.

I wasn't about to get caught in that trap, though, not with my best friend missing. Besides, my nowhere-near perfect marriage to one Paul Backman left me leery of anything long-term.

ELEVEN

For a hundred yards or so the road curved back near the water. The pond was black with pre-dawn darkness, and left me hopeless. Nothing made sense.

The west side of town seemed bound toward the future with big box stores lining the two-lane highway, which led travelers off the interstate. A few miles west, the four-lane narrowed to two and became Main Street.

There, I was surrounded by its past. The sign at the edge of town boasted a population of twenty thousand. As we drove down the street, I remembered the furniture store, the beauty parlor, and the place we sought.

A halo of light from the street lamp fell on a flat wooden sign, its paint peeling from each corner, pointed out the entrance to Sadie's Diner. The place was clean, but showed a lack of interest in the march of time or diet fads. A billboard on the interstate advertised it as serving the best food in four counties. If you liked burgers, barbeque, fried chicken, plus a few other Southern delicacies, Sadie's was the place.

The bell on the door announcing our arrival startled me, still a little gun shy from our adventure in the woods in the predawn hours. It held a hometown charm as though, on purpose, the owners had made no updates for half a century. Blue-checked café curtains covered the front windows to match the baby blue walls on the interior. Original Formica covered the counter and tables.

To my left, a glass domed display held pies, some topped with whipped cream, others with meringue and bottomed with real lard crusts, as advertised on the dulled, raised, yellow and green metal placard on the wall behind the counter, "Just like Sadie Jones made 'em in 1922." The sign included a likeness of Sadie herself. The passage of time had caused the black paint accentuating her heritage to chip, leaving the bent metal face a dull gray, but no one seemed to care.

A slender black man frying eggs and bacon on the same grill surface with a generous dab of what I assumed was real butter hollered, "Order."

The woman behind the counter moved as though hers was the most important job in the world, speaking to each customer as she made her way to the grill. She held two plates while the man filled them with breakfast. She presented them to two customers sitting on stools at the counter next to where I was standing.

I got her name off the blue badge pinned to her apron.

Cami Littleton caught me gazing with lustful hunger at the pies in the glass display. She set a single-sheet, laminated menu on the speckled blue and white countertop. Her voice came through as syrupy as I imaged a few of the pie fillings to be. "Ya'll wanta try one? I got blueberry, strawberry, peach, apple, and pecan." Of the last, she accentuated the long 'e' and the last syllable sounding like a container for vegetables and soup.

"Folks say they're the best in the state, though I doubt anybody 'round these part's ever tested that theory." Her laugh was one of sheer delight. "And don't be worried about calories in my pies. I make sure, when I cut 'em, those little buggers escape." She laughed again, pulling a pen from behind her ear and her check pad from the pocket of her apron.

I ordered a slice of pecan and a cup of coffee.

Carmichael said hello to a few customers and then settled on a stool at the counter. He called out to make it two. I couldn't bring myself to call him Jack. Too intimate after our encounter.

"Good choice." With her eyes on her task, Cami cut a generous slice, and then another while keeping the conversation flowing. "It's my favorite. Just can't get enough of them pecans. I swear I eat half the shipment when they come in from down south. And they show up down south too." She patted her hips and snickered.

Cami leaned on the counter, her deep brown eyes relishing in my enjoyment. I didn't disappoint, releasing a moan of pleasure when the first bite hit my tongue. I was starving and downed the slice in no time. With no other customers needing her immediate attention, she didn't budge until I scooped up every last bite, including every crumb of crust with my finger.

She admitted she'd heard about Ranger Jack's ward but no one could recall a name. "I'm Cami Littleton. The man behind the grill is my husband, Sam, and you are…?

I stuck out my hand and shook hers. "Sue Allgood Backman. Friends call me Sue. My best friend was the one kidnapped out at the pond." I raised my voice toward the last so to stop the whispering from everybody in the place. The last of the crumbs came off my mouth with my index finger and thumb. "So, remind me again how you're related to Sadie?"

She poured a cup of coffee for herself and refilled my mug. Her gaze wandered past me, over my shoulder, taking a quick inventory of tables and booths full of patrons. Each table carried its own bronze-colored carafe of coffee so all must have been content. She resumed leaning on the counter, cupping the mug in both hands. "She was my grandmother. Memaw we called her. When Granddaddy Connie died in World War II, he left Memaw widowed at the age of twenty-five with Mama in diapers. So she took his army pension and bought this place."

One of the beauticians from the shop across the street came in for two sodas to go. While Cami filled two Styrofoam cups with ice and soda she indicated me. "This is Sue. It's her best friend went missing up at the point."

Great, I thought, why not just alert the newspaper. Carmichael had tried to warn me. I spun on the stool to see where he'd gone. He was leaning in a booth speaking to four men. One I assumed to be the former chief of police. The one after Bill's dad.

When I spun around again, the beautician was waiting for her change. Her smile stated how little she cared who I was; she took the sodas and exited without a word.

Cami flapped her arm in the direction of the door. "Don't pay her no mind. Carol gets like that sometimes. Mrs. Forrester's probably coming in later for a bikini wax or a pedicure." She leaned closer. "The old gal is seventy-two, you know. Got some kind of skin condition." She cringed, her jaw tightened, drawing her lips into a disgusted frown as though she had sucked a lemon. She added a shiver for emphasis.

"So, anyway, where was I? Oh yeah, when Memaw fell down the cellar stairs and shattered her hip, some new doctor in Montgomery told her she'd have to give up the diner, and since Naomi—she's my mama—since she already had The Boondocks, Memaw turned this place over to me, and here I am." Her toothy grin returned.

"Don't get me wrong, I wouldn't give it up for anything. I get paid for hearing all the latest gossip and baking pies." Cami slapped her hands together just like my mother did when she was finished rolling dough and needed to brush the flour off her hands.

She grabbed the glass coffee pot from its place under the drip spout and started to pour my cup full for the fourth time, but I moved my hand over it. "I drink one more cup and I'll be awake for three nights running." I paused to slide the cup toward her. "Mostly in the bathroom, if you get my drift."

Time was becoming a precious commodity for Ruthie. I decided direct speech was the best approach. "What have you heard about trying to by up what was Ruby's land?"

"All kinds of rumors 'bout it." She puffed on her cigarette.

"Like what?"

"Like how Cousin Roy is riling everybody up about the will again."

"So you believe John Pennington signed a will giving his slave one hundred acres facing the pond?"

She grabbed the coffee carafe and refilled my cup despite my refusal only a moment ago.

141

I left it untouched.

"Oh yes, Ma'am. That was big news back in the day." Her brown eyes flashed a quizzical glare. "Funny how it got all hushed up when Papa John bought Cyrus from Grandma Elizabeth's family to be his father." She gave me a stern look. "How'd you know about that?"

I almost laughed. "In a way, I'm your..." I tried to figure out the genealogy in my head but I needed one of those charts. "Distant cousin, I guess.

She stepped back and stared twitching her mouth. "Sure, you're Roy's mama's sister's daughter."

My lip twisted in between my teeth and one eye closed. "Virginia is Roy's mother and Gladys is Virginia's sister, so yeah."

Sam and I were out at the pond for the revival three nights running this week. Your little boy stood up defending that bat the last night. Didn't see your husband this year though."

"Paul and I are divorced." My voice dropped to a whisper, though no one sat within five stools of me. I changed the subject and retold the story of the potty trip. "That's where some man tried to grab me."

"Yep, we heard rumors 'bout that first thing this morning when Bart came in." She pointed to the table where Carmichael stood. "One of the men, the really big one Ranger Jack is talking to, is Barton Harris, former Chief of Police. He came in telling 'bout how Mama went to Sheriff Bill saying Daddy'd disappeared last night, but he was busy with your friend's kidnapping and didn't pay her no never mind, so she went over to the police." She sounded out the last word with a long "o."

She cleared away my plate and fork and set them on a lower counter by a deep sink. "She told Bart she was thinking about suing the sheriff's department for their lack of interest especially when she heard about Deputy Duffy dying. I declare, I think somebody out there's gone plumb crazy."

Carmichael joined us at the counter. "Now, Cami, don't be scaring the woman more than she already is. You know as well as I do, your daddy likely ran off to avoid the law catching up to his selling lightning again."

Cami waved a hand in his direction like she was tossing him away. Then she snapped thumb and forefinger of the same hand. "By the way, Jack, Roy was in here a little while ago claiming he saw Vernon rowing toward The Boondocks this morning with two others."

Carmichael chuckled and rolled his eyes at me. "That would have been us." He pointed between the two of us.

The bell over the door jingled, and Cami moved with the older couple to the far end of the counter, and then waited while they settled on stools. The man removed his baseball cap with the logo from a national seed company and set it on the stool beside him, as if it were his most precious possession.

The distraction left me time to wonder why Cousin Roy would have been out at the pond before sun up, but I didn't say anything to Carmichael or Cami. I'd ask the man myself. I took out a five and flattened it on the counter. "How much do I owe you?" I called down to her.

Cami waved the guest check pad in the air. "It's on the house." She looked Carmichael up and down as though sizing him up. "Now, I don't want you letting anything happen to that nice lady, Ranger Jack. Just found out we're kin." She motioned for me to lean close so she could tell me something without him hearing what she said.

"You know, y'all make a mighty fine looking couple." A roar of laughter seemed to start at her waist and emerge from her wide-open mouth. Gold crowns reflected the fluorescent light.

The enormous former Chief of Police everyone called Bart waddled in our direction. "Don't be giving him ideas, Cami Jo. Jack's been doing just fine until now. He doesn't need your matchmaking to mess up his life." Bart nodded in my direction. "No 'fense ma'am." Roly-poly cheeks wanted to swallow laughing eyes the color of the gulf on a seaweed-free day.

"None taken, Sir." I looked in Cami's direction and rolled my eyes. "Believe me, getting hooked up with anyone right now is the last thing on my mind."

She giggled behind her hand.

Carmichael caught up to me and grabbed the door handle just as I did. "Allow me and don't pay them any mind. Cami's been trying to set me up with somebody since I moved here." He stood with the door open, despite Cami's comment about letting out all the cool air. "Don't get me wrong. I miss a woman's company every time I have to walk in that cabin alone, but I just don't think it'd be fair to subject her to the isolation of living so far from town."

"I guess not, but maybe you just haven't found the right woman yet. At least, out at the station, there's nobody nosing around in your business all the time."

"Nope." He wiggled his pursed lips side to side. "There's already enough of that in town."

Before I headed out the door, I leaned in and asked Cami one last question. "Since the courthouse burned, can you think of any other place where there'd be a record of the sale of Twelve Oaks?"

"Memaw told me one time that somebody in the family had a copy, but I'm afraid it's disappeared."

TWELVE

The sun ballooned off the trees into a lemon yellow ball. I made the mistake of staring into it while still chewing on Cami's information, and my eyes watered to tears. I closed them, but the image of the sun still burned against my retina.

When I opened them again, I glanced at Carmichael. A deep vertical line dug into the space between his eyebrows and met horizontal ones the same depth. His lips were pursed in concentration.

"I'd like to go back to the Palmer's and maybe take a nap. Spend a little time with my son." What I really needed to do was get to the park at ten. "But first I need to go to The Boondocks and get my car."

He just kept driving. "I was given strict orders to keep you in custody. If someone did grab Ruthie, then his next logical move would be to come after you. Bill and I discussed the situation and he's afraid you'll do some fool thing like go back out to the point all by yourself."

I took in and released a breath saturated with anger. I was growing weary of his arrogance. "I'll be fine. My mother, The Reverend, and Mr. Palmer will see to it. I won't leave the house. I promise." I held up three fingers. "I'm perfectly capable of taking care of myself. And I'll handle Bill, so don't worry. I'll tell him I threatened you if you didn't take me to John Earl."

He turned a corner so fast the tires squealed, and I knew he was not happy with my decision. I suspected an ulterior motive. After all, he had already complained about the loneliness, and he'd attempted physical contact. He didn't say a word while he dropped me off by the Taurus, but I could tell he was fuming. The tires on his Jeep spit gravel at me.

An orange early morning sun illuminated the front porch decked out with rail boxes filled with geraniums across Palmer's house was like a smile welcoming me home. Lee Palmer's car was not in the driveway. I found The Reverend in the study and asked him about Mr. Palmer's absence.

"Lee's in a relationship with the widow Linden, and I believe they are out posting flyers with Ruth Ann's picture in some of the neighboring towns."

At this hour? but I didn't say it to The Reverend. Let him keep believing the man is one step away from sainthood. "Good, at least he's not moping around in this house with all its reminders of Ruthie and Mrs. Palmer."

The Reverend hummed agreement the way he did when he was busy and didn't want to be disturbed any longer. The pages in his Bible crinkled with his turning them.

I was sure The Reverend didn't want to speak to me about Mrs. Linden and Mr. Palmer since I was sure their relationship had stirred up a batter of new gossip. I wondered if Ruthie knew. If she did, she probably liked the idea of her father stirring up trouble.

She'd done plenty of that as a kid. When we met, Ruthie had a mop of curly red hair she hated. So, when we were eight, she convinced me to cut it to within an

148

inch of its life. I thought Mrs. Palmer was going to have a coronary when she saw Ruthie's beautiful curls heaped on their bathroom floor. I was certain she was going to banish me from the house and forbid me from speaking to Ruthie ever again. Not Mrs. Palmer; she always forgave and forgot, no matter what mischief Ruthie and I invented.

Ruthie didn't date much in high school. Or, at least that's what she'd told me. She'd always said she liked the money she earned babysitting. And when she wasn't watching someone's children, she was with me. We spent so much time together in school, one boy in our class called us lesbians, and even though at the time I didn't know what it meant, I'd punched him anyway.

Later, I found out that she'd attended several parties and had dated several guys without her parent's knowledge—or mine. Then she'd had the gall to use me as her alibi. She'd told me not to look for her in Heaven because St. Peter wouldn't approve some of the things she'd done.

I wondered if she was up to her old tricks. I realized I was crying. What if some of those things had gotten her into serious trouble? What if I never saw her again? Never heard her quirky laugh?

A nasty case of heartburn told me this all had something to do with Cami's tale of our extended family, but what?

The front screen door sprang open, ending my disturbing venture down memory lane. Gladys headed my way with arms outstretched, but John Earl came around her and ran to me first.

149

"I missed you, Mama. Where you been all night?" Those giant brown eyes showed bright with question and concern. "And why hasn't Aunt Ruthie come home yet? She promised me that, after the revival was done, she'd take me fishing out on the lake."

Kneeling, I scooped him up in my arms and fought with everything I had to dam the waterworks. "We think maybe she ran away." I hated lying, but I was not about to scare him any more than the man at the point already had. "How would you like it if I take you fishing instead? Just you and me, the catfish, and a can of worms. But you gotta promise to take a little nap first."

John Earl almost burst with laughter. "You don't know how to fish, Mama."

I stood and pressed my fists into my hips. "I'll have you know, your great-uncle Daniel taught Thomas and me to fish when I was about your age. Just because I haven't done it in a while doesn't mean I can't."

When I looked up, away from my son's face, my father's stern stare met me from the porch. His voice stole my smile. How different he was from his brother. Uncle Daniel had always laughed and told jokes. "I just received a telephone call from the ranger. He told me not to allow you or John Earl out of my sight."

I remained standing where I was with my fists pressing hard against my hipbones. "What Ranger Jack Carmichael doesn't know won't hurt any of us. I'm not about to let some— "I'd almost said "crazed lunatic," but I didn't want to rouse John Earl's curiosity "—other man's disappearance scare me. And we don't know what happened to Ruthie." I made a quick nod toward John Earl. "So let's not assume the worst."

When he asked what I meant, I whispered to him that I would explain later.

The Reverend's soft-soled shoes made little noise across the wood porch. The screen door slammed. I was sure he'd returned to the house for some research into scripture he could spew to persuade me not to go fishing. In his own always prim and proper way, he was worried about John Earl and me.

Gladys came out for a few minutes and sat next to me in the soft grass warmed by the morning sun. Her maternal instinct switch remained on at all times. "You and John Earl are going to need a slathering of sunscreen if you plan to spend the afternoon down by the pond. And bug spray. Maybe Jedidiah should go along just in case."

"We'll be fine, Mother." Her hand was outstretched in the grass and I reached for it.

John Earl promised to make us lunch, querying on what kind we wanted. "Come on, Mama, you can help. That way we can get out to the pond quicker." He grabbed my hand and tugged until I stood and followed.

We made a half dozen each of tomato with mayonnaise, and peanut butter and jelly. When I asked why so many, he said we could use some for bait, or snacking. He cut off the crust and we jammed them into a plastic sandwich bag. "Daddy says bread balls make the best bait."

He scrambled off the stool he'd been kneeling on at the counter and went to fetch Mama and The Reverend for lunch. Peanut butter and jelly stuck to the roof and sides of his mouth while he complained about desserts at the Palmer's house. He swallowed the remainders of

151

the impairing sandwich. "Mr. Palmer's only got store-bought cookies. Somebody needs to make him some." Then he proceeded to gobble up three of those store-bought cookies.

"Sue, John Earl hasn't slept much. Don't you think fishing could wait?"

John Earl stood beside me, tears welling and his bottom lip protruding in a pronounced pout.

"We'll both take a short nap and then we'll go."

He tried his best to convince me he didn't need a nap to fish, but he could not dissuade me.

"Nap or no fishing."

He agreed but hung his head low. It bounced on his neck with each step. I could hear footsteps stomping up the stairs on the thick Persian runner.

I called for my parents, making my way across the polished oak floor running the length of the house. I found both The Reverend and her in the study.

"Mother, how much do you know family history?"

Her stare gave me the willies. Was she ashamed of the family? "Why?"

"Cami, Naomi's daughter, owns the diner downtown, and she was filling me in on the unofficial branch of the family tree. Did great-great-great granddaddy John bed one of his slaves?" I gave her a minute to react. She didn't.

Instead, the Reverend stood. "That's just a nasty rumor started by town folk jealous of the Pennington money. I won't have anymore said of this subject."

"Actually, Jedidiah, I've heard that story too," Mama said.

He would have nothing of it. He returned the discussion to the matter at hand, John Earl's and my safety. His Bible, pages loose from years of use and abuse, remained open on the desk. He stood over the desk pointing to the open Bible lying there. "Read this, Sue, and recite it while you and my grandson are out of mine or the sheriff's reach."

The verses he chose were the first two of Psalm 59. "Deliver me from my enemies, O my God, protect me from those who rise up against me, deliver me from those who work evil, and save me from bloodthirsty men."

"Daddy, I promise nothing is going to happen." I didn't slip into that little girl thing I usually did when speaking to him. "I'm taking John Earl to the dock on the north side of the lake. Do you really think I'd take him anywhere near The Boondocks?" My conscience screamed, "Liar."

Relief swept over my parents' faces.

After I went to see whoever it was with information about Ruthie, I knew of a special spot for the best fishing halfway around the point. Besides, what could happen in the middle of a gorgeous July afternoon?

* * *

I couldn't sleep, but John Earl slept a good two hours.

While I was upstairs lying beside him, Gladys and The Reverend had a soft, but lively discussion about Pennington/Fielding family history.

By the time I went down to the study, Gladys returned to the worrywart I knew and loved. She said John Earl's exhaustion from worrying about me the night before was a sign from God saying we shouldn't risk going back out to the pond.

John Earl came dashing down the stairs. His puppy dog frown almost brought me to tears when I suggested we postpone, and I would go back to search for Ruthie alone.

"Come on, Mama. I'll protect you from that bad man." He put up his fists the way a professional pugilist did at the beginning of a fight.

Gladys stood behind him, watching me and waiting for my reply. When I looked to her for guidance, she just shrugged and smiled.

As Ernest and Julio Gallo would say, "Thanks for your support."

I ignored the warning. I had to. I had to meet the mystery caller. What had been a scoop of orange sherbet sun hidden by storm clouds became a lemon drop in a pure azure sky. John Earl and I packed up two rods and the bread balls in the car. "You must be excited about going fishing. It'll be the first time in a year."

He kept his eyes fixed straight ahead, climbing in and buckling up. "No it won't, Mama. Daddy and I came down here the last time it was his weekend." He turned toward me and stared as if I should know this. "We met Aunt Ruthie at that really good hot dog place in Montgomery."

I started the car and pulled out of the drive, steadying my voice so I wouldn't sound surprised or startled. "And what did y'all talk about?"

"Daddy and Aunt Ruthie did most of the talking. Something about her building a house near here."

I didn't press the subject because I didn't want to worry him or have him think he had done something wrong. We rode the rest of the way in silence. A cool wind blew in one car window and out the other and raised goose bumps on my bare arms, until we arrived at our destination.

We'd be safe, I reassured myself. With search teams combing the area, the kidnappers would have to be pretty stupid to remain in the area.

The Reverend would call Bill the minute Mother told him where we were headed. Soon, every member of law enforcement in Elmore and Autauga Counties would be on the lookout for the Taurus. I wasn't ready to be found, so I didn't pull into the parking space in the lot. I followed the signs to the new boat launch. I unhooked the chain across the service road entrance and pulled in as far as I could. Kudzu drooping from the tree branches camouflaged the car.

John Earl asked why I didn't just park in the parking lot. "Daddy, Ruthie, and Pawpaw would have."

I explained to him how much time parking where I had would save for fishing in the special spot I wanted to show him.

He accepted the explanation but dragged behind, looking for frogs, while lugging the fishing pole we found in Palmer's garage, his bait, and tackle box. "Mama, you sure you know where you're going?"

"Yes, I'm sure. I've been here many times." We stood on the incline of the concrete boat launch, turned right, and headed toward familiar territory. We made our own path for the first hundred yards, following the curve of the shoreline. Straight ahead, waves slapped the muddy shore, while a green heron remained a statue until we moved close.

We both jumped at the movement. Instinct made me reach for John Earl.

He pointed at the ascending bird. "Just a giant bird. Looks kinda like a pterodactyl, doesn't he, Mama?"

I watched him fly to a nearby island and alight where he assumed his pose.

Two hawks soared on the morning air, backed by clouds, moments away from bursting with rain. They must have been searching for prey. There must have been plenty of tiny, furry creatures to be had on the islands captured by the flood.

I fixed my gaze on The Boondocks. It appeared to be sleeping after a rough night. Levered windows, opened the previous evening, were shut tight. How surprised I'd been to find Thomas there. Questions about a possible relationship with Naomi coiled around all the others snaking through my brain, including ones concerning Ruthie's and Archie's disappearances. Intuition told me the two were tangled together.

John Earl and I dipped our lines in the muddy water and waited. Daylight shrouded with storm clouds transformed the surface of the dark pond to pewter. It glinted on a shiny object about ten feet off shore.

As a child and a PK—Preacher's Kid—I'd learned tricks of subversion used to tease Thomas, such as making small undetectable movements. I glanced over at John Earl. Once convinced he was concentrating on the hawks, I cast my line toward the object and reeled it in.

What I hooked brought gurgling to my gut. Ruthie's handbag, a clutch really, soaked through with muddy Pennington Pond. Bill needed to see it right away, but I didn't want to alarm John Earl so I tucked it down the back of my jean shorts and baited my hook again.

The sound of Bach's "Jesu, Joy of Man's Desiring" coming from my pocket signaled a call on my cell. No caller ID just meant it wasn't Gladys, Paul, or the school.

"I thought I told you to come alone."

Before I could respond I heard, "Sue, you gotta come and find me."

Ruthie's voice trembled with terror and was barely audible.

"Where are you?" I didn't say her name so John Earl wouldn't get excited.

"I don't know. Someone grabbed me last night from behind, blindfolded me, and dragged me to a boat. He threw me in and rowed for a while. I don't know how long. Then he dragged me out and threw me in a car." She was breathing into the phone. "Oh no, he's back.

And as quickly as she had come on the other end of the line she was gone.

John Earl ran past me, back to where the path widened and led back to the car.

"John Earl we need to go. Now."

Silence.

I ran in the direction he'd headed. "John Earl Backman, you answer me."

"Shh." He grabbed my arm and tugged until I squatted alongside him, tucking Ruthie's clutch deeper in my pants. My gaze scanned the underbrush for the crouching man.

157

John Earl pointed toward the pond. "Somebody in a boat and it's coming this way."

It was aimed toward the deepest part of the pond. A dark figure lifting oars, throwing them into air so thick you could ring it out like a wet shirt. Then down again they went into choppy waves.

At first, I thought it might be Vernon, but he'd hunched when he sat on the barstool next to me earlier. Unless it was an act to get people to pity him, all the while carrying out devious acts like kidnapping and other things too horrific to consider. The person in the boat sat tall, rowing with even, strong strokes, obviously an old hand at it.

Several yards in front of us, the rowing stopped.

John Earl squeezed his eyes shut. "Is it a man or a woman?"

I craned my neck long to get a better view. "Can't tell; whoever it is, is facing the other way. They've got on baggy raingear and a hat." My drumming heart caught in my gullet. The jacket looked identical to the one Thomas had been wearing at The Boondocks, but the distance was too great to be certain.

John Earl stood up just as the person in the boat pushed a large bundle over the side. The splash threw water up the side of the tiny boat and then the bundle sank, sending silent ripples over the black lake disturbed by rain drops.

The unnamed person threw his or her head to the left, then the right, peering over a shoulder in our direction. I couldn't make out a face under the hood. Then the figure turned again and began reverse strokes toward the far side of the lake.

It was my turn to pull John Earl back to the safety of the underbrush. "Stay perfectly still."

I don't think either one of us inhaled, until we no longer heard the sound of the oars slapping the water.

I sprang up with a jerk. Another boat passed the rowboat, and its driver waved at the person in the boat. His cap gave him away as a local I'd seen at The Boondocks the previous evening. This was our chance to escape undetected. Then I decided I didn't want to escape. "Grab the stuff and let's go." I took several steps toward the path.

"Where we going, Mama?" John Earl grabbed the unused tackle and pole and followed me.

"To visit a friend." I waited for him to get in front of me and hustled him back to the car.

We threw the fishing gear in the trunk and, after a slightly treacherous time getting out of the car's hiding place, we were pulling out of the parking lot and curving along the road around the point toward The Boondocks.

"Granddaddy and Grandmother aren't going to like it when I tell them we came here."

I turned off the engine and turned my shoulders in his direction. "Who says you have to tell them?" Any cheer remaining in my tone dropped. "Listen, John Earl, Aunt Ruthie is missing, probably kidnapped, and if we leave it up to that sheriff, well I'm afraid we'll never see her again. The lady at The Boondocks knows something about everything that goes on in and around her place. I think it's time we had a chat."

I took Ruthie's clutch out of the back of my pants and tossed it over the seat into the back while John

Earl seat-belted himself in. Bill would get to see it soon enough and I could tell him about the call.

The gravel parking lot across the road from boat ramp used by The Boondocks customers was empty. Naomi might not even be there. Frustration began to seep in.

John Earl jumped out as soon as the car stopped. "I'll row across." Always good to have a willing male around.

I couldn't stop a tiny snicker when he tried flipping the boat. Instead, he dragged it to the water's edge and looked up at me in disgust. "You gonna give me a hand or you gonna just stand there laughing?"

I serious-upped and helped him flip the boat to its bottom in a way that gave him the impression he was doing most of the work.

I'll give him credit, the young man gave it the old second-grade try to row, but the oar was just too heavy for him. With a little help from me, we traversed the twenty-yard strait to Boondocks Island. I lifted him out of the boat and followed.

We were about ten yards in when I thought I heard footsteps behind us. I spun pushing John Earl behind me. "You stay back and don't say a word."

The person following us made no attempt to mask the sound of acorns and pinecones crackling underfoot.

I decided to sound brave, even if my heart was fluttering and I was sweating a cold sweat. "Whoever you are, be assured I have a gun and I know how to use it."

John Earl pushed against my legs so hard I thought I might topple forward.

Vernon stepped out of the shadows. "No need, Ms. Sue. I don't aim to harm you." He smiled, then spit a wad of tobacco on the ground.

I rested my hand against my chest until my heart slowed to normal pace. "Vernon, you just shouldn't sneak up on a person. Especially these day."

He hung his head and mumbled, "Sorry."

John Earl tilted his heard around me and stared at Vernon. "Are you gonna hurt us, Mister?"

I scooped him up in my arms and hugged him, but he refused to take his gaze off Vernon.

"This is my friend, Vernon, John Earl. He won't hurt you."

Still unsure, John Earl clung.

"I swear on the Bible, I won't hurt you." He put one hand out as though placing it on a Bible in court and raised the other palm out. "My name's Vernon Fielding, what's yours?" He reached for John Earl's hand.

My young son gathered his courage, clambered out of my grasp, grabbed the man's hand and shook. "John Earl Backman, Sir. Do you know where my Aunt Ruthie is?"

"No I don't, John, and I've been to every island on the pond and down river."

I've always been a proponent of believing someone who looks you in the eye, and Vernon's gaze never wavered from John Earl. "We were headed to The Boondocks to speak to Naomi. See if she's heard anything. You're welcome to come along."

Vernon shook his head. "No need. Naomi isn't there. I just saw her putting some stuff in the boathouse, then that man came and she drove away with him."

Disappointed and perplexed, I took John Earl's hand and started back to the spot where we left the little boat.

161

Vernon followed.

"Do you remember what the man looked like, or what kind of car it was?"

"Sure, I've seen the man 'round plenty of times. Every time he comes to town, he and Naomi go into Montgomery."

Thomas? "Does he have brown hair like mine, longer, over the collar?"

"No. This man has light hair. Color of John Earl's." He anticipated the next question and answered it before I asked. "He was driving one of those fancy sports cars. Porsche I think." I must have stared in disbelief because he chuckled and said, "Ranger Jack lets me borrow his car magazines. He's teaching me all about them. I love Porsches and Lamborghinis, but Mustangs are my all time favorite. Ranger Jack let me drive his once before he sold it."

John Earl stared at him with a quizzical look. "You can't read?"

"Never learned. Daddy said it wouldn't do me no good anyhow, living out here on the pond."

"Cool, you live here in the park?"

Vernon grinned as though someone had presented him with a great compliment. "All my life."

It was my turn. "Vernon, who supports you?"

I was his turn to look quizzical. "I don't know what you mean."

"I mean who supplies the money for food, clothing, and such?"

"Aunt Virginia." Another grin. "She gives it to Naomi and she buys clothes. I just eat at The Boondocks when Archie and now Tom aren't around."

162

"Tom isn't mean to you, is he?" I was getting mad at Thomas and I'd only seen him for a few minutes in twenty-years.

"He doesn't like me coming round when he's there. Told me he's on some secret mission." He put his hand to his mouth away from John Earl like he was going to divulge some top government secret. "He treats me like I'm John's age, but I know what's going on. He's sweet on Naomi."

I needed to assess the information Vernon had provided, but first, I wanted to get a look inside the boathouse for any clue what Naomi had left there. As we approached, I asked Vernon if he had a key.

"Oh, it ain't locked. Wouldn't help anyway. That old thing's about to fall down."

Vernon was right, the latch had held a padlock at one time, but the rusty thing just hung there. The doors swung open with a teeth-gritting screech. Clouded sunlight on the interior revealed numerous rowboats in varied stages of disrepair with a few better looking ones toward the front.

"One last question, Vernon, then John Earl and I need to go before Bill and the entire sheriff's department arrive to arrest us."

He tilted his head and frowned, questioning, but I didn't explain. Instead, I asked, "Did you see someone rowing across the pond earlier and dump something in the water?"

"No, Ma'am. I was visiting Ranger Jack before I saw you heading here."

He was lying and I wasn't sure why, until I watched him row toward another island. He was hunched over the oars, so he wasn't the person rowing earlier, but he was surely protecting that person.

The most horrific thought I'd had since Ruthie's disappearance occurred to me. I grabbed John Earl's hand and we headed for the car.

"Where we going now, Mama?"

"Back to the house. I'm going to drop you off and then I need to speak to the Sheriff."

THIRTEEN

I was shocked not to find an army of police and deputies surrounding the car when we returned to it. I opened the trunk and took the fishing rods and tackle from John Earl. We climbed into the car and for a few minutes, we said nothing.

"What'd you want to tell me, Mama?"

His innocent voice grated my nerves. How could I explain what had happened to his honorary aunt without scaring him? I started slowly. "John Earl, you remember I said someone had kidnapped Aunt Ruthie? Do you know what that means?"

"Sure, it's when somebody takes somebody else without their permission. One of the kids in the fourth grade got kidnapped by his father." He spoke with the same calm he used when doing his spelling.

My heart thumped one hard pump against my chest. Okay, now for the tough part. "Well, Aunt Ruthie has been kidnapped."

I waited for a reaction, a question, but John Earl sat mute, mulling over what I had just said. "Also another man is missing too."

"Mama, do you think the same person took Aunt Ruthie and the other man, too? And do you think the man who grabbed your arm took them? Is he the same person we just saw in the rowboat?" Fear lengthened his face. "Or is it Vernon?"

"I'm not sure yet, John Earl." I started the car and pulled the purse from out of my waistband. "This is Aunt Ruthie's, and Sheriff Halvorson needs to see it."

He begged me to let him go with me, but I refused. For a while, he sat, arms crossed over his chest, fuming. His lips tightened into an angry circle, but soon he calmed down, and filled my head with questions.

I could supply few answers. Suspicions about the parcel dropped in the lake floated around my cranium, but I was not ready to speak of them. I didn't even turn off the ignition in the driveway. "I want you to go in and tell your grandparents where I've gone, but don't tell them where we went or about the purse. Can you keep a secret?"

He nodded, glaring in my direction, hoping I'd change my mind. The ploy often worked, but I didn't have time to deal with him and, even at seven, I think he understood. He climbed out, slamming the door behind him.

I made sure he went in before I pulled away from the house. I was halfway out of the driveway when he came rushing back out of the house waving an umbrella in the air. I opened the window and took it.

"Grandmother said you're going to need this real soon." I watched him run back inside, telling God I'd do anything to protect him.

Then I sped toward the sheriff's office with my news. Every five seconds I checked the rearview mirror, certain The Reverend was following and would pull me over, demanding I return to Palmer's.

Dollops of rain began to splash the windshield and came with more frequency a few blocks from downtown.

The clouds cracked open when I opened the car door. I made a mental note to thank Mother. At least I wouldn't again appear the drowning puppy in front of Bill. The blue umbrella popped open and I hurried up concrete stairs, past a bare flagpole, and through two sets of electronic doors.

I was headed into his office when Martha's words of warning came through the grate in her window. "I wouldn't go in there for all the tea in China. Ranger Jack is off searching for you. Bill and Bart are in there waiting for your father to call, saying you and your son have returned home safe."

I thanked her for the warning and walked into the office. I recognized the chief of Police filling the chair across from Bill's desk. "I hear there's an APB out for me and my son." I dropped the purse on the desk.

Bill tried to act mad, but the worry lines around his eyes gave him away. He masked a sigh of relief with a cough. "Sue, what kind of lame-brained idea is going off to the pond with John Earl? And what the hell is this?"

"I took him fishing." It was not an apology but a statement of fact. "Look, you can yell at me later, but I have news. We had quite the morning. First, I found this floating in the water near the point." I nodded at the purse on his desk. "It's Ruthie's. For a moment, I waffled about telling him the other part, but decided it was time. "Second, she called. And third, we saw somebody drop something big enough to be a body over the side of a rowboat in the middle of the pond."

He motioned for me to take the extra chair. "You, sit and start talking."

167

I repeated every detail I could from Ruthie's call, her tone, and the person in the boat with the heavy load.

Bill leaned forward in his chair with his forearms resting on the desk. "All of that furthers our suspicion of a murderer and a kidnapper on the loose. If he thinks you can ID him, Ruthie's as good as dead, and you and your entire family are in extreme danger."

He pointed a stubby finger at me and shook it. "Now, I'm going to call your father. Tell him I've put you in protective custody again, and Chief here's putting a man on round-the-clock watch until this lunatic is caught."

He sat and slumped with his forearms resting on the desk. He stared at me, and his eyes gave him away. He was mostly scared. "Off the record, why didn't you ask me? I'd have been glad to take you and John Earl fishing. After we find Ruthie, I'll take you two to my favorite spot." He sent one of his silly sideways grins, and I knew the anger and fear had faded. "There's a little hidden cove across the river between two islands. Best place in Alabama for striped bass."

Bart Harris snickered. "Think I'll be going now that the emergency has been averted. I'll just leave the door open so Martha doesn't get the wrong idea and go telling everybody ya'll were doing something improper during his shift." He snickered and pointed at Bill. "You need any help, you know where to find me."

Bill shot him a dirty look, crumpled a note, and tossed it across the room.

Martha's voice came through the static in the speaker on Bill's desk. "Sheriff, the suspect is being released. I need your signature."

He rose, and the light from the barred window hit the creases in his uniform. It never dawned on me that he hadn't slept or showered since Ruthie disappeared. Guess he cared after all. He grabbed the bag and took it with him.

I'd been waiting an hour for Bill to return to his office when my phone rang. I didn't know who or what to expect. Was it Ruthie again? Maybe her kidnapper again with more instructions. I pulled it out and flipped it open.

"Mama, when are you coming home? I miss you." John Earl's squeaky voice faded.

Before I could answer him or reassure him, Paul's bass blasted across the connection. Great, just what I needed, the ex stirred in the mix. "Your father called me, Sue. Told me about Ruthie and the possible danger you were in. I think it best, and The Reverend agrees, that I should take Johnny for a while."

"Don't you dare. I'll be right there."

I shut my eyes, reeling from the words and the anger rising within me. The last thing I needed was Paul. I wanted to know how he'd gotten there so fast, but I didn't ask. He'd probably never left the area, just waiting for an excuse to take John Earl. A notion snaked its way into my thoughts, but I dismissed it. He wouldn't.

I went in search of Bill to tell him I was going back to Palmer's.

He was standing in the outer office speaking to a group of men. Bill nodded, acknowledging my presence and held up one finger. "I can't hold him any longer, but remind him not leave the area. I may have more questions later."

169

One of his deputies nodded, and we all watched him disappear down the corridor toward the cells.

I squeaked Bill's name.

All four men turned in unison, similar to a team of synchronized swimmers.

"Have you arrested someone in Ruthie's kidnapping case?"

Bill took my arm and walked me away from the others. "Could only detain him. Seems he has an alibi."

"I need to get to the Palmer's ASAP. My asshole of an ex-husband wants to take John Earl." I shoved my cell phone in my front pocket. "Well?" My hand came forward, palm up. "You can drive faster legally with your siren and lights on. He is breaking the law, after all. I have full custody."

He started toward the door. "What are we waiting for?"

This time, I didn't give my protector the chance to open my door. I ran to the Crown Vic, climbed in, and fastened my seat belt. "Hurry, please. Paul'd think nothing of just lying to my folks, telling John Earl I said it was okay to take him, and go." Tears formed in the corners of my eyes as I glanced over at him. "If he does, I may never see my son again."

Bill sped, lights flashing on the dashboard, and sirens screaming. He ran two red traffic lights and released a quiet curse swerving to miss an elderly couple crossing a street.

When we approached the house, I recalled how much I once loved the Palmer's with its red brick exterior. Its arched covered porch always seemed to be inviting me in. Now it held nothing but my fear for Ruthie, and my escaping ability to hold onto my son.

A clearing sky did nothing to brighten my state of mind. The Reverend would side with Paul. Past disputes proved the men always agreed, and whether right or wrong, assumed each knew what was best for John Earl and me. It escaped reason why either believed it gave him the right.

Mother would weigh both options with her usual thoughtfulness. I prayed she would understand my conviction that a boy John Earl's age needed to stay near his mother. I added in for God to remind her of the threat Paul had made after the custody hearing to avenge the pain he'd claimed I'd dealt him. Somehow he'd forgotten my suffering his two affairs. Okay, I'd had one, too, but on the scoreboard, he was up two to one.

Urgency weighed heavy in the car. Breaths came in short spurts, an attempt to calm my accelerated heartbeat thumping behind my uvula. Still, Bill didn't break the silence. The several block drive from the station dragged on.

When we rounded the corner, the drama I dreaded as much as finding out some harm had come to Ruthie was taking stage in front of the house.

Paul's 4Runner was parked askew at the curb in front of the house. He'd obviously been in a hurry, trying to avoid confrontation with me. He was helping John Earl into the back seat.

Bill pulled the car around in front of Paul's vehicle, preventing him from driving away without backing up.

I jumped before he put it in park. "Hold it, Paul."

John Earl climbed out of the seat, ran around his father's legs and into my arms. "Mama, Daddy says it's his turn to have me now, but I don't want to go with him. You need me with you."

I stifled a snicker. Then anger swelled again. "You heard him. He's staying here with me." Through our years of marriage, I could count on one hand the number of times I'd spoken up against Paul, and I don't think, for the moment, he knew how to react.

He gathered his gumption and approached. He would have grabbed John Earl and run, but Bill stepped forward, flashed his badge and Paul stopped. "You haven't even been here to look after him, Sue." His whining grated. "You've been off gallivanting with the sheriff here." He ran a mocking gaze over Bill's tan uniform. "Or that fancy-dressed park ranger your father told me about."

To Bill's credit, the lawman stood his ground. I doubted Bill Halvorson backed down from anyone these days. Why would he at six-foot-three, and sturdy as stone?

"Look, Mr. Backman, there's no need for insults. I'm just doing my job. Your wife may have seen the man we believed killed one of my deputies and kidnapped Ruthie Palmer. I appointed the ranger to guard her and that's all either of us has done."

Oh, to be a little girl again, and get away with sticking my tongue out at my ex, adding a raspberry for emphasis. But I had to be the adult here. Paul certainly wasn't. He was prepared to defy my full custody rights and take John Earl, by force if necessary. I wasn't about to let that happen.

"Wait a minute, Paul. The Reverend would've had to have called you before dawn for you to get here now, and he wouldn't have known then that Bill was going to put me in Carmichael's custody." I moved to within inches of him. "Are you following us?"

Slick as a weasel, the man presented a logical answer. "I had business in the area and I was in Montgomery when your father called my cell."

I glared, thinking of ways to get the truth out of him until the strangest of all things happened, for that moment at least. Then it dawned on me; he fit Vernon's description of the man in the rowboat. But the vehicle was different. Could the sports car have belonged to Naomi?

A pickup truck I didn't recognize pulled up behind Paul's. The door opened and Thomas emerged from the driver's side, wearing a short-sleeved tee shirt with a screen-printing of a German Shepherd on the front, and large oval sweat stains under the arms. If Thomas was in on Ruthie's kidnapping, and it was Ruthie's body John Earl and I saw thrown out of the rowboat, he wouldn't have been the one in the boat. One thing I remembered about Thomas; he hated rowing. In fact, he wasn't all that fond of water at all.

He grabbed Paul by the arm and spun him so that the two men stood face-to-face, inches from each other. "I think it's time you go home, Backman. I'm not going to let anything happen to John Earl or Sue."

Paul yanked his arm out of Thomas' grasp and rubbed it.

Thomas caught Paul's chin with a right uppercut.

Paul touched the wound with the back of his hand, withdrew it, and stared at his own spilt blood for a split second.

I'm always amazed at how much head wounds bleed, considering there is little but skin and skull.

John Earl hid his face in my shoulder.

Paul took a swing at Thomas, but my brother was ready for it, leaned back just far enough so the fist just missed landing a blow on his cheek.

Thomas punched Paul in the gut.

Paul fell to the ground in obvious pain. Yes, my ex is a wuss.

Thomas leaned forward, ready to grab Paul by the collar, but Paul slid away and then rose to his feet. He dusted the dirt from his jeans.

Bill never made a move to stop the scuffle. He just stood back, wiggling his mouth to keep from grinning.

Paul rubbed his chin. "I'll go, but I'll be back with a court order giving me temporary custody of Johnny. No judge in the state will deny my request when I explain how you've put my son in mortal danger."

Satisfied of his safety, John Earl climbed down. He clung to my leg, squeezing his face into a defiant frown.

I stood with Thomas and Bill on either side. "Go ahead; try it," I said. "Guess I'll just have to tell that judge how you tried to kidnap your own son while I wasn't here."

We all watched while he backed up enough to maneuver around the vehicles and drive away. My wonderful ex-husband would go off somewhere to lick his wounds like an animal, but his return was eminent.

174

I hoped Bill and Thomas were around to protect the little guy from his bastard father then.

"Mama, why is daddy so mad?" John Earl stared up at me, innocent and still scared. "And who is that man?" He pointed to his uncle.

"It's okay now, John Earl. Nobody's going to take you away." I nodded toward Thomas. "This is your Uncle Thomas. Guess you two have never met before."

Thomas knelt to John Earl's level and shook his hand. "It's nice to finally meet you. I've heard some pretty neat things about you."

John Earl beamed. "You fight real good."

Bill stuck out his hand to Thomas. "Sorry about this morning, but you were a person of interest."

"Don't worry about it, Bill. Sure isn't the first time I've seen the inside of a jail cell."

I stared at Bill. "Is Thomas the man I heard you talking about back at the station? You arrested him?" I tried not to laugh. "You actually think he's somehow involved with Ruthie's disappearance?"

"I didn't arrest him; I only detained him for questioning. Sales records showed he owns a Remington." He tilted his head to the left, face crooked with forlorn. "See this anonymous tip came in early this morning. Someone claiming they'd seen a woman fitting Ruthie's description at The Boondocks Friday night. I suspected Ruth had put two and two together about him and Naomi, and they decided to get rid of her and Archie."

"What changed your mind?"

"Information from those other two men in the office earlier." The little lines deepened around his eyes, which told me he wasn't going to say any more, but he continued. "One was a from the forensics lab. Tests confirm the shell that killed Cody came from a rifle made before 1970."

"I told him mine is probably still in The Reverend's basement." Thomas was gloating. "He didn't have any other evidence so he had to spring me."

I moved my questioning gaze to Thomas. "How'd you know to come here, now?"

"I knew there'd be trouble. I saw Paul a couple of days ago. Thought he might cause trouble knowing you'd be back in town for the revival. I thought you might welcome the back up." He wrapped his arm around my waist and tugged me close. "Remember, I'm the one who warned you about marrying him in the first place."

"Don't remind me."

I wanted to ream The Reverend a new one, but I found out he was out with Mr. Palmer searching for Ruthie. Chicken. He knew Paul was on the way, but he didn't want to be here for the fireworks.

Gladys wrung her hands. "You know how he is. He told me he didn't think it was right you exposing John Earl to your activities with the ranger or sheriff. Honestly, I think he was hoping you would turn to Paul for comfort and perhaps reconcile."

I wanted to scream, curse, bang my head against a wall, but I knew it'd do no good. The Reverend would never change. "It'll never happen, Mother. You know I wouldn't take that slime bucket back if he came crawling on his hands and knees. For your peace of mind, my activities with Carmichael included a visit to The Boondocks to ask Naomi Claremont a few questions, and then to Sadie's to meet with the former police chief. Bill and I have spent little time in his office with his receptionist right outside. That's all. Despite Paul's innuendoes, there's nothing going on between us."

Bill turned to John Earl. "What can you tell me about the boat or the person in it?"

John Earl twitched his mouth back and forth, while he thought about the question. "The bottom half of the boat was dark...black or green...well mostly, anyway. The top half was white. I think it was wood because part was kinda gray, like a lot of the paint was peeled off." He squinted, thinking hard. "But it could have been aluminum. The person was wearing a dark blue rain jacket with the hood pulled up." He looked up at me, looking for assurance that he had done well.

I smiled and winked. "Better description than I could've offered."

"I'll get a couple of deputies on it right away." He started for the gate. "Sue, can you remember hearing any strange noises in the background when Ruth called?"

I chewed my lip while considering the question. "Maybe an airplane or a big rig? Hope that helps."

His smile reassured me they'd find her alive. The small amount of hours of afternoon and evening sunlight remaining afforded him a more hours to search the woods again and he would speak to Vernon again. "Also, got a crew coming from Montgomery to drag the pond."

Thomas frowned, sending me a silent, "What's that all about? You keeping tabs on Bill now?"

I just smiled. I wasn't even sure yet. Whenever he was around, I felt safe.

Gladys and I moved inside. "Forget Bill Halvorson. What's this about speaking to Ruthie?"

A check outside assured me that John Earl was out of earshot. "While John Earl and I were out fishing, she called." I fell into her arms. "Mother, she sounded terrified."

She patted my back. "Let's give thanks that she's alive and pray that Bill finds her before that crazy man decides he's had enough." She glanced at a clock inside a rooster on the wall. "Your father and Lee will surely be home soon. I think fried chicken for supper would be just right."

Thomas wanted to take John Earl to the backyard to play and get to know him, but I told them that John Earl needed a nap first. He protested, saying he'd already had one earlier, so I gave in and told him to at least go up and try to rest a while. Thomas said he would go with him and promised he'd stick around for a little while. I knew he wanted to avoid The Reverend.

So while Gladys gathered buttermilk, flour, and her secret seasonings, I pulled two frying hens out of the fridge. She poured buttermilk in a bowl and flour on a plate. "Okay, it's time you knew. My secret ingredient all these years has been Lawry's Seasoned Salt." She shook some on the flour and tossed it with a fork.

I heard John Earl call and Thomas said he'd go to him, giving Gladys and me a few minutes alone. "How'd you know Thomas was in town? I thought The Reverend forbade any contact with him."

178

"Thomas called me about a year after he left home. He was broke, unemployed, and living with some girl. He wasn't ready to set the past right with The Reverend, but he asked me to forgive his supposed sins. I just couldn't throw my son out like a bag of garbage, though Jedidiah insisted it was for the best."

She chopped up the chickens into pieces, then soaked them in the milk. Next, she dredged them in the flour mixture and laid six in hot oil in a black iron skillet.

"I can't wait to see The Reverend's reaction when we tell him about how Thomas kicked Paul's butt. Or Lee's when I tell him I'd spoken to Ruthie."

Gladys forked each chicken piece, and the oil crackled and spit when she turned them. "You can't tell him that Thomas was here. I'll never hear the end of it."

I couldn't deny her request to protect her or Thomas. After all, I'd done the same thing for him the night before.

Even with all my persuasiveness, Thomas refused to stick around long enough to see the old man, but promised John Earl he would play a while.

Mama returned to her spot at the window over the sink. A yellow bulb in the porch light sent a warm glow over the area. "I pray every night for The Reverend to forgive Thomas and his rebellion." Sadness echoed in her voice. "But your father is a proud man."

I joined her. "Don't I know it."

She put her arm around me. "Someday maybe he'll be able to talk about his past. It explains a lot."

John Earl came slopping in the back door, every exposed inch covered in mud. Beneath a layer of caked Alabama red clay, I could see his eyes twinkle, his nose wiggle as though preparing for a sneeze, and a toothy smile. "We made a mud slide. Uncle Thomas told me ya'll used to do the same when you were my age."

Thomas stood in the doorway laughing, until Mother sent him one of her looks. She played the part of the meek minister's wife most of the time, but a person in her path should be advised to avoid her anger at all costs. Sort of like the Martian from "My Favorite Martian" who shouted, "Danger, danger," warning the humans.

The boy took only one step off the mat by the back door before I stopped him. "Hold it right there, young man. You're going to strip down here and have a bath before dinner."

He let out a loud, "Aww, Mama. Do I have to?"

Amused by the situation he'd caused, Thomas let out a guffaw. "Better do what she says, Johnny. I've see her when she's really mad, and you just don't want to." He glanced at his own mother, still riled. "Kind of like her mother."

That got him another one of Mother's stares, and a gentle slap on the arm.

Clean pink skin appeared from underneath John Earl's tee shirt and shorts. Then he scooted between Mother and me, and we heard stairs creaking from his weight. He got to the top before calling back, "You gotta help, Mama. You know you won't let me turn on the hot water by myself."

"Be right there." I turned to Thomas now picking at a piece of hot chicken on the oblong patter. "Stay for a while. We need to talk." I tried to duplicate Mother's formidable gaze, but failed at the attempt.

Mother found some of Ruthie's bubble bath and, soon, John Earl was creating the Appalachians in bubbles. He pushed a little boat around the water, making motor noises between pursed lips.

I was oblivious. I replayed the confrontation with Paul and Thomas' sudden appearance. Another fight with Paul appeared inevitable, until Ruthie was found and this nightmare came to an end.

And eating at the back of my thoughts was the Pennington family tree. What was I missing?

And Ruthie. She'd sounded weak and terrified. I couldn't imagine what she might be suffering at the hands of Deputy Duffy's killer. He was the same man she and I had seen in the woods. Was he the same person who tossed the bundle over the side of the boat? It had all happened so fast. Was I wrong? Was Thomas that person?

He cleared his throat, alerting me to his presence. He leaned against the doorjamb and winked. He looked so natural standing there, like he'd been a regular part of the family, instead of the missing black sheep.

I laughed.

"What?"

"Just reminds me of when we were little and Mother used to make us take a bath together."

He rolled his eyes, then snarled, "Like we needed to conserve water or something. I hated being put in there with a girl, especially my sister."

I let out a nasal chuckle. "You were what, nine? I was five. What difference did it make?"

"None, I guess. It wasn't so bad, except when Uncle Dan babysat us. He used to make fun of my...." He stopped, embarrassed at his inability to say the word. Even at our ages, neither of us could just say penis to each other.

My anger sifted through. I didn't understand it, but I had to consider John Earl, so I stepped out in the hall where I could continue without impressionable ears eavesdropping, getting the wrong idea about his uncle. Despite my misgivings, I didn't want to sully Thomas in John Earl's eyes, but time was passing, and Ruthie was still out there somewhere at the hands of a murderer.

"Thomas, I need to ask you something." I searched his face for reluctance. "Did you have anything to do with Ruthie's disappearance? I mean I know you've been vindicated of killing Duffy, but if you know anything you've got to tell Bill."

His dark glare made me quiver.

With a sudden jerk, he spun and descended the staircase, two at a time. Without saying goodnight to the folks, he exited the house into the waxing evening, just as he had eighteen years before.

I didn't understand his differences with The Reverend then; I just knew he'd been coming home drunk every night, picking fights, and keeping me awake. I'd been a senior in high school and trying to keep up the grades, so I would be accepted to Auburn with Ruthie.

I'd been too young then, too wrapped up in my own little environment, to understand Thomas' pain.

The Reverend couldn't understand it either. It seemed, from his point of view, the world was white or black, good or evil. It wasn't possible for a good man to lapse into what he considered debauchery, if only for a short time, and then realize his mistakes. Thomas had surrendered to the devil, and The Reverend's solution was throwing prayer and scripture at it to keep it from invading one's life.

But Thomas wasn't evil, then or now. I needed to believe it. I should've gone after him that night back in 1987, when he stormed out of the house on Chestnut Street, with a gym bag containing all his precious belongings slung over his shoulder.

I should've gone after him minutes ago, too. After all, he'd rescued my son from his father's clutches.

I owed him. How could I have suspected him of harming Ruthie? He'd loved her once.

John Earl came into the hall dripping, wrapped in a towel. "Where'd Uncle Thomas go? He promised he'd read part of *The Three Musketeers* to me."

A single tear trickled down my cheek. "He had to go." Again. Sadness swelled with the possibility of never seeing him again.

"Why, Mama?"

My reverie ended, and I turned to find John Earl staring up at me, waiting for an answer. "I wish I could explain it so you could understand."

"I'd understand. I'm not a baby anymore."

"Your uncle used to be a great baseball player. Even won a State Baseball All-Star Trophy for pitching a no-hitter in the final game of the state championship. I think if he'd gone straight to college instead of choosing the Army, he might have gone on to the Major Leagues."

"Why couldn't he have done both?"

He was moving into territory even I didn't understand, so I fudged. "It just wasn't the right time or place, I guess. The country was in the middle of the Vietnam conflict, and we needed every able-bodied man the US could spare. He must have felt pressure to serve."

Had he left because The Reverend pressured him to choose the conscientious objector status, so he wouldn't break the seventeenth commandment?

My answer to John Earl's question about Thomas' sudden departure placated him, because he scooted off to the bedroom we shared while visiting for the revival. It'd been Ruthie's room when she was a girl. He hated all the girly things. Antiqued furniture, including frilly twin beds, filled the pink room. He dressed in a clean pair of gym shorts and a fresh tee shirt.

I studied the room while he dressed. Its familiarity increased the heartache of Ruthie's kidnapping and her possible fate until it overwhelmed me. I'd spent the better part of my high school years in that room, gossiping about other girls and dreaming about the boys.

I crumpled to the floor and wept.

John Earl slipped his young arms around me and rocked me as I had him so many times. "It'll be all right, Mama. Uncle Thomas promised me he'd visit us again. Oh, yeah, I remember something else. Right before Daddy got here, I saw a truck like Uncle Thomas' drive by the house."

I ran down the stairs and got Thomas' cell number from Gladys. "John Earl said he saw you drive by the house early this morning." I held the phone with my ear and picked at my cuticles.

184

"Yeah, so."

I took the phone and shouted, "Thomas, what's going on?"

"Just be careful, Suz. There's stuff going on you need to steer clear off." He hung up.

FOURTEEN

I sat on the floor in Ruthie's bedroom and cried until I slept. When I awoke, the sun was gone. We'd finished dinner hours ago, and still The Reverend and Mr. Palmer hadn't returned. Ruthie was still missing. I refused to open my eyes, until I head John Earl's voice.

"Mama, it's gonna be all right."

Gladys stood in the bedroom doorway watching John Earl patting me. Tears washed away the face powder from her cheeks and pooled it at her chin. She had a way of shedding tears, void of red blotches around her eyes or her cheeks, the traveling make up being the only evidence a tear had been shed.

She fascinated me. She was never without a handkerchief. In winter she tucked it in her sleeve; in summer, in her waistband or pants pocket. Gladys Mae Allgood wouldn't be caught dead in shorts.

Now, she dabbed her lower eyelid with such a delicate touch, she never disturbed her minimal eye makeup. Then it dawned on me. How stupid, wasting time thinking about her crying ability while Ruthie was missing, and if Bill's suspicions were true, John Earl's and my lives could be in danger.

She stepped into the room and moved around to the other side of the low bed. A wet curl stuck to John Earl's forehead and she swept it back. "Uncle Thomas said he was going out on his own search for Aunt Ruthie, but told me to tell you he hadn't forgotten his promise to read to you."

Gladys could alter the mood in the room with her presence. Her voice skipped in, a cool breeze on an evening like the one shaping up outside. "I came up to see if ya'll were up for a dish of vanilla ice cream for dessert?"

John Earl shot out of my lap and ran past her. "Ya'll coming? I'm starving." I called after him, but John Earl's bare feet had already taken him down the stairs and into the kitchen.

I searched Gladys' eyes for answers.

"There's nothing more you can do for Ruthie tonight. I'm sure if your father, Bill or that ranger had heard anything they would have called. They're doing everything they can." Gladys put her arm around my waist, laughing. "Now you heard; let's not leave the man waiting. He'll starve to death for sure. A dish of ice cream never hurt a tired child's ability to sleep. Besides, I had an ulterior motive. I don't get to see you two enough any more."

John Earl had the container out on the counter, scoop in hand, waiting for one of us to dish. He started to complain when I stopped at two scoops, but I believe the boy had sense enough not to push my buttons.

We took our treat on the back screen porch. Fireflies blinked, and a single cricket serenaded us from somewhere past the sandbox. The waning moon appeared behind stringy clouds, a beacon of protection in Palmer's backyard. If not for the evil happenings the night before at Pennington Pond, the town would be at peace.

My mind wandered away from the calm of the back-yard. The same questions still weighed heavily. Since my gut feeling about a person was rarely wrong, and Vernon was innocent, why would anyone else want to kidnap Ruthie, especially Thomas? What connections, if any, existed between Thomas, Ruthie's and Archie's disappearances, the man in the woods, and the man in the rowboat? Were they all one in the same? Maybe I was way off base, and it was Vernon or just some maniacal killer, hiding under the guise of a revival attendee.

I felt a weight pushing against my side, and I pulled away.

John Earl was leaning against me, his mouth open wide with a noisy yawn.

"That's it, young man, you've had all the excitement a seven-year-old needs in one day."

For once in his short life, he didn't argue.

John Earl was already in bed when Gladys and I stepped into Ruthie's room. We watched him fall into slumber, but his mouth was taut.

I smoothed the hair away from his face. "I know he's worried about Paul returning and mad because Thomas left without reading."

"He'll be fine, Sue. He's too young for all that."

I shook my head. "No he's not, Mother. Too many times Paul told him he'd bring him a gift from whatever city he was visiting that week but never came through. Now the man thinks John Earl should just go with him no questions asked. He's a fool if he thinks he'll get away with it."

The expression on his face on any given Friday haunted my thoughts throughout the divorce proceedings. It was what fueled my convictions during the custody battle."

"You've got to stop doing this," she told me. "Scratching at old scabs is painful and wastes time. You need to concentrate on keeping yourself and John Earl safe."

The contents of my stomach tumbled. She was right. Here I'd enjoyed ice cream on her back porch, while a kidnapper and murderer was roaming free. What if he was my own brother? Or my ex-husband?

The fear churned the ice cream another turn. After Paul discovered my affair, he became violent. Subconsciously, I rubbed the spot where he'd grabbed my hair. He'd threatened to kill me.

The straws I was reaching for were miles away, but it wasn't out of the question that Paul was Ruthie's secret man. John Earl had said Paul met Ruthie at The Boondocks during one of his custodial visits. What if she'd crossed him and he'd done what he threatened to do to me?

I spun so fast I almost knocked Mother over. "I gotta go. I gotta go look for Ruthie." Before I realized what I had said, or how it would affect John Earl, I blurted out, "She is in mortal danger."

He awoke with the sound of my fear.

My stomach flopped a second time.

"What does that mean, Mama?"

I couldn't answer. I didn't have one. I ran out of the room, calling back to him. "You stay with Grandmother, John Earl." I looked to her, my gaze begging forgiveness. "If Carmichael or the sheriff calls or stops by, tell him I've gone back out to the lake."

Gladys came to the doorway and sent me the, "You'll do no such thing," look. Her eyes appeared over the top rim of her glasses while her head tilted forward toward the room. Lips formed a tight line. She leaned her head toward John Earl. I got her telepathic message loud and clear. "You are neglecting your son again."

Then, in an instant, her expression changed. Instead of admonishing my leaving she said, "At least call one of them to come and get you, and escort you out there."

"I think I can make it to the pond and back without incident." I turned and walked out the door, not allowing a response.

"Sue, it's pitch black out there."

"I've got a flashlight in the car." I crossed the living room and grabbed the door handle.

"What do you expect to find?"

I heard a noise from upstairs and, when I looked, John Earl was peaking between the oak spindles of the upstairs railing.

I couldn't say the words out loud, not with him listening. Guilt ended my march. I was leaving Gladys in a precarious position again. John Earl would bombard her with a hundred questions about Ruthie and what dragging the pond meant. Nevertheless, I couldn't help it.

My mouth opened wide with a yawn, and I realized I hadn't slept in two days. I just couldn't sit around being comfortable while my best friend was missing, or worse, but I wasn't doing her any good wandering around in the dark in an exhausted daze. I'd done enough of that already.

191

Through the open windows came the whistle of the grain train from the tracks north of town. When we were kids, Ruthie and I would run to the crossing at the end of Main Street and wave at the conductor.

I began to cry. This was my fault. I should have insisted John Earl use the port-a-potties near the tent. Not that I blamed him.

"Sue, are you going?"

I shuffled back up the stairs. Slumped and exhausted, my feet stumbled up them. "I decided to get some sleep first."

Even in the dim light, I saw the relief relax the muscles of her face. We walked back into the room together and I scooped John Earl into my arms. For one night, I would concern myself with him and leave Ruthie to Bill, Carmichael, and the FBI.

FIFTEEN

Thomas was standing over me, laughing, while I struggled to escape. Water splashed against the pilings inches below my toes. I was pleading for my release. Then I heard John Earl. I sat up.

Moonlight spread through the window. My arm was heavy and I saw John Earl's head inches from mine. I slipped my arm out from under his head and sat on the side of the bed. Beads of sweat trickled down my neck and between my breasts.

He yawned. "Mama, you all right? You were crying and mumbling about being let go."

I lay back down and pulled him into the crook of my elbow. "Just a bad dream. Let's go back to sleep."

Morning sun slipped between the slats of the blinds and awoke me the second time hours later. It created linear shadows on everything in the room. Conditioned air moved the blinds, and those same shadows danced on the far wall, reflected by a mirror on a dresser.

John Earl was already out of the bed and downstairs, probably bugging his grandmother to make pancakes or French toast. The growing boy was a food abyss.

I stepped across the hall into the bathroom and a hot shower. I scrubbed with Ruthie's puff until my skin glowed red. Back across the hall, I dressed in a clean pair of Capri pants with a sleeveless loose-knit shell. With cleanliness and sleep came renewed hope.

I skipped down the stairs. If not for the missing Ruthie, it was looking like a perfect summer day.

Mama poured a cup of coffee for me, and I promised John Earl I'd join him in the yard the minute I finished the pancakes on the plate. Then reality threw a slider and I couldn't consider food.

"She's out there, Mother, hurt or maybe dead now, and it's all my fault."

"How, Sue?" She scraped the batter droppings out of the skillet and tossed them in the garbage. "Because your son acted like a little boy and ran off, forcing you to follow as any mother would?" She stopped scraping and shook the spatula at me. "You didn't kidnap her or make Archie Claremont disappear. So stop blaming yourself."

She leaned the skillet in the sink and filled it with hot water. "Jedidiah left before dawn. He says Bill is convinced she's out of the county by now. All those men have been out there searching for more than twenty-four hours and they haven't turned up anything."

I shook my head, maybe a little too vigorously. "She's out there on that pond."

John Earl appeared at the back door and pushed his nose against the screen door. "Mama, you promised you'd come out and help me build a sand fort."

I couldn't resist that pouting face already caked with wet sand. Either he'd found the garden hose, or it'd rained the night before. No moisture on the porch proved the former. He'd emptied a corner of the sandbox of sand and filled it with water.

When I realized John Earl didn't want my help as much as he wanted my presence, I returned to the

194

house, phoned Bill and waited through four rings. I was forming the message I would leave when I looked through the front window and realized my car was missing. *I'll bet you anything The Reverend took it thinking if I didn't have transportation, I wouldn't leave the house.*

Bill finally answered with deep puffs of breath. "Hi, Sue. Hey, I was just about to call you. Seems your story about something being dumped in the pond had some merit. The crew just found it."

I whispered an expletive before the out of range alarm beeped on my phone. "Listen, Bill. My phone is acting up. Stop by Palmer's to pick me up, okay? The Reverend has absconded with my car."

The phone went dead, and I never heard him answer. I hurried back in the house and tried calling from the landline, but I got his voice mail. I slumped. What if he ignored my request? I had a feeling he would make sure I stayed away. I called his phone again from the landline.

No answer.

I told John Earl I was going out front to wait for the sheriff and he was to stay put.

"Mama, don't go this time." He knew how much I hated whining, but I couldn't scold. I heard fear tremor in his voice.

"I have to, John Earl." I grabbed his little hand and kissed his gritty fingers. "I have to be there when they find Aunt Ruthie."

Gladys Mae Covington Allgood owned a sense of just the right moment to appear. She gave me a glare of disapproval that said if we were alone I'd get it. Her voice was that of a grandmother. "We don't need her around, John Earl. We'll make those cookies I've been promising."

He made a dash toward the house, but she stopped him. "Just hold those horses, young man. You're not going anywhere near that kitchen until I see clean."

He faced me, shoulders drooping in disgust. "Do I have to take another bath, Mama?"

I looked at Gladys and back at him. "I think a good scrubbing in the hose will get most of the crud off. Then you can scrub those hands at the kitchen sink."

Both she and John Earl nodded agreement and they were off for a morning of baking.

I walked around the house and plopped down on the front steps inhaling and exhaling my frustration. Clouds had invaded the pure blue morning sky, and it was sprinkling rain, but I didn't care. My elbows dug into my thighs and my chin rested against my fists. What happened next switched my mood from glum to glummer.

Lee Palmer pulled his Buick Century in the driveway. He greeted me with a shaky voice. "Sue." He hurried up the porch stairs, but I caught him before he opened the door.

"Mr. Palmer...Lee I need a favor." I turned and stood in a single move.

"I can't right now, Sue. They've pulled something out of the pond. I may have to identify Ruth Ann's body, but I thought I'd come clean up a bit before going down there." He muffled a sob. "The sheriff suggested I go to his office to wait but I can't. I have to know now."

"I want to come along if it's all right." I felt like a little girl again, standing on that front porch, but the

196

question then had been if Ruthie could come out and play. She might not ever play again. *Stop it,* I scolded myself, *it is not her.* It just couldn't be. I wasn't ready to say goodbye.

I told Gladys about my conversation with Bill and asked that, if he called, to tell him that Mr. Palmer and I were on the way. Just in case, I left him a message that we would be at the pond in twenty minutes.

Standing on the kitchen stool at the counter, John Earl brushed my cheek with a quick good-bye kiss. He was smiling, or doing a good job of faking. I took it as a good sign; God saying all right, young lady, let's get down to the business of finding Ruthie and the reason for her kidnapping.

Mr. Palmer dragged himself to the car. He'd shaved but was wearing the same clothes he'd had on since the night before. He said nothing. His hands shook. He was one step from falling apart.

I grabbed the keys from his hand. "Allow me to drive, okay?"

Stiff-armed, my tight fists gripped the steering at ten and two; my right foot pressed the pedal to the floorboard. I was hoping Bill would allow me the first peek, saving Mr. Palmer from the dreadful task. I couldn't imagine one more horrific than having to stare into the face of John Earl's corpse, and though I disagreed with Lee Palmer on many topics, I'd never wish that distress on him.

I pushed the car to fifty miles an hour around the rain-soaked roads. The image of Ruthie's bloated flesh surfaced and brought bile into my throat. I swerved toward oncoming traffic, until I heard a car horn and

197

squealing tires and realized Lee was steering us back into the correct lane.

My foot came off the accelerator at the parking lot, and I angled the car into a space by the old docks. The front bumper scraped against the concrete parking block.

Blue and red flashing lights coming from the Coroner's van, three county cars, and Bill's Tahoe reflected on the grassy field where the circus tent had stood two days before, the last place I'd seen Ruthie.

Lee stopped, staring at the tree line where we'd first started looking, and where that search might be coming to an end. I forced a smile and grabbed his arm. "It's not her, you know. She was alive yesterday." Hand-in-hand, we walked the path toward the water rescue team.

Curiosity seekers gathered on the floating docks, crooking their necks, and whispering about us, until Bill met us and escorted us to a small open area. "I thought I told you to meet us at my office."

"Bill, this was all so unnecessary. I talked to her yesterday afternoon."

He pointed at me. "You're the one who told me you saw someone toss something that could have been the size of a corpse over the side of a rowboat. Now, I've got two missing persons, and I needed to eliminate your parcel as Ruthie or Archie.

At the mention of her name, Lee shrugged, the same mindless movements I'd seen the day Mrs. Palmer passed. I wasn't sure he could survive losing Ruthie too.

It lay on the muddy shore, a still plastic cocoon. The person responsible for dumping the body had taken great care to wrap it in several black garbage bags and

198

secured both ends with duct tape. I couldn't take my eyes off it. I couldn't bring myself to cry, although my best friend's remains might be inside.

"Sue, is this what you and John Earl saw tossed over the side of a rowboat yesterday afternoon?"

No words would come. I closed my eyes tight and managed to nod. Bile rose from my liver into my throat.

The coroner and his assistant loaded the parcel onto a folded gurney and we all watched while four deputies hauled it up the path toward the county van.

The Reverend was suddenly beside Mr. Palmer. He caught Mr. Palmer as he sank to the ground, weeping. "Now Lee, I know this is upsetting, but we don't know if it's Ruth. Let's wait and see what the coroner has to say."

I marched up to Bill, my face crinkled into a sour, angry frown. "How could you do that to us?" Anger gave way to a crescendo of frustration and I began to weep.

He tried to embrace me, but I pulled away.

"Listen, Sue, I have to follow procedure. This is a murder investigation; if those are the remains of a human in there, then we must allow the coroner to establish cause of death before notification of next of kin. How do I know Lee didn't get mad at Ruth for not showing up until Friday? Maybe he considered it a personal affront."

When I wrinkled my face into a disbelieving frown, my eyelids squeezed tears out and they ran down my cheeks. I caught them with my tongue. "Lee Palmer? He wouldn't know how to murder someone, even if he wanted to." I wiped my nose on the sleeve of my tee shirt. *Enough of the frail woman act,* I told myself. *Remember*

199

you are Gladys and Jedidiah's daughter. Have faith. "Ruthie's still alive. That is not her."

He moved to within inches of my face. For a second, I thought he was going to kiss me on the forehead, and I realized I wouldn't have minded it. Instead he whispered, "We can hope."

I slipped away from him.

The Reverend and Mr. Palmer stood next to each other on the shore. Mr. Palmer's strained tenor pleaded with God for the body in the bag to be someone or something else besides Ruthie.

The Reverend added a strong, "Amen."

Many of the people I'd seen at The Boondocks gathered a few yards away, trying to comfort Naomi. Thomas was mysteriously absent. So many notions and assumptions about him swirled like the cinnamon and sugar in one of Gladys' morning buns.

He was most likely back at The Boondocks, avoiding a scene with The Reverend. Maybe he couldn't stand the thought of seeing a corpse. Or maybe he was the kidnapper slash murderer and was whisking Ruthie away to another locale.

Bill made an attempt to disperse the crowd, but folks remained, milling around, whispering about the contents of the bag. Some said it was probably just Vernon's garbage. One woman speculated the chance it was Archie Claremont.

Then I admonished myself for wishing the man dead.

The Reverend stepped forward. "You heard the sheriff. Go home, everyone, and pray for this poor departed soul and the family."

Bill placed his hand on the small of my back and, thinking it belonged to The Reverend, I leaned back against him. His whisper came from his lips, low and husky. "I didn't mean to upset you before."

I took a step forward and spun. My cheeks turned every shade of red from bubblegum pink to crimson. "Sorry, I thought you were my father."

He licked his lips, and I found myself yearning to taste them. Movement behind his head distracted me, thank God.

The crowd hadn't listened to The Reverend. Little girls giggled, and their mothers tried to hide their eyes as divers stripped to their shorts and redressed. As Gladys would say, "Right there in front of God and everybody."

As they gathered their equipment and climbed into a Suburban marked Elmore County Search and Rescue, Bill let out one of his guffaws. "That'll teach those biddies to hang around trying to dip their noses in official police business."

Carmichael approached with his one-sided grin in place. God, how I'd come to hate it. Where had he been all morning, anyway?

He put his arm on Bill's back. "One of the searchers found some spent shells at the point. I went back to Vernon's and borrowed his rifle for comparison, but Bill I swear he didn't have anything to do with Duffy's death, or anything else going on around here."

Bill took a deep breath. "Wish I could be as convinced as you."

Carmichael elbowed him. "By the way, you're going to be getting at least one call, or a letter, telling you your

201

department is going to Hell for exposing sweet young things to the sight of practically nude male bodies."

"Yeah, and I'd bet they're not as sweet as their mamas would have you believe. Every single one of those little girls has sneaked a peak at her brother or father, and vice versa. I know my sister and I did as kids." He glanced at me with dancing eyebrows.

The two men continued to laugh, but the noise grew weak, as I drifted up the path away from them. I couldn't take part in their levity, not until I was certain Ruthie wasn't the corpse in that bag.

But talk of girls sneaking peeks warmed my cheeks to a blush and hauled me back to our eighth grade year. A sly grin pressed my lips together. Ruthie and I'd just finished track practice and were on our way to the locker rooms to shower before heading home. She'd double-dog dared me to sneak into the boy's locker room, and being the go-along-with-anything dummy I was, I'd done it. I'd snuck around the corner to find the best-looking boy in school butt-naked. I'd tried to move, but my feet had stuck to the tile floor until he asked me if I was going to leave or wait until Coach came back and found me staring at his privates.

I jumped when Bill tapped me on the shoulder. "Where'd you go? You were a thousand miles away."

More heat of embarrassment spread over my collarbone. "Just thinking about something stupid Ruthie double-dog dared me to do when we were in school."

"You mean the time you got caught staring at Mike in the boy's locker room?" Bill had an amazing, albeit, annoying memory. "Well, while you were daydreaming, I decided it would be best if you stayed with me. Jack's going to accompany Naomi back to The Boondocks and sniff around over there. There's going to be reporters from every little newspaper in the south waiting there and at Palmer's house. I figured you didn't want to get caught up in a media feeding frenzy, so I'm offering my office as a safe haven. Besides, I can't trust you to stay put if I'm not around." He held out an arm giving me space to move.

"Mother would never expose John Earl to her anger, but when I left, she was still boiling just under the lid like a kettle of potatoes on a stove. And we all know what kind of mess they make when they boil over. I'm not ready to have to clean it up, so I graciously accept your offer."

Bill released a laugh, and the tension of recovering a body from the pond dissipated, but only for a short while. "I got to tell you, Sue, I enjoy your company. Just wish it was under better circumstances."

I'd always liked Bill, even as a gawky kid, but I didn't have time for his suggestive manner. We had to find Ruthie. Besides, I was a divorcee with a seven-year-old son. I wasn't about to moon over a man just because his eyes sparkled and I liked his smile. He was just another one of those guys who knew he was charming and used it to get his way.

Since The Reverend was driving Mr. Palmer back to his house in his car, I followed Bill in my car, so I could have a getaway vehicle in case Gladys called me back to the Palmers'.

I'd spent too many years under the incorrect assumption that I had no control over circumstances surrounding me. Ruthie had always enjoyed more fun than I, because she figured it outweighed the consequences. She was in trouble, and I wasn't about to let some out-of-the-way sheriff and his Barney Fife park ranger friend bumble through until they discovered her cold, lifeless body at the bottom of the pond or out on one of the islands that grew out of it. Or in a body bag at the morgue.

A block before the bridge over the Coosa, I turned left and made a U-turn. I was going back to my son and wait out whatever news came. I kneaded the braided muscles in my neck when I saw cars and vans marked with television and radio call letters and numbers. I wasn't ready to answer their questions so I kept driving, circled the block, and completed the trip to Bill's office.

Martha sent me a look when I walked in and asked her to buzz Bill. By her expression, she'd pegged me as some evil hussy casting my spell on him. Well, she was wrong. The search for Ruthie remained the only reason I shared his company.

I didn't wait for his reply. I knocked at his door and walked in. He was on the phone and waved me into the chair. I pressed my face into my hands and prayed for help. I glanced up and found Bill standing over me with a cup of coffee in his hand waiting for me to take it.

"Where'd you go?"

My hands shook when I took the coffee from him. "I decided to go back to Palmer's to check on John Earl, but you were right. The street and lawn are lined with news vans. The Reverend can handle them. He's accustomed to dealing with difficult people."

He watched me take a sip. "Is it okay?" He'd fixed it just the way I liked it with cream and sugar. "I know you're worried, Sue, but it won't do any good, I promise. Waiting is all we can do now. Craig Hodges is the best there is for a coroner."

Three soft knocks at Bill's door and Martha appeared with sandwiches. "Cami sent these over." She looked down over her readers at me. They were attached to a pearl chain. "Didn't figure you been eating much since your friend disappeared." She set the platter on the corner of the desk in front of me, turned on her heel, and hurried out.

What did she expect to see, Bill and me in some compromising position? I shuddered with the idea and of putting anything in my stomach.

"Better do like she said." Bill nodded with that easy chuckle. "Martha doesn't cotton to folks not eating. Besides, you don't want to be sick when we find Ruth."

God, that all-lip grin. And now, those sparkling eyes I'd found so attractive hours ago were becoming condescending, just like The Reverend's. What was it about the older men I knew, which made them think they knew more about me than I did?

I refused to eat. Instead, I sipped coffee and watched Bill fax a photo of Ruthie to the surrounding county sheriffs and one to the FBI office in Birmingham. The dark-brown liquid burned my empty stomach.

He seemed nervous and started telling me personal things I bet never came up in any other casual conversation. The leather recliner in the corner of his office was his lonely night chair. A place he rested weary bones, read, and watched TV while on late duty.

I curled one leg under my butt and slipped back against cool leather on a long sofa adjacent to him, sharing a rustic coffee table in front of us. When I told him I liked the furniture, he explained he had inherited it from the last regime.

When I asked where his ranger-boy friend was, Bill sent me his official stare, head back, chin tucked. "He's out with my deputies searching, while I'm stuck here waiting for word from Craig, and baby-sitting you, since I can't trust you to stay put at Palmer's."

"I'm sorry, Bill, but she's my best friend." I started to cry when my stomach announced my neglect with a loud growl.

"Sue, it's going to be okay." He pushed part way off his chair, then reversed the move. "Better have one of those sandwiches. Like Cami said, bet the only thing you've eaten since Ruthie went missing was a piece of her pecan pie."

Martha buzzed.

He stood, walked out of the office and was gone about five minutes.

I leaned on my right elbow. The angle allowed me to see him and hear his conversation. I pulled out my phone and found Paul's office number in my contact list. "Debbie, Sue here. Did Paul have business in Montgomery this week?"

"Yep. He was meeting with some guy about some land near there."

"Thanks." I heard her talking, but whatever she had to say wasn't worth hearing, so I clapped my phone shut, ending the call. My lips twisted the way they always did when my synapses were filling those gaps. Paul dealt only in large residential real estate, and the only land that fit that bill belonged to the mother's family, the land Naomi and Vernon claimed and the state park had once been part of, their three-hundred acre plantation.

I was so deep in thought, my head slipped off my hand. A foul odor emanated from the trashcan. The source was a ball of foil near the bottom.

Bill screeching into his radio distracted my attention from it. "What do you mean you can't reach him? You try the station? Okay, call over to The Boondocks... never mind. I'll do it myself." He stormed back in the office.

"Problem?"

He fumbled with the phone on his desk. "You bet there is. Jack's missing. After he dropped Naomi off at the bar, he told one of my deputies he was going to row out to one of the islands, but that was an hour ago, and no one's heard from him since."

He punched numbers. "Naomi, is Jack there?" He sucked in a breath. "May I speak to him please?"

"Jack, what the hell are you doing still there? I thought you were going to lead a search team?" Less than a minute passed before he dropped the receiver on the cradle.

He leaned on his desk. "If I wasn't so mad, I'd laugh."

"Why?"

"He was searching the little dab of land near Elizabeth's Island, the one The Boondocks is on, when he saw someone rowing over there and went to investigate. Turns out it was Vernon, and he lost him between two islands on the far side of the pond."

"Good; with one problem solved, maybe you can explain the smell in here." I pointed to the trashcan.

He bent down and dug out the foil ball. "The last of a roast Emma Brown brought me a couple of days ago. I say it was a thank you for getting her cat, Barney, out of the downspout on her garage. Fool thing probably chased a squirrel down it." A twitter of a nasal laugh leaked from his nostril. "Martha swears Emma's trying to hook her claws in me. Calls her desperate for a man. I'll just take care of this. You eat." He pointed to the plate of sandwiches and left the room with the trashcan. The odor remained at the door after him.

I picked at thin slices of turkey piled between two slices of whole wheat bread, slathered with mayonnaise.

When he returned, the can was empty and the smell had dissipated.

"Bill, can I ask why you told me all about Carmichael before?"

His bottom lip rolled out. "I don't know, I thought I saw some attraction between you two."

Somehow I managed a grinning frown. The concept was funny and ridiculous. "No way. Finding Ruthie is the only reason I'm still here." I bit off a hunk of sandwich. "Look, I'm eating, and the only place I want to go right now is back to my son. I'm ready to deal with the media."

"I can't do that. I don't trust you."

"Fine." I took another bite, and for several minutes, neither of us spoke. The tension grew until I'd had enough. We'd talk. "What about you, Bill? What'd you do after we graduated?

"You sure you want to know? I'm not all that interesting."

I nodded.

208

"I joined the Navy right out of high school. When I got out, I went to Wallace Community College in Selma to study law enforcement."

"Apropos, since you father was once the chief of police."

Bill stood and retrieved a pack of Winston Lights from his breast pocket and offered one to me. I declined, but he said I'd have to accompany him. He really didn't trust me.

He pushed the button on the phone and reported to Martha our intended movements. We stepped out of his office to the left and followed a hallway to the end of the building. Outside the door, butts floated in rainwater in a rusted coffee can.

He pulled out a cigarette and lighter, and it flared. Puffs of gray smoke rose between us. "Okay, so continue."

He leaned against the building holding the cigarette, but it never made it to his lips. "I got a job as a deputy in Bedford, Tennessee. That's where I met Margie. She was a waitress in a truck stop in Shelbyville. We were married right away and were happy for fifteen years. We have two sons."

He stared past me at a yellow-white sky of early afternoon and took a long drag. "When I told her I was applying for this job, she said she wasn't moving. Her entire family still lives in Shelbyville."

Gurgling erupted from consuming nothing but coffee. "You about done with that? My stomach is telling me it would like to be fed more."

Back in Bill's office, I took my seat and I reached for another half a sandwich. "What about your sons? Where are they?"

209

He grabbed the other half of the sandwich. "Bill, Jr., lives in Birmingham. He's an insurance agent." A proud smile pushed his ruddy cheeks to his eyes and, for the hundredth time, I noticed how blue they were. "John moved to Nashville to be near Margie. He works at a chemical plant." He stopped talking.

I didn't want a lapse. Too much silence only brought back the possibility of Ruthie being the corpse in Dr. Hodges' morgue and Thomas being her killer. "How are your parents?"

He chattered away between bites. "Mother lives in a gated retirement community in Naples, Florida. Even after having both hips replaced, she plays golf every day with what I call her 'gaggle of widow friends.' Dad passed away two years ago."

He reverted to a little boy before my eyes. He dropped his head, and his voice grew mouse-quiet. "He dropped dead on the golf course." For only the second time since becoming reacquainted, Bill's eyes glistened with tears. "They didn't have a defibrillator on site, and the nearest ambulance was half an hour away."

He dropped his head into his hands. "He always seemed so healthy. A man like Bob Halvorson shouldn't have had any medical problems. I mean, yeah, he was big, but he didn't seem fat. At least not to me."

I just wanted to scoop him into my arms and rock the man like a baby. His father's sudden death, and the fact that he hadn't been nearby when it happened, left the man no way to say good-bye.

We had that in common. If Ruthie was dead, I'd lost out on a chance for closure.

The telephone rang and he reached for the receiver. The familiar Sheriff Bill Halvorson returned, steel-eyed and ready for a challenge. "That's correct. We've got one missing and two dead. The first, the victim of a shooting at the state park, was my deputy. I gave you guys a photo of the missing woman two days ago. We've heard nothing about the bar owner. Now, that's all you're going to get." He hung up growling about damned reporters.

He leaned back in his chair and his gaze was so intense I thought he was sizing me up. Did he suspect me?

The buzzer on his phone came as such a shock, I dropped the sandwich into my lap. I scooped it up and tossed it back on the stack with the others. My stomach cramped. I never should've tried to eat.

"Okay, I'll tell her." He sat up and leaned across the desk. The gleam in his eyes returned. "That was Martha. Craig just phoned to say that the body in the pond was Archie Claremont. Naomi's there now."

I jumped out of the chair and cheered. My hand held my chest in relief. At the same time I realized I was cheering for Archie's death, Bill came around the desk, lifted me up and swung me around until I became dizzy. When he set me down, his intense gaze settled on mine and again I thought he was going to kiss me.

I'm not sure I didn't want him to. His index finger on one hand ran in small circles on my back. The other stroked my hair as we rocked together. Then, with a move so subtle I hardly noticed, he grasped my lower cheek, pulling me closer to him.

I squeezed my hand between our bodies and gave him a shove. "I told your friend Carmichael not to do that again, and I'm telling you the same thing."

He backed away hands up, surrendering to my request. "Sorry, guess I got my signals crossed again." The sparkle in his eyes went out, a dying oil lamp.

"It's not that, Bill, it's just I feel like I need to stay focused on Ruthie. And, in a way, we just danced for Archie's murder."

He leaned against the edge of the desk and crossed his ankles. His thin, but muscular, arms crossed over his chest. "I want to ask you a question, and it's gonna be a tough one, but I want you to give it some thought before you answer."

I shrugged. "Okay."

"Do you think that brother of yours could have anything to do with Ruthie's kidnapping or Archie's death? From what Vernon told Jack, he's a mean one and, just because we don't have solid evidence that he wasn't the one who nabbed her, doesn't mean he's not involved."

I wasn't about to tell Bill my suspicions about Thomas until I got a chance to speak to him first. "No way, Bill. Thomas used to be in love with her. The only reason they broke up is because he found out she was seeing somebody else on the side." Okay, I didn't really lie. I just didn't tell him everything Thomas told me.

"What about revenge?"

"After all these years? Doesn't make sense. That was back in high school. Besides, I think I would have recognized my own brother if that had been him in the boat." I unfolded my legs and stood. "If that's all, I want go now. John Earl is probably worried."

My cell phone rang from my Capri pants.

Mother was on the other end of the line. If I didn't answer, she would suspect I was learning the Horizontal

Rumba from the County Sheriff whether it were true or not.

I heard her voice without any trouble, but her words were garbled. I almost went through the roof. I checked the screen and found four bars, plenty of signal strength.

I thought maybe she'd heard the news about Archie, so I screamed into the phone. "Did you hear, Mother? It wasn't Ruthie at the bottom of the lake."

Then I realized, she was screaming in panic.

SIXTEEN

"He's gone, Sue. I turned my back for one minute to check the cookies we made and he was gone. I'm so sorry."

I didn't have to hear any more. I swallowed hard, barely forcing down the bile, the bite of sandwich, and the coffee.

Someone had stolen my precious John Earl. I didn't know what to do first. I trembled from head to toe and my skin tingled until all the hairs stood up.

Bill saw my reaction and grabbed me by the shoulders. "Tell me what's wrong and what I can do to help."

"I have to go, right now." I struggled out of his grasp. "Someone's taken John Earl out of the Palmer's backyard." Tears dammed in my eyes as I stared up at him. "He's been kidnapped too, Bill."

His professional calm settled in the room. "Do you know that for sure? Maybe he just wandered down the street. Maybe that husband of yours came back for him, only this time he didn't wait for anyone's permission."

Even in my panic, I took exception to his inference. "John Earl knows better than to just wander away. Especially now." I was sobbing. "And if Paul was going to take him, he'd make a big deal with a court order, after the way he was sent away beaten up and ego bruised."

He asked the question I'd been dreading. "How would he know not to leave the yard? Have you given him details? Have you actually said the word kidnapped in his presence, or does he just think Ruthie wandered too far into the woods?"

I snapped. "Yes, I have said the word kidnapped in to him. We discussed it as a matter of fact. I thought the best way to keep him from being scared, if he did hear talk, was to tell him myself." I ran out the door and stopped on the porch. "Shit. I'm shaking too hard to drive."

Bill was behind me jingling the keys to the Tahoe. "Let's go. I'll radio my deputy on the way to the Palmers.'" His arm went around my waist and, with a tiny bit of force, he pushed me toward the vehicle. "You call your husband."

I stood in the doorway, frozen in my tracks. A heavy dread seemed to hold me in that spot. "I can't."

He gave me another shove. "What do you mean you can't?" His voice reeked of panic, too.

I looked him square in the eye and said, "Look, I've just been fooling myself for two days. You and I both know what happens to victims of kidnapping, especially little kids." The tears began rolling down my cheeks, caught on the tip of my nose, and I swiped at them with the back of my hand. I couldn't stop the onslaught of horrors weaving their way across my limbic system. Images that could make even the stoutest constitution go weak.

Moving those away, I fell into self-pity.

Bill listened to me rant without a word for a few minutes.

"First, my marriage fails, then my best friend is kidnapped, and now my son. There's no way the person in

216

the boat saw us as he threw Archie Claremont's body over the side of a rowboat." Another swipe and a loud sniff. "Hell, I don't even know Archie Claremont, much less anyone who'd want him dead."

"Are you finished?" Squinting eyes shot rockets of rage at me. "Because if you are, we'll eliminate the obvious. If you have one, I'll need a picture of Paul and send out an APB."

I nodded.

"And if Paul doesn't have him, then we have a very scared little boy out there somewhere who's wondering why his mama hasn't come looking for him." He slipped past me and called from the driver's door. "Are you coming, or are you just going to stand there like some frightened pup? The Sue Backman I've grown quite fond of is a woman who wouldn't let this scare her. She'd be... well, pissed off."

Bill was right, of course. I was not about to let some lunatic just take my son without a fight. And if Paul had grabbed him, I was going to...I wouldn't allow myself to think the words. God was listening.

The mindbender of emotion did a one-eighty back to semi-calm. I got in and slammed the door. The damned seat belt refused to cooperate at first. After three jabs, it finally clicked. This time my heart was doing the Mamba against my larynx.

The sun was high and burning moisture off the pavement from rain the day before, but no amount of heat could compare to the tongue-lashing I was in for from The Reverend. This time I deserved one. He would find an appropriate scripture concerning harlotry, even if nothing inappropriate had happened.

217

Truth was, The Reverend couldn't believe it possible for a man and a woman younger than he to act appropriately without escort. I had to stop worrying about what the old fuddy-duddy thought and concentrate on Ruthie and John Earl. My tears blurred the pines and oaks that stood taller than every house in town, and standing so thick along the road, I couldn't see the river. I wavered from fuming anger to near hysteria so fast my heart pumped two beats away from tachycardia. "I'm shaking so bad I don't know if I'll be able to stand when we get back to the house. If Paul did grab him, he might have a case for child abandonment."

Bill looked me in the eye. "Don't fall apart now. I'm not going to lie to you. If Paul has him, you'll get him back. If he doesn't, your son's life is at stake. You're going to have to keep it together. And if Paul doesn't have him, my guess is that well-meaning father of yours has called him and he's on his way back."

He was right and I hated it.

* * *

City, County, and State Police cars lined the usual quiet Second Street where Lee Palmer lived. With no curb to stop them, tires sat on soggy lawns after the morning rain. Jack and two important looking men were on the front porch talking to Mother when we arrived.

She was trembling and sobbing, twisting a hankie between nervous hands.

I jumped from the car before Bill had a chance to bring it to a complete stop and ran toward the group.

218

She swallowed me into her arms as she had countless times over the years, but this was different. I stiffened with her touch. Some man I didn't know had stolen my son from her care, and with Bill's urging I was furious.

She backed away, masking her hurt and disbelief.

"I'm sorry, but I can't fall apart in your arms right now. John Earl is out there, somewhere, in the hands of some maniac, or his father, and I don't have time for a break down."

Her pride halted the flow of tears, and she pursed her lips in a prideful grin. Piercing green eyes twinkled. "That's my girl." She followed me to the group of men.

A taller man wearing a short-sleeved dress shirt and slacks posed the most pressing question to Mother. "The sheriff has filled us in on the situation. Do you think the boy's father has him?"

She shook her head.

I moved in front of her and butted in. "I'm Sue Backman, the boy's mother. His father, Paul, would have come to the front door. Like I told Sheriff Halvorson, he'd have returned with a document signed by a judge giving him parental rights and claiming I'd abandoned him."

My mind roared into the next gear and I began firing questions at them. "What's our first move? Are we absolutely sure this is related to the Archie Claremont murder? Why haven't they started looking?"

Bill put his two bear paws on my shoulders to stop me, the same hands that had consoled me less than an hour ago. He returned to being Sheriff Halvorson. "Listen, Missy. I've allowed you a lot of free reign around here, because I thought you could help us find Ruth, but this is different. You're too close. I've got guys canvassing the neighbors, asking if they saw any suspicious people or vehicles. Let us handle it."

I took two steps forward. "Like hell I will. That's my son out there, Bill, a seven-year-old little boy. You can't even find a grown woman and you let somebody murder Archie Claremont. How can you expect me to assume you can find him?"

Gladys grabbed my arm and dragged me into the house. "Susan Marie Allgood Backman." I knew I was in trouble when she used all four of my names. I bit my bottom lip in anticipation of the verbal wringing out I was about to receive. I fell into an overstuffed chair in the front room.

She stood over me, just as she had when I was a little girl in trouble for causing a ruckus at church, or playing what she considered too rough for a proper young lady. "Now you listen up. I know you're scared, no…terrified, and madder than Aunt Penny's hen, but going off half-cocked and cursing at those trying to help will do more harm than good." She pointed toward the street. "Your father has just returned, and I want you calm when you tell him about John Earl."

"Me?" I gathered control and stared up into her stern face. "You're the one who lost him." I sucked in a breath, hoping the words would come with it and slapped my hand over my mouth to keep them there. Of all the times for me to insert my size eights, this was not it.

Without a word, she spun on her heel and walked through the doorway that separated the living room and kitchen.

I should have gone after her, apologized, and comforted her, but I wanted to know Bill's plan.

"Sue, what has happened? Sheriff Halvorson tells me that someone has taken my grandson." His voice was loud, his tone accusatory.

Bill walked in and stood next to me. He looked over the rim of his sunglasses, and his head did an almost undetectable shake, saying, "Back off, Sir."

I hung my head. I couldn't look The Reverend in the eye. I knew if I did, he would know I'd spent the last several hours pretending to be helping in the search for Ruthie. That little voice that was my conscience began teasing. *You were just spending time enjoying the company of the good sheriff.*

I recounted how my intent for spending time with Bill went solely to finding Ruth. I began stammering. "Mother called while I was waiting with the sheriff for news from the medical examiner." I almost slipped and called him Bill. So what if I had? He was a classmate before he was sheriff.

The Reverend would have surely quoted. One of his favorites came to mind. Mark, Chapter 14l, verse 38, "Watch and pray that you may not enter into temptation; the spirit indeed is willing, but the flesh is weak."

I searched his face for compassion. "She said John Earl had disappeared from the yard while she was checking on the cookies they'd fixed."

I prepared for the third degree about where I'd been, but it never came. Instead, he asked where she was. When I told him about our conversation and the horrible thing I'd said, I expected a tongue-lashing. It never came either. The Reverend touched my arm.

221

"I'll speak to her, Sue. I'm sure she understood that you were upset and all has been forgiven." The expression on the man's face took me by surprise. It was so loving and tender, his tearful smile not at all the staunch tight-lipped face I'd grown up looking at.

I can tell you there is no feeling lower than having to call your former spouse to ask if he's the one who's taken your child. No, not having a clue where his was, and having not been there when he needed you, trumps everything.

Paul's bimbo secretary said she wasn't sure where he was. Between the gum-smacking, she asked if I wanted his voice mail.

I hung up. This was no subject for a voicemail, or a text message, no matter how little I liked the man. He didn't answer his cell, so I did leave the message for him to call me right away.

Bill and three other men were just standing, chit-chatting, doing nothing to return my son. My approach was less than subtle. The ground quaked as my legs took me in their direction; my fists dug into my hips. "Gentlemen, is there a reason why ya'll are still standing around instead of trying to find John Earl?"

Bill hissed an introduction. "Sue, I don't believe you've met Walker Crowley, Prattville's current police chief. And you haven't officially met Special Agents McCoy and Linton from the Missing Persons Division of the FBI in Montgomery. They are coordinating Walker's office with mine on Ruthie and John Earl's disappearances, and Archie's murder."

McCoy reeled off information with a professional ease I found irritating. "Photos of tread marks from the pavement in front of the house are on their way to the lab for analysis, along with all the fingerprints on the fence, the swing set, the sandbox, and the back porch. In addition, we are waiting for a list of all the child molesters living in the area. Now if you can provide us with a recent photo…"

My phone rang before I could apologize or question why Bill didn't call it what is was, a kidnapping.

"Okay, so what's so important?" Paul's demanding voice scratched at my eardrums.

I wanted to scream into my cell, but I knew it would only exacerbate the situation. "Did you come back for John Earl this morning?"

"No. Why?"

"Then I think you should get back here right away." I didn't know how to say it delicately so I just blurted out the words. "He's been kidnapped."

Paul shot questions I wasn't prepared to answer.

"Just get here as soon as you can." I slapped the phone shut.

Bill took my arm and gave it a gentle squeeze. "I'm gonna get going back to the office." His expression was different somehow—vulnerable, jealous maybe, guilty for allowing this to happen. "On the way, I'm going to go downtown, see if anybody's seen anyone with a scared little boy in the last couple of hours. Call me right away if he turns up." Then he grabbed me by both biceps and cocked his head. "Pray if you can. We can use all the help we can get right now."

Jack cleared his throat and we realized he stood behind us.

Bill released me with a jerk. "Where have you been? Never mind, right now I need you to coordinate a new search at the park. This time for Sue's son, John Earl. I need for you to speak to Vernon again. Tell him about the new search parties and make sure he doesn't interfere. And tell him to be on the look out for John Earl."

"You got it, Bill. Anything I can do to help." He turned to me, took both my hands in his. "I promise we'll find him." Then he ran to the Jeep.

I stood on the lawn for several minutes watching the flurry of activity. The Police Chief's big 'ol sedan headed back toward downtown, while Jack led another driven by one of the FBI agents in the other direction toward the pond.

Lee pulled in. "Did they find her?"

I broke down and wept against his chest. "Whoever has Ruthie has John Earl now."

"Take some comfort that he's not alone, Sue. Ruthie's with him, comforting him." He jingled his keys. "I'm going to shower quick and then I'm going back out there, myself. Gotta keep busy or I'm going to go nuts." He kissed my forehead as he had many times when I was little. "We'll find them, Sue, I promise." He took my hands and squeezed them.

His words brought a moment's reassurance. I pitied Mr. Palmer before, but now we were kindred spirits. We had the most to lose in this tragedy, and yet we were powerless over it. If I didn't know better, I'd swear the man had aged a year in two days.

The Alabama sun beat down on me and all the humidity that came with it surrounded me. I should've been drenched in sweat. Yet, a chill ran the length of my spine. My emotions were in a pile like pieces of a jigsaw puzzle just after being poured from the box.

I needed to know why anyone would want Ruthie or John Earl. Whoever it was set a higher priority than my happiness, and my emotions couldn't take much more. Thomas came to mind, but the boy I remembered wouldn't do this to a member of his family. He wasn't a good enough actor to play innocent while underneath hiding a cold-hearted murdering kidnapper. Besides, I couldn't fathom his reasons.

All those years I denied God even existed, now I was pissed off at him for allowing this crazed idiot to put my best friend and son in grave danger. I couldn't be mad at Ruthie or John Earl. Being mad at Gladys or The Reverend made even less sense. I believed in God enough to think He was the only one left to blame.

There was the person in the woods. I wasn't sure anymore that it was a man. He or she must have thought Ruthie saw something she shouldn't have and that same person must have seen John Earl and me watching him or her toss Archie Claremont's body over the side of the rowboat. Reason said it was a man. A woman wouldn't have the strength to lift Archie into the boat and then out again on the lake unless she had help.

Vernon hated Archie but he'd never hurt Naomi that way.

My thoughts returned to Thomas. If Cami was right about those two being an item, maybe they'd decided to get Archie out of the way.

Maybe Ruthie had gone to The Boondocks Friday night and had seen Thomas with Naomi. Maybe Thomas kidnapped and murdered her so she wouldn't tell anyone and knowing Vernon would be the best suspect. I couldn't allow myself to believe that he'd harm John

Earl even if he was the man in the boat. They'd gotten along so well during his visit to Palmers. I bowed my head, closed my eyes. "Lord, forgive my anger. Please protect my friend and my son from this maniac. Let the men out searching now bring them home safe." Then I looked to the sky. "And God don't let it be Thomas."

"Amen." The Reverend's voice came from the porch. "But why would you include Thomas in your suspicions?" He reached into his pocket, pulled out a pressed red handkerchief, and dabbed his forehead and neck.

Confession time. "He was at The Boondocks Friday night when I went looking for Ruthie."

"Couldn't be Thomas." Mother stood in the doorway. "Nothing you say will ever convince me he's capable of such abominable things." She waved her hands in front of her face. "Now come in out of the sweltering sun and join us for a glass of tea and some of those cookies John Earl mixed up earlier. I suspect you haven't eaten much in the last two days."

Sweetened tea cooled my dry throat, but the taste of the cookies sickened me. Fact was, with each passing minute, the likelihood of seeing John Earl alive again grew as cold as the ice tinkling at the bottom of the glass. The plate of fresh baked chocolate chip and pecan delights brought images of his small hands scooping up the dough and rolling it into misshapen balls. I could imagine him popping one into his mouth without Mother seeing, just as I had done as a girl. Then he'd squish them out with a dough-covered fist laughing with a delight.

I needed to hear his giggles again. My head came to rest on my forearms on the table and I sobbed. "If he's not found soon, I'm going to lose my mind."

Gladys stroked my hair and, when I raised my head, she cupped my cheek with her other hand. "Have faith, child. God is watching over them."

The Reverend glanced at me and, with only a slight bob of his head, he told me not to mention my doubts about God's role in this turmoil. He was right of course. It was stupid to blame God. The real problem was my frustration and guilt for asking Ruthie to go with John Earl and me, and for not being here with John Earl.

"I should've made sure Ruthie was behind us when we came out of the woods. And I should've been here with my son. I should've known he'd be in danger."

Her gaze met mine, and tears ran down both our faces. Then, as if she couldn't look at me anymore, she stood, gathered the cookie plate, and took it to the sink.

She stared out between chintz curtains at the spot where she'd last seen him. The palm of her left hand pressed the window glass. "He was right there…in the sandbox. I should have been out in the yard with him instead of being so worried about whether the cookies would burn in Lee's damned oven."

The Reverend stared in horror at Gladys' outburst and her cursing. "Gladys Mae."

She faced him, donning the prettiest shade of red, as though at any moment she might burst into flame. With her chin tucked to her chest, she mumbled an apology. I wasn't sure where it was aimed— at God for using that word or me for her carelessness as a sitter.

I never blamed her, not really. Since Paul and I'd split, John Earl had become a mini-man. I just assumed if confronted by a kidnapper or any other bully, he would know to run.

Guess I'd been wrong.

SEVENTEEN

The back door hit the counter beside it and I dashed like a wind out of nowhere. The urgency to be in the same area where John Earl had last been grew to gargantuan proportions. Touching what he had last touched, I hoped to click on a maternal extrasensory link to his location. I ran my fingers over the same wooden swing set and play tower that Ruthie, Thomas, and I once fought over. The wood was split and gray with age, and my fingers caught several splinters, but I didn't care. John Earl had touched it last.

Memories of long ago and those more recent swirled like chocolate syrup in milk. John Earl preferred his finger to a spoon so none was wasted. The image brought a smile, but when my tongue reached past my lips I tasted the salt of my tears.

I grabbed a glob of sand from the box. The top dry layer sifted between my fingers, the fine grain equal to the time remaining in my best friend's and my son's lives. A stick from the maple tree that shaded the box lay in the sand. A drawing for his grandmother was scrawled beside it. My eyelids fluttered closed, and try as I might, I couldn't control my ragged breathing. I might never see him or one of his pictures again.

Remorse and anxiety bubbled into panic.

"Stop it," I said. "Stop thinking like that. He's coming back and so is Ruthie."

A car stopped in the drive, and I ran to the front anticipating news from either Bill or Carmichael. Disappointment and fury swallowed me when I saw Paul climbing out of his Jaguar. Again, I asked myself how he'd gotten back to town so fast, unless he was in the area. None of that mattered. Our son was missing, and I stiffened, ready for Paul's accusations. Deep breaths rose in my lungs.

He walked right up to me and grabbed my arms, like shaking me would force the truth from my very being. "What the hell is going on?"

The Reverend and Mother stood on the porch. "That's enough." The Reverend took two long strides toward him. "Sue doesn't need your scorn, Paul. We must join as a family now in this hour of despair."

His head dropped and he pushed his hands together behind his back. He took two steps back. Paul was actually cowering with my father's warning.

Thank God for parents.

"Just tell me what happened." Paul's green eyes glazed over, trying to intimidate me, a trick he had mastered early in our married life. He took on this look of superiority and stared without relent until I gave in. During the later years of our marriage, he'd taken every opportunity to second-guess and belittle every decision I'd made. I truly believed he thought me equal to John Earl.

Gladys took up my sword. "It's my fault, Paul. I left him alone in the backyard while I was futzing around in the kitchen with the cookies he'd helped me make. I thought they'd make a nice treat for the men searching for poor Ruthie."

Her voice wavered, the dam on her tear ducts leaking but not breaking, and she held fast. She knew Paul's trickery as well as I did. Her eyes could melt a person's heart, or as they did then, go cold, become icy emeralds. They stared him into veritable mush.

Paul apologized for his rudeness, and the next question came with a mouth full of accusation aimed at me. "Where were you?"

I got the message in his tone with complete clarity. This was my fault because I'd left John Earl with mother. "See," he was thinking, "I told you he would have been better off with me."

I stood firm, curling my toes against the inner soles of my shoes for balance. "It just so happens, I was waiting with the sheriff on the identity of a body they dragged from the pond." *So there.* Okay I didn't verbalize, but I thought it.

Paul's eyes twinkled with lewd undertone. "And what else have you been doing while under the sheriff's protective custody?"

Oh sure, I could have defended myself, but why should I? Let him make the same assumption my parents had. I told the truth. "We were at his office waiting for word from the coroner about the identification of the body they found in the pond."

None of them believed me. Paul lifted one eyebrow, a habit I hated. He was mad at me because I'd abandoned John Earl. My parents, on the other hand, stared with a pallid shameful glower, as if it were not bad enough that the maniac had wrenched John Earl from the loving arms of his family; I was somehow to blame because I was sinning while it happened.

I let them have it. "I know what you're all thinking, suspecting me of some afternoon tryst with the sheriff, but do you really think I'm so weak and desperate I'd be doing the horizontal boogie under these circumstances?"

I pointed first to Paul, then at my parents. "Our son, and your grandson, is missing. Kidnapped most likely by a man who killed a deputy sheriff, took Ruthie, and killed Archie. Don't you think our time would be better served concentrating on them rather than making idle accusations?"

Saying the word again and relating it to John Earl brought a stomach full of acid indigestion, the same one I got whenever I ate Mexican food. My son was missing. I had to get him back or die trying. I swallowed the fear, and the resolve to find him returned. I got pissed off again. I stormed off to the backyard under an arbor laden with the same red blaze climbing rose bush Mrs. Palmer had planted the year Ruthie and I graduated from high school.

Paul came up behind me and stopped so close I could feel his breath moving the hairs on the top of my head. "Whatcha doing?"

"Looking for evidence." I turned around and stepped on his foot.

"Don't you think local forensics guys have gone over this place already?"

I took careful steps, searching the ground for what I didn't know. "Yeah, I believe the police did their job, but this is John Earl we're talking about, and my baby is out there somewhere, with someone he doesn't know. Over the past two days, I've become a woman who doesn't

232

leave everything to the authorities. After all, I know my boy better than anybody."

I pointed toward the house. "I got a question for you? Where'd you get enough money for the Jag out front? I can't imagine real estate development being lucrative these days. It can't be Debbie's. You don't pay her that much. Never mind. I have a better question. Are you cooking up some real estate scheme with my cousin Roy?

He just stared.

Then we heard it.

Tires wailed, no doubt leaving tread marks on the street out front. Folks living in larger cities might hear it every day, but not on Second Street in this small town where everybody on the block knew everybody. Nobody sped down its streets, especially during those afternoon hours when seniors and infants napped, and children walked home from school.

I led the charge back through the house, but by the time we reached the front door, the offending vehicle had disappeared. No wonder, it must have been going fifty or more in a twenty-five mile-an-hour zone.

The screen door yawned open with a moan. A sealed manila envelope fell flat at my feet. It had been hand delivered. It wasn't sealed and there was no return address.

I bent the tabs back, opened it and pulled out a typed note on a piece of yellow lined paper. Paul, the Reverend, and Mother asked me to read it. I couldn't say the words aloud so they looked over my shoulder while Paul read.

233

"I have your son and I'm coming for you. It is already too late for your friend. Call off the police. If you understand, your signature at the bottom will be your sworn oath. Return this note to the envelope and leave it on the porch by midnight. I will contact you soon with further instructions."

A lock of hair taped to the bottom of the page produced a sensation I'd never felt. I reeled. The acid in my stomach whipped into frothy terror. The slip of hair had been snipped from John Earl's head. My hand trembled as it went to my mouth and I swallowed the scream lumped in my throat. My knees buckled and I sank to the floor sobbing.

Paul grabbed the envelope away from me. "That eff'ing maniac."

Before he exited the house, Paul began shrieking at my parents. "If you'd kept your opinions and advice to yourselves, we'd still be married, and my son would be safe with me." He shook his finger at my parents.

The Reverend refused to back down. "Just a minute, Paul..."

Paul spun and his finger with him, like the needle in a compass. It pointed east at me. "And if you'd just agreed the other day, he'd have been with me, alive and safe on a boat in the gulf. If they harm him at all, it'll be your fault." The spring on the screen door stretched to its limit when he flung it open and stormed out of the house. He hopped off the porch without using the steps.

I caught the door before it shut and followed him out screaming at him. "You have no right to speak to my parents that way. And if anyone has to take blame, why not start with you? Your little fling with Ditzy Debbie is what did-in our marriage." I screamed louder. "And I'll never give up custody."

Paul waved a hand, dismissing me. When he reached his car, he sank into the seat and the engine roared on. He swerved just in time to escape flattening Lee's mailbox and surrounding flowerbed.

When I returned to the house, several flies and mosquitoes came in, clinging to my tee shirt and buzzing past my head. Then, in an effort to escape the house, they directed their flight pattern to a front window.

I wanted to warn them.

They were doomed. See, Gladys Mae was a wizard with a fly swatter. And as strange as it all seemed at that moment, she went to the hall closet to retrieve it. It seemed silly to be worried about them now, but she believed in keeping busy during a crisis. Idle hands and all that.

The Reverend was still holding the note. He forced a calm tone. "We have to tell the police, Sue. This maniac has John Earl. He's all but admitted to killing Ruthie. And this is our only evidence."

Deep in my gut I knew he was right, but I wasn't ready to give up the only thing linking me to having John Earl returned in one piece. The thought of someone hacking up my son sent me running up the stairs to the bathroom, where I could only produce a dry heave. A sad figure of a desperate woman, half her hair pulled back in a ponytail, the other half flying willy-nilly around her head, stared back from the mirror. Mascara darkened my lower eyelids. "You are a sorry sight. Remember what

Bill said? Where's that anger? Scream. Do something to stop this rollercoaster of emotions."

The pep talk ended, and I returned to the porch where I took the envelope from The Reverend's hand. "I have to sign it and put it back on the porch before midnight. Then I'm going to come up with a plan to trap the person who comes to fetch it and threaten him with everything I've got to get John Earl back."

Gladys and The Reverend stood, arms touching, both staring at me, as though I had just spoken in tongues and informed them I was the lost however-many-great granddaughter of Satan himself.

Ten minutes later, Bill pulled the Tahoe into the muddy driveway. A second county vehicle pulled up to the lawn, but the deputy stayed in the car.

I wanted to run into his embrace, but a lifetime of living with my parent's belief in restraint at all times prevented it. All I could do was tuck my head and hope he got my telepathic message of apology for pushing him away earlier.

Then I panicked. What if the kidnappers were watching? They'd see Bill and assumed I'd called him.

"What's the news of Ruthie?" I invited him into the house. Safe within the walls of Palmer's sanctuary I shoved the note at him.

He released a frustrated breath, closed his eyes, and tilted his head back. "I tried to warn you…"

I cut him off. "Sheriff, I don't need a lecture on putting my son and me in danger right now. I need for you to listen to my plan." I rubbed my chin. I twisted my mouth and chewed the inside of my cheek. Ideas rolled over the hamster wheel in my head. "Would it be tampering with evidence if we made a copy of the note, taped John Earl's hair to it and sent it back to the kidnappers while forensics goes over the original for prints?"

"This is a matter for the FBI." The lack of urgency in Bill's voice irked me. "I'll call Agent McCoy and see what he thinks." He excused himself and slipped into the dining room to make the call.

For the umpteenth time in the past two days, I twisted like a line full of the day's clean laundry in a tornado. I hated myself allowing his charms to sway me, and at the same time, thankful he was around to support and comfort.

Paul would be no help in that department. Who knew what he was planning? He'd probably hire a private detective just to show Bill, Jack, the FBI, and me who was smarter. I had a sneaking suspicion Bill Halvorson had dealt with the likes of Paul Backman before and wouldn't let his big-city machismo get in the way of solving the crime at hand.

A meat cleaver couldn't have cut the tension in the air with The Reverend and Gladys staring me down. His brown and her green eyes bore holes to my core in disapproval.

I touched my forehead, making sure I hadn't developed one of those running message boards across it announcing my attraction to the man.

Bill returned with good news. "McCoy likes your idea. Says he can take the note to their lab in Montgomery. They can make a copy, then run the original for fingerprints and trace. Said he was going to call and have the technician waiting. He'll have it back before midnight.

Plus, I called the Department of Justice about an Amber Alert going out on John Earl. I need a picture."

He reached for the letter, but I held tight. I was not ready to relinquish my last connection to John Earl. "I want to go with McCoy. I want to make sure nothing happens to this."

Before The Reverend could remark, Bill gave his own reason why he wanted me to stay put. "You need to keep an eye out for anyone hanging around watching the place."

"Mother and The Reverend can do that." I caught myself whining and cleared my throat. I looked out the window. "Besides, that deputy sheriff is here to watch the house."

He grabbed one arm with a gentle, understanding touch. "Look, Sue, you're the only one now who can identify the guy who grabbed at you at the pond." He gave me a squeeze and a stern look. "Stay here with your parents. I swear I won't let anything happen to the letter."

I gave him John Earl's second grade picture from my wallet.

His cell rang and once again he excused himself.

I watched him through the window. He climbed in the Tahoe and started it up. Once again, he'd left me to The Reverend and Gladys. This couldn't be good.

The lace curtains hanging in the fifteen-foot window moved with the breeze. I never was much for omens, but my green eyes stayed on those curtains, hoping that breeze would bring me news of my missing loved ones.

Were they already dead and our search was for naught? Or were they tied together, duct tape strapped around their mouths so they couldn't scream and couldn't alert the hundreds of town folk searching the underbrush? What a pitiful life I'd led until this point, watching far too much television.

I walked back through the house, past Mother pouring a glass of tea in the kitchen, and stood at the sink staring out the window. She came up beside me and reeled me in with one arm. "It's going to be all right, Sue. The good Lord won't let anything happen to them."

My gaze remained fixed on the last place anyone had seen John Earl. "He already has." Tears rolled down my cheek as I continued to stare. "For all we know, they're already dead."

* * *

Gladys tried to convince me to eat something. I guess it's a mother thing. I picked at a tomato sandwich, but the tomato only stirred the acid in my stomach. I paced the parlor awaiting Bill's return.

Half an hour later, he pulled up in front of the house.

I ran out to meet him. The air was so thick with humidity I began sweating the second I stepped out on the front porch. "Any word?"

"McCoy should have delivered the note to the lab, by now. I asked him to call on his way back to town. I could stay with you and wait or I could get back to work."

I wanted him to stay, but The Reverend assured him we'd be fine. "Allgoods come from sturdy stock, indentured farmers and even a few horse thieves, according to family lore. The clan always managed to rally in hard times, and we will persevere in this our most horrific time. With His help, of course." His gaze lifted skyward, his eyes closed. "Lord, look over our lost sheep and guide those brave men and women who continue the search." Then he looked at me and said, "Amen."

We all followed suit.

"Then I'll get back to the office." Bill spoke to the group, but his gaze sought mine. Those eyes were trying to comfort, tell me everything was going to be all right.

The Reverend offered to join a search party, but Bill nixed the idea. "As a pastor, you realize the need for a level head. I need for you to see that Sue stays here. I don't need her going off half-cocked again, thinking she should venture through the park searching alone."

His stern gaze pierced me with his words. "She already risked her life and put John Earl in immediate danger with that subversive fishing expedition."

He stepped ahead and blocked the steps. He was gruff. "I mean it now, Sue. I want you to stay put this time. The person in that boat knows you and John Earl were out there, and I don't need another missing person." His voice softened, and I thought I saw fear in those blue eyes. "Got it?" The red SUV backed up the drive and disappeared up the street.

I stood with my hands in the back pocket of my Capri pants contemplating my escape the minute he left.

Downtown Montgomery was a less than a thirty-minute drive. Taking into consideration traffic on Interstate 65, and time in the lab, McCoy should've had plenty of time get there and back.

Forty-five minutes passed before Bill called to say he'd just spoken to Jack. "He was out on Highway 55 just east of town when he came across McCoy's car in the ditch. The agent told him somebody'd run him off the road, but not to worry, because Jack's going to drive him to Montgomery."

"Is McCoy all right?"

"According to Jack, he's got a banged up arm and a bump on his head, but other than that he's fine." Bill drew in one of his nasally breaths. Something else was wrong. "Sue, Paul stopped by the office a little while ago in a tirade. Brought Martha to tears, which is something I thought near impossible to do. Seems he called the entire department incompetent. He told her he was going to the capitol to have me recalled as sheriff." His attempt at laughing off the matter failed. He was pissed. "Could you call him, or get The Reverend to? I'd sure appreciate a good word."

"I'll try, Bill, but Paul Backman is the most stubborn man I know after The Reverend." The laugh came with a pinch of melancholy. "In the fifteen years I've known him, I can only remember one time he changed his mind and that was being married to me."

I hung up the phone, muttering. "Christ Almighty."

"What was that, Sue?" Gladys walked in, looking like she was ready to lecture me on the second commandment.

"I said Christ Almighty, and before you start the lecture on taking the Lord's name in vain, I apologize." I passed along the sheriff's tale of Paul's activities in his office. "The last thing I needed now was for Paul to go off half-cocked and bring charges down on the sheriff because some insane idiot has snatched our son."

The Reverend joined us in the living room. He wasn't the looming figure he'd been for so many years. Worry over Ruthie and John Earl was shrinking the life out of him. The knit shirt he wore hung off his shoulders, and the trousers bagged at his waist. Lines dug trenches around his eyes and mouth as I watched him speak.

"Paul's just worried, Sue. His son is out there. Who knows where, with who knows whom? I think we should pray." He reached for my hand and Gladys', but I drew away.

"You and Mother pray. You're good at it." I grabbed my purse and my keys off the secretary. "I'm going to find my son. I hope I see Paul, too. I have a few words for him about common courtesy to those trying their best to find John Earl."

I heard them calling my name while I backed toward the end of the drive, but I paid no attention. The patrol car pulled forward across the end of the driveway impeding my progress. I rolled down the window. "What gives?"

"Just doing my job, Ma'am. I was given orders not to let anyone enter or exit the drive."

I wasn't about to let this guy stop me from searching for John Earl. I pulled forward, jacked the steering wheel to the left with a jerk, and across the yard. When I checked the rearview mirror, the deputy was speaking into his shoulder two-way. I was now a fugitive. It didn't occur to me what a pain in the behind I was being for Bill.

Thunderclouds stained the afternoon sky concrete gray. Habit brought my hand to the visor and I checked my hair in the mirror. Increasing humidity turned it to something similar to copper wire so, while I steered with my knees, I pulled it back in a pony tail with a holder I found in my purse. Then, I tossed it over my shoulder.

The clouds, burdened with too much water, burst and the storm let loose. Thunder rolled a symphony of timbre drums and cymbals. Rain hit the windshield with such force that, even at the highest speed, the wipers couldn't keep up.

I should've backed up, turned around, and gone back to my parents. I should've waited for Agent McCoy to return with news from Birmingham, assuming he'd been there and was heading back when the jackass side-swiped him.

But I didn't.

When we were kids, everyone said Thomas was more stubborn, but I was about to prove them wrong, or die trying. I'd been the sensible kid, sitting back and waiting for someone else to try something first.

I pulled into the utility road. Dollops of rain disturbed the top layer of dust on the path near the wood post as I unclipped the chain from it and tossed the chain aside.

Standing there beside my sensible car, wearing comfortable tennis shoes with arch supports, I found strength to seek out and confront the man we'd seen in the woods, the man who'd taken from me two of the people I loved the most. I'd find him, and if he didn't confess and tell me where John Earl was, I was prepared to kick his sorry ass.

I hurried through the old part of the park. Sphagnum moss hung off the branches of pines and oak standing three stories tall, cutting the partial sunlight to almost nil. I could see where John Earl could have confused them with monsters.

I ran along the shoreline to the pavilion where the path along the pond became impassable. There, I climbed the hill near the new restrooms. At the end of a split-rail fence in the new section of the park, I climbed down the embankment and found the continuation of the path along the shore east toward the golf course.

Nothing moved except the rain on the pond's surface. It pummeled my face like wet BBs shot from an air rifle. I hadn't thought to bring rain gear. Only a few minutes passed before tee shirt and Capri pants clung like a wet second skin.

I started to run, sobbing and calling John Earl's name. I lost the path at the curve and low branches whipped my head. Keeping it down and watching where I stepped, I still stumbled on rocks and exposed roots made slick by the ungodly weather.

As a kid, I believed The Reverend carried the power to control Earth's ebb and flow, the yin and yang of the universe, because whenever he became angry with Thomas or me it rained, or it seemed that way, spoiling one outdoor activity or another. Later, I'd realize how irrational that belief had been. Pushing my way around Pennington Pond, I wasn't so sure.

With only water-leaden rays of late afternoon daylight to guide my steps, I couldn't decipher direction until I came upon the new marina. Then I saw him. He was rowing toward the nearest island. He kept rowing until he was on the far side and out of sight. I stumbled back through the brush I'd just traversed trying to spot him again.

I kick something hard. Then a sunbeam glinted on the corner of it. Under vines and scrawny trees lay a small boat with an oar hidden underneath it. I dragged the boat to the water.

Extra light would've come in handy since sundown was less than two hours away, but I'd left the flashlight in the glove box. I shoved the boat into the shallow water and fell in. I hadn't noticed my ankle swelling until I planted my foot to push while rowing. No amount of pain was going to deter me.

The island in question sat in the middle of the river beyond the actual limits of the park. Great place to hide a terrified forty-year-old woman and a frightened seven-year-old boy. The hairs on my neck stood with my dander. If Ruthie and John Earl were there, they were leaving with me.

Rowing with one oar became a chore, especially with a bum ankle. Wind drove the rain across me, and for the last half of the trip, I rowed with my eyes shut, guessing the direction. When I did look, I was only yards from the island.

Thunder followed a bolt of lightening, which lit the sky and, for a split second, I was afraid the man would see me. The water level on the northwest side of the island was knee deep. Drenched clothes weighed heavy, but the water eased the load when I climbed over the side and in. I waded to shore dragging the boat behind and using the oar as a crutch.

Overgrown kudzu hanging in the scrubby trees tickled my neck. I moved saplings aside and walked toward the center of the island. Fading light hit something dark at ground level and I stopped. My heart palpitated. Every muscle tensed. Every sound intensified.

245

It appeared I had discovered the foundation of a large house. Part of the front porch was still intact, but with a hole in it large enough for an adult to climb in. Down there in the ruins sat a small propane cook stove and a pile of clothes.

I almost jumped out of my skin when a dog barked in the distance. Probably one of old Mr. Skinner's hunting hounds.

My feet couldn't run fast enough back to the boat. When I slowed to catch my breath and stretch my shins before I got splints, I realized I'd run the wrong direction.

Something rattled the limb overhead.

My gaze darted skyward.

A shadow came at me from above. I screamed when he landed on me, knocking me to the ground. Twice my weight, he had me pinned beneath him. The depth of the woods and the lack of sunshine kept us in shadow. Those two things and the mud packed on his face disguised his identity for a time.

He covered my mouth with a bear-sized dirty hand. "I don't like folks on my island."

I bit his palm and he let out a yowl that echoed off the trees. "Vernon, it's me, Sue."

"You shouldn't be out here." He moved his hand so I could speak.

"I've come to talk to you about Ruthie and John Earl."

He climbed off me and yanked me to my feet. He made no attempt to rid his face of the mudpack.

"Vernon, you almost scared the sh… out of me."

"You shouldn't be out here in the middle of a thunderstorm." He removed a handkerchief and made a swipe at his face.

"John Earl has been kidnapped, too, and I'm worried sick." I began to tear up, and he offered his rag, but I shook my head and held out my palm facing him.

He shrugged and stuck the muddy thing in his back pocket. A crack of thunder, followed by a flash, allowed me to get a better look at the man. He was older than I remembered with a tight, sour mouth.

Three more cracks of thunder shook the ground, then dissipated and continued to roll across distant hills, leaving just a steady straight rain.

His smile did little to sway my fear and I began to babble. "Whoever it was just grabbed him right out of Lee Palmer's backyard." I yanked my tee shirt out of my slacks and dabbed my eyes with the tail. "He's just a little boy; he doesn't know anything. He didn't see anything. I had to come looking for him." My hands caught my head and hid my face. "I just want my best friend and my baby returned safely."

His lips tightened, and mud slipped into the lines around his mouth. Vernon's eyes darkened. "I wouldn't know anything about that."

I didn't know what to say, what to think. He was lying, but gut instinct told me not to provoke him. Only one question climbed aboard my train of thought. Had he killed that woman a couple of years back and stashed her out here on this island? Is that what he was trying to protect?

The rain slowed to a drizzle, and a haze of stifling, humid air settled over the park. I squirmed as a bead of

247

perspiration ran between my breasts and soaked into my bra. "Well, time's a wasting. I've got some investigating to do."

Vernon stood. "A word of warning." His face moved to within inches from mine. The reek of chaw drifted up my nostrils. "Don't go over to The Boondocks. Seems Naomi's new man's kinda taken up over there since Archie passed on, and he's a mean 'un." He gave his head a nod in the direction of the bar for emphasis. "Told me to stay away from now on."

A filthy, grown, uncouth man stood before me, yet I couldn't suppress maternal tenderness. I rose on tiptoe and kissed his mud-smeared cheek. "Thanks, Vernon, I'll watch myself."

EIGHTEEN

I took several steps and turned back. Vernon had already disappeared deeper into the woods, escalating his enigmatic aura. "Hey, Vernon?"

He reappeared in a flash. "Yeah, Sue?"

"Isn't that the foundation to Twelve Oaks?" I pointed in the direction of the porch and foundation. I wanted to find out what he knew of the area.

"Yep, that was the old Pennington mansion. Belonged to my great"—he started counting greats on his finger—"granddaddy. Somebody burned it down."

I contemplated his words for a moment, then asked, "Why would somebody want to destroy such a magnificent home?"

"Cause of the skeletons in the closets. Aunt Virginia knows all about it."

"You can't mean Virginia Covington Pennington, Vernon. She died in that fire."

He frowned. "No ma'am, Roy has her over in the old folks home just the other side of town. I've seen her."

He had to be mistaken, or lying.

My mouth twitched from side to side, while I watched him disappear into the forest. "Hey Vernon, you got any idea about who took Ruthie and John Earl?" No need telling him about the note or the killer's admission to killing Ruthie. If he didn't have anything to do with Deputy Duffy and Archie Claremont's murders, I saw no reason to scare him. If he did, there was no reason to tip him off.

His shoulders straightened, as he came forward again. "Well, I been watching The Boondocks since I was told to stay away. Kinda keeping an eye out for Naomi, and I'm not sure, but I think something's going on over there. Could have something to do with those two being missing."

I pushed. I had to. He could be my only hope in finding Ruthie and John Earl. "What kind of something?"

"I think Naomi's man is doing something illegal, maybe even making shine." Those blue eyes grew steely. "Maybe even killed Mr. Archie for his recipe."

Everything he said made perfect sense. "He's not competition, is he? I mean you're not running shine are you?"

"No ma'am," his answer came back firm, without hesitation. "My deal with Jack is that I can live out here in the park for the rest of my life if I don't do anything like that again." With another definitive nod, he turned and made his way back into the forest.

The deepening of his brow and the look in his eyes told me he would be more than just a little peeved if he ever discovered a still on one of the islands, which didn't belong to him. Judging by the respect he'd shown Carmichael, he was keeping his end of the bargain. Still, the park was his territory, and he must be aware of all the activities going on. He might not be the most liked man in the area, but his freedom to roam gave him the best sense of the temperature of it. If the heat was on, so to speak, Vernon Fielding was the most accurate thermometer.

He turned and hollered over his shoulder, "Gotta go. Got work to do." And he was gone into the underbrush like an apparition.

"Wait, Vernon, one more question. Have you ever heard about John Pennington's will giving your side of the family one hundred acres?"

He returned but spoke in a whisper that barely carried the space between us. "Heard of it, I saw it. The original got burnt up in the house and the second's lost somewhere."

One ring and Bill answered, announcing his rank and name. "Bill, Sue Backman. I just met up with Vernon out on one of the islands..."

I pulled the phone away from my ear when he yelled, "Officer called a while back. Said you escaped across the lawn. Mind telling me what the hell you're doing out there?"

I waited for the tirade to subside. "I've decided not to wait until this maniac decides to go off the deep end and kill John Earl and Ruthie. I'm going to find him, or them, even if I have to do it all by myself." My pride lasted but for a moment.

"Now you listen up, Sue, and you listen up good." His voice strained so he barely held his composure. "We've got a force of trained professionals checking every lead to track Ruthie and your son. You see, I'm convinced they're alive." He drew in a loud breath.

"Do you want me to tell you what historically happens to parents and friends of missing persons who decide to play hero and go out on their own?" He stopped and waited, and when I did not venture to guess, he answered for me. "They end up missing, or injured, or

251

worse. Now, I'm ordering you to go back to Lee Palmer's house to wait with your parents." The call ended.

Well, I was not about to let some backwoods, know-it-all, woman-hating lawman order me around. Before I hung up, I said, "By the way, I've got an idea why Vernon's been lying." Then I slapped the phone shut, climbed in the boat, and started rowing toward the point.

I rowed until my arms ached and the pain in my ankle spread up my leg. Then I rowed more until the boat hit the shallow shore near the point. My steps took on a more definite rhythm. My feet came high off the ground as I marched, angry and more determined to find answers to the nagging questions. I could add a new one. If Thomas was Naomi's new guy, then why was he being so mean to Vernon?

The rain had come to a temporary end, and a hazy sun brought sweltering temperatures that threatened to melt me. It did a number on my resolve. I started to second-guess all my decisions of late. If John Earl and I hadn't made the drive back to the revival, he would be all right. But Gladys had expected us. And I've never been able to turn her down.

A smidgen of guilt spilled in. Paul had been bugging me for extra time this summer so he could take John Earl fishing in the gulf. Now, all I could taste was heart-wrenching, gut-knotting remorse for being too stubborn and childish to put aside my own opinions or numbness about him without thought about what was best for John Earl. If I'd just let him go, my baby would be safe somewhere off the coast of Florida, far away from two murders and two kidnappings.

Tears clouded my vision, and I tried to wipe them away. They were coming so fast now, I couldn't keep up. Everything in front of me blurred. I was rowing close enough to the north shore that, when I stopped, I noticed movement in the underbrush along the nearby shore.

Someone was following me.

Nothing but silence swallowed the forest.

A solid shadow formed. Someone was watching, and it couldn't be Vernon. As far as I knew he hadn't left the island.

I began power rowing, and a searing pain soared up from my right ankle to my knee. I screamed and dropped the oar in the bottom of the boat. Birds fluttered from the treetops screeching their annoyance at me.

No one around, not even an evil maniac.

I waited. I reached for my cell phone but it was low on power. I couldn't even call for help, and dusk loomed. I twisted my mouth the way I do when I am considering a heady subject.

So, Sue, I thought, *are you just going to sit out here hoping Vernon comes back to claim you, too? Carmichael isn't going to rescue you when he's not even in town. Bill's in his office. Stop wallowing in self-pity and start rowing to The Boondocks for help.*

There really was no choice. Thunder in the distance answered the questions. Another wave of storms was headed my way. I wasn't about to lie there in that boat and get soaked again. I leaned down and grabbed the oar.

253

According to my best guess, rowing with all my parts intact would take five minutes.

It took me an hour. The next batch of storms came about half way around, soaking me through, again. I didn't need a mirror. I knew I looked like a drowning rat. Better yet, a drowning rat that had crawled out on the highway and got hit by a semi.

NINETEEN

The bow of the boat bumped against the T-shaped pier, and I tried standing, leaning on one oar while leaning forward to steady the boat. My first three attempts failed, and I ended up pushing the boat farther away.

I caught a post with the oars just before the boat floated out of reach. I yanked, crashing the worn aluminum rowboat back against the wood. As I crawled out, I held tight to the post, and hoisted myself forward. I didn't care where the boat landed.

Creosol and fresh cigarette smoke burned my eyes. A fresh butt floated on the water's surface then disappeared under the pier. Perhaps it had belonged to a lookout, and Naomi and Thomas had been warned of my arrival—or the man I'd chased over here, assuming he was the man I'd seen in the woods. Or was that Thomas too? My mind tried to envelope these thoughts while my body attempted its first step on the stairs leading to the front door of The Boondocks.

My ankle ached but I never questioned my reasons for coming. I wanted to watch and listen, and with any luck pick up a clue or two about Ruthie and John Earl's whereabouts. Bill's words concerning the man lying about Ruthie's death brought some comfort and hope.

I clung to the railing, limping up the steep steps slick from the recent rain. The screen door announced my arrival with a bang that echoed throughout the bar. For a Saturday afternoon, it seemed quiet, then it dawned on me that no one wanted to venture out with what was happening in the area. The locals stared up from their beers. With a defiant eye, I stared them down, one by one. Most went back to sipping without another thought of me or my sorry appearance.

Naomi appeared from the kitchen. "Sue, whatch ya'll doing here in this kind of weather? And what happened to your foot?"

My ankle had swelled up around my shoe and reminded me of the Uncle Fester minister, his collar digging into his thick neck. The sight intensified the pain threefold.

I sank into the nearest chair and pulled another close for my foot. I motioned for her to lean close. I reached for her hand. "My condolences for the loss of your husband."

She mumbled a thank you. "Now you gonna tell me how your foot came to look like an overgrown eggplant?"

I had to laugh, for sure enough, that's exactly what it looked like. "I was wandering around the point, hoping to see something that might lead me to clues about my friend, Ruthie, and my son John Earl. Caught my damned foot on a root and wrenched my ankle."

"Yeah, I was awful sorry to hear about your little boy going missing." She turned and walked toward the bar. Her hips swayed with a swing that would interest any male.

She returned with a shot of tequila and an ice pack. "Help the pain and the swelling."

I squelched a scream as she laid the ice over the offending upper ankle. I downed the shot and shivers ran up both legs, and fanned throughout my body.

"Sorry." She shrieked. "I thought it would help."

"I'm not sure anything can help me right now." The shot warmed me to the gizzards.

Naomi pointed at the empty shot glass. "Want another?"

"No thanks, just a diet something. Whatever you got in the gun is fine." The ice began its numbing effect on my leg, and besides my paranoia about my appearance. I was beginning to feel okay. When Naomi returned with my diet soda, I stung her with the question that had been foremost on my mind since my chat with Vernon.

"So, I hear there's a new man in your life? Kinda quick after Archie's death, don't you think?"

She stopped dead in her tracks, as they say, and turned back so fast I thought she might slap me. "You been talking to Vernon, haven't you?" Her brown eyes grew sharp. "Ain't nobody's business who I see and who I don't." Then, quick as a wink, she friendlied up, and changed the subject. "Bill got any good news about the kidnappings?"

"Nothing." I choked back the tears. "Naomi, he's just an innocent boy. He doesn't have a clue what's going on." I spoke loud enough for everyone to hear. Even these self-absorbed bar flies might own up to seeing somebody with the boy if they knew one had been kidnapped. "The last time anyone saw him, he was wearing athletic shorts and an Atlanta Braves tee shirt. And Ruthie Palmer is my best friend. Her only mistake was

257

going out in the woods with John Earl and me at the revival."

None of the men at the bar even flinched. Well, it was worth a try.

Naomi sat in the chair across from me, but soon called back at her patrons lining the bar. "Ya'll need something, just holler."

Each of the four men acknowledged with the wave of a hand and returned attention to the game on television. Atlanta Braves playing the Houston Astros was a bigger deal than most any local news, even a kidnapping. John Earl loved his Braves.

My head sank to the table. I couldn't hold the tears at bay any longer. "I can't keep doing this. I've got to keep my wits. Falling apart will not help the sheriff find Ruthie or John Earl."

My head came off the table and I pushed damp curls away from my face. "Naomi, is it true that Aunt Virginia is alive and Roy's hidden her away at the nursing home?"

"It's complicated." She stood, placed both hands on the table and leaned close. "See, after the fire she went a little nuts." Her scent was a familiar cigarettes and grease smoke, but the flowing pants and matching top she wore revealed her to be a woman more worldly than the owner of a bar in the foothills of Alabama. "How about I fix you a bite to eat and get you a real drink? Food in the stomach always makes a body feel better." Her smile produced almost perfect white teeth. "You can't be going too far on that leg anyway. If somebody don't come looking for you in a while, I'll call Sheriff Bill."

I had to see for myself that Aunt Virginia was still alive. I had to know the reason for the lies and secrets. I was going to that home and stand outside her room until she opened the door. I'd force my way in if I had to.

While Naomi was gone, I rested my head on my arms crossed on the table, trying in desperation not to think about the pain in my foot, my son, or the fact I was in the most dangerous place possible at the time. Fact was, any one of the eight men or six women at the bar, enjoying a late afternoon brew, may have kidnapped Ruthie and John Earl, shot Deputy Duffy, murdered Archie, and dumped him in the lake.

I raised my head just far enough to peek at my watch. Four forty-five. Had to think clearly. Jack and the FBI agent were back in town. Bill knew I'd been in the park. He'd assume I'd come here to talk to folks and look for clues. It was comforting to consider the man knew me so well. Confessing to him the possibility someone was following me terrified me. He'd probably return me to protective custody.

I couldn't think about that. I had to focus on Ruthie and John Earl.

Naomi set a plate in front of me with more food than I ate in a day. The burger was at least a half a pound piled just the way I liked, dripping with cheese, ketchup, mustard and, when I bit in, the condiments oozed out. The lettuce was cold and crisp, and the tomato ripe. Crisp fries, lightly salted, released steam, causing a flush in my cheeks. She set a bottle of beer in front of me from a brewery in Birmingham.

I'd told her I didn't want anything alcoholic, but Naomi just giggled. "Lordy, girl, beer ain't much alcohol." Then she waited, as an artist would, for a critique.

I raised my thumb still holding the drippy burger.

"Brought you a couple of pain killers, too."

"Next time you come by, you want to bring a pack of Marlboro Light Menthols?"

"Sure thing, Honey, but you sure don't look like the smoking type."

"You'd be surprised what type I really am." I sent an impish grin and swallowed two aspirin with my beer. My ankle ached along with my head and my heart. I wanted my friend and my son returned. I wanted Paul to retreat into what's-her-name's arms and leave me alone. I wanted my life to return to normal. I didn't see those few things being too much to ask.

The painkillers kicked in with the last of the first beer. With my belly full and my foot less painful, I settled back, hoping Thomas would arrive and waiting for Bill to fetch me.

By five-thirty, I'd downed three beers, three more than in the past year. Added to the shot of whisky for medicinal purposes earlier, a good buzz had developed. My vision blurred The Boondocks grow more crowded. Patrons stood two and three deep at the bar, and a din of multiple conversations arose. I was wasting time, sitting at the back of the room, but I was afraid the pain would return if I put pressure on the foot. Still, distinguishing between conversations required I move closer.

I pushed up on my one foot and steadied myself. Balancing between tables and stools along the way, I managed my way around the bar near the back deck.

An almost cool breeze off the lake rattled woven wood blinds rolled to the ceiling. I sat at a table by the back door and lifted the sore leg at the knee, placing it with care on a chair next to me.

Naomi noticed my move and came to question me. She brought the pack of cigarettes I'd requested.

"It was getting a little stuffy in the corner. Thought moving over here by the deck might help." I ripped off the plastic and the silver paper off the top of the pack, tapped it on my palm and pulled out the first. Naomi lit it for me.

My answer must have satisfied her, because she returned to her position behind the bar. Was she keeping track of my every move? Was she concerned about my safety? Or was she more concerned I was spying? I chose to believe the first until Thomas walked in.

The bar opened at both ends, so when he walked in the door, he stepped right behind it and pulled Naomi into his arms. He nibbled on her neck, whispering something that made her giggle. She responded by pushing him away and pointing at me.

In an instant, Thomas stood over me. "What the hell are you doing here again? And when did you start that nasty habit?"

I was not about to allow my older brother to chew me out, especially since, until twenty-four hours ago, he hadn't given a rat's ass about my well-being. "I could ask you the same question. And as for this—I took a long drag just for him—I've been smoking since I was in college." It was a lie. I started long before that. Ruthie and I used to sneak Mr. Palmer's Winston Reds when we were in junior high.

261

He sat without invitation. "Is your car in the parking lot? If not, I'm going to call you a cab and row you back to shore."

"You'll do nothing of the sort." I sat up letting my swollen foot drop to the floor. I cringed. "Look, Thomas, in case you haven't noticed, I'm not a little girl anymore. I'm a grown woman, right now missing a kidnapped best friend and son."

"They've got John Earl, too? Christ, why didn't somebody call me?" His volume caused a momentary silence in the immediate area.

I almost told him about the note, but my distrust loomed like an umbrella over his head.

He stood and held out a hand. "You shouldn't be here. Let me take you back to Lee's and promise never to come back here again."

I pointed to my swollen foot. "I'm not going anywhere until the swelling goes down a bit. Besides, the sheriff should be here soon to fetch me."

Thomas flew into a rage. "You called the sheriff? What'd you go and do a stupid thing like that for?"

How about for my safety, Doofus? "Why did you scare a sweet man like Vernon and tell him to stay away? Don't you know Naomi sometimes feeds him the only meal he gets in a day?"

"I don't trust him. He sneaks around, peeking in the windows." His answer came too quickly.

"How in the hell does he sneak around out here in a rowboat? Besides, what do you have to be worried about? You and Naomi carrying on some kind of secret affair, are you? Or worse, doing something illegal?" "Did you off Archie so you could have her all to yourself?" I was joking, but he didn't share my humor.

Please tell me what's going on so I can help you. If you know something about the kidnappings, I'll go with you to see Bill" Then, I did the one thing I promised myself I'd never do in front of him again, I started crying. "It's Ruthie, Thomas, and my baby."

He didn't answer the question. Instead, he leaned on his hands and moved to within an inch of my face. "You'll stay out of my business, Sis, if you know what's good for you." He pushed away from the table, made his way back across the room, and took a spot at the far end of the bar, near the front entrance where I'd found him that first night.

He acted as though I wasn't even there and we'd never spoken. He spent the next hour flirting with Naomi, and she with him. If I wasn't so angry with him for his comment about knowing what was good for me, I would've been happy for him.

He and Naomi were hiding something. I had to admit, I knew little about Thomas' activities over the past few years. What if he'd become involved with some gang or the mob? The mob, what was I thinking? There was no Mafioso in central Alabama. Especially working out of a place located so close to a state park. Not with Bill and Carmichael so close.

Still, I found myself trembling. A barmaid, a younger version of Naomi, came to ask if I needed anything else. Beer filled me to the gills. "A vodka and tonic, with olives please." She started to walk away but I added, "Oh and, Miss, just wave the tonic over the glass. Don't want to waste a good buzz."

Days and time swirled around me like a sweet cooling breeze. I reached for my phone to check the date and day of the week on it but remembered it was dead. A calendar on the wall behind the bar did the trick. Saturday, remember.

Ruthie had been missing for twenty-four hours, John Earl, five. I scoped out the place, not only hoping to take my mind off the pain in my ankle, but convinced if I sat there long enough the kidnappers or someone who knew something would give themselves away.

There was no one distinct group of clientele. Men who worked with their hands, skilled tradesmen, plumbers, electricians occupied stools along the long end of the bar best for viewing whatever sport was on one of the six televisions. Younger business types stood at high tables wearing swim trunks and tee shirts with the names of places they'd traveled. The women wore shorts and poofy tops. Chatter was loud and lively.

The young woman finally returned with my drink. "Sorry 'bout that. As you can see, we're getting busy and there's only the two of us waiting tables."

"No problem, I understand, believe me. I worked my way through college as a waitress." I held my glass in a sort of sisterly toast and downed the contents. Its strength made me wince.

Then I set the glass back on her tray. Her name tag read "Dee."

"Dee, do me a favor and lighten the next one by about a third?"

First she frowned like she thought I was nuts. Then she shrugged and nodded. "I suppose so, but I'll have to charge you full price."

"No problem." I hoped my smile convinced her I knew what I was doing. "And tell Naomi I'd like to buy a drink for that gentleman at the end of the bar."

"You mean Tom?" She held the tray high in his direction. "I don't want to tell you your business, but I don't think that's such a good idea."

My tiny chuckle came in a puff. "That's okay, hon.' He's my brother." I downed the contents of the glass.

Her reaction was as I suspected it would be— simple, straightforward shock. "Oh," was all she could muster.

I sat back and watched Dee work her way to the bar to follow my orders. Naomi pointed at me. I smiled and waved. She leaned over the bar close to Thomas. Then she poured his tumbler to the rim with clear liquid out of a tall bottle from the back of the bar.

He held it high in a silent thank you.

My lip curled into a frown and I bit it, staring at the scene. I asked myself when Thomas had started drinking vodka. I blew him a sarcastic kiss. "Kiss my ass, you jackass."

TWENTY

In a sudden burst of motion, a hand the size of a child's catcher's mitt, and covered in wiry red hair, grabbed the chair my foot was resting in, spun it around, and before my eyes sat a man best described as the second coming of Erik the Red. Eyes the color of the Caribbean I'd seen only in magazine photos, stared from behind eyebrows resembling copper wire and matched beard and mustache.

"Hi, name's Charlie Wilson. My friends call me Cannon, but that's a story we should save for our second date." He grinned and tiny lines collected around his eyes when the eyebrows and mustache tried to touch. "Can I buy you a drink?"

I guessed the reason for the nickname. My first instinct was to laugh, my second was to run for my life. And since the Redneck from Hell had dropped my ankle with his spectacular chair trick, running would be out of the question. I was trapped. I stared at him, shaking my head side-to-side so fast my teeth rattled in my mouth.

Thinking I was married might deter Cannon, so I used Paul as an excuse. "No, thanks, I'm waiting for my husband." The attempt failed.

"I don't see no wedding band on that pretty little finger." He reached for my hand, but I drew it away and pressed both into my lap, hiding the trembling from him.

Don't panic, I thought. *He's like a mad dog. If he sees your fear, he'll attack.* My purse was locked in the car, but the cell was in my shorts pocket. I knew it was dead, but hoped he couldn't hear its silence when I opened it and pretended to call Paul.

"Honey, where are you? I'm at The Boondocks, and I've already had a drink." I paused what I thought was the appropriate amount of time for a response. "Okay, see you soon. Love ya."

"Now do you believe me?"

"No ma'am. Just 'cause I look dumb, don't mean I am." A claw finger pointed at my hand. "I never saw any lights. Means your battery's probably dead."

Okay, so I'd been caught in the act of faking out a less-than-promising date prospect. Wait until I tell Ruthie. Crap, I forgot again. I melded into thoughts of shared confidences when Cannon's voiced boomed.

He pulled his cell out off his belt. "Want to try mine?" Okay, so I'd been caught in the act of faking out a less-than-promising date prospect. Wait until I tell Ruthie. Crap, I forgot again. I melded into thoughts of shared confidences when Cannon's voiced boomed.

He reached to his belt and slipped it out of its leather case.

I punched in Paul's number and waited for him to answer. I didn't give him a chance to say anything. "Listen, Paul, I just want to apologize for not listening to you when you wanted to take John Earl. I realize now how selfish and stupid that was." Whew.

"A little late for that now, don't you think? Maybe if you'd convinced Johnny that going with me was a good thing, he'd be safe, fishing in the gulf. Or maybe I could've gotten us tickets to the Braves game tonight. You know how much he loves going to the games. And maybe if you'd tried a little harder when we were married we still would be."

He was torturing me with all this, but his last statement stung the worst. I could've cried but I didn't. Years of his crap made me strong because I grew remarkably calm. "Never happen. My parents taught me not to lie. Unlike yours. By the way, were you at The Boondocks recently? Maybe talking to Thomas?" A click and dial tone.

Cannon stared at me with green puppy eyes behind wiry eyebrows. "You look like you could use a drink." He motioned for Dee and minutes later she set a tell glass of what looked like tonic water and lime in front of me. The last thing I remembered was walking back to the table. Someone put real vodka in my vodka.

TWENTY - ONE

The eye facing the ceiling rolled around in its socket for a minute. An attempt to open it was the pain, I imagined, the pulp of an orange experienced during the peeling process if it had a nervous system. At that moment, I wished I didn't.

Even lying still as a corpse hurt, and no matter how many times I swallowed, the sandpaper that formed on my tongue refused to relinquish its reservation.

Birds chirping outside the window ricocheted against the interior of my skull, causing the most excruciating sensation of all. When I did manage to get one eye open, I saw The Reverend standing by the bed, King James in hand, shaking it over me.

"Proverbs 14.34 'Righteousness exalts a nation, but sin is a reproach to any people.'" He flipped a few pages forward just for the dramatic touch. "Chapter 24.9, '…the devising of folly is sin and the scoffer is an abomination to men.'" His fist began a fierce vertical motion over my body similar to the knifing scene from the movie "Psycho." "And let's not forget what Paul wrote in Romans 6.12 'Let not sin, therefore, reign in your mortal bodies to make you obey their passions.'"

He completed the tirade with his favorite when speaking on the subject of drink, Jeremiah 25.27. "Then you shall say to them 'Thus says the Lord of Hosts, God of Israel: Drink, be drunk and vomit, fall and rise no more, because the sword which I am sending among you.'"

I raised my head off the pillow, creating an unbearable pain. "What about the letter? Did McCoy and Carmichael return it before midnight?" The guilt of not being there worsened the headache and the nausea. My voice seemed to originate from somewhere outside my body. I whispered, raspy.

He nodded, still in Repent-or-be-damned mode.

"Reverend-Daddy, I'm sorry. I went to The Boondocks with the best of intentions." Tears came equally from the pain and the guilt, and rolled out of the corners of my eyes and into my ears.

He remained, lording over me, glaring down over his spectacles with superiority shining in his eyes. "How could going to a bar, getting so drunk you had to literally be carried home by the sheriff, be the best of intentions?"

"I went looking for information on Ruthie and John Earl's kidnappings." I sat up and realized someone had exchanged the tee shirt I'd worn the night before with one of my nightshirts. I no longer wore a bra.

I wrestled with two possibilities. Bill had seen me half-naked, a thought that sent terror into my gut; or Gladys, a slightly more comforting, but still embarrassing prospect, had changed my clothes.

"Sue you have got to act more responsibly, more careful." The Reverend sat on the edge of the bed. His voice softened like it did when I was a kid and he would come into my room to say goodnight.

The pain in my brain throbbed from its stem to temporal lobe. My eyelids smashed together in a sort of sympathetic gesture. My teeth hurt, and yet, I couldn't help wondering if we were on the verge of a Hallmark Moment, The Reverend and me.

"When little John Earl returns, he's going to need his mother here for him, not to discover she was kidnapped, or worse, because she was too stubborn to listen to the advice of experts and stay out of their way."

I fought the urge to scamper to the bathroom and empty my stomach of its contents. My arms curled around my bent knees and my chin rested between my kneecaps. "You're right, as usual. I just thought I could go over there and maybe dig up some criminal activity that might lead us to Ruthie and John Earl."

The Reverend rose off the bed and did something I hadn't seen in ages. He chuckled. "Sue, you have quite an imagination. I give you credit for your resolve, though. Many a woman, and man for that matter, would have folded in like the old revival tent after a meeting."

A compliment coming from the man is a treasure, like finding the secret decoder ring at the bottom of a box of cereal. My stare as he left came with pure shock. "Thank you, Sir."

And with that, he departed.

My gaze didn't leave the doorway until Gladys came in carrying a tray with black coffee, dry toast, and a tall glass of milk on it. "What's going on? Did he quote the sins of the flesh to you on a hangover?" I straightened my legs and she set the tray on my lap. Then she turned back. "I'll go have a talk with him if he did."

"He's fine, Mother. He quoted a few lines. But then he made me understand how much I need to hold on for John Earl's return."

I didn't want to get caught in that emotional upheaval again. My aching body couldn't take any more for a while, so I downed the milk in one swallow. There is nothing better for a hangover than a glass of cold cow juice. It eats away the cottonmouth and coats the stomach. Following that with fresh-brewed coffee gives a person the jolt needed to get going again, and the dry toast helps to settle the stomach.

Gladys watched my activity with the gaze of a concerned mother caring for a sick child, only my sickness was self-inflicted. That fact didn't matter to her. I was hurting and therefore, the responsibility fell to her to make it all better. She waited until I finished the toast before springing the news. "Now you'd better hurry. Sheriff Halvorson will be here soon. Said something about taking you to breakfast."

I handed her the tray, flipped the covers off me and sprang out of bed. Dizzy with a gut-wrenching pain, which started at the base of my skull, I goose-stepped across the top, and then felt my ankle, and grabbed the bed. "When, when did he call? Why didn't you tell me right away?"

I sank to my knees. Panties, bras, tank tops and jean shorts came out of the suitcase and flew in the air. See, I pack by outfit, not by type of clothing.

Gladys began collecting the items and refolded them. "Bill told me not to wake you, and if you think I was about to interrupt your father in the middle of a good scolding sermon...well you should know better." A smirk lifted the right side of her face and enunciated her crow's feet.

College taught me a multitude of things, and none more important than the ability to put on and remove a bra while wearing a shirt. After the bra was in place, I tugged the nightshirt over my head and replaced it with a sleeveless tee shirt John Earl had given me for a birthday. Then I yanked on cropped pants I found under some other clothes.

She started for the stairs, carrying the tray and giggling like a girl. Gladys Mae was a devoted wife, but she knew Jedidiah to be overbearing at times. Her innuendos to that end were our little secret.

I hobbled to the bedroom door and called to her. "Mother, thank you."

She'd flashed that smile before. She sent it when her heart overflowed with pride. "You're welcome, but I haven't really done anything. Just brought up a little coffee and toast."

I rolled my eyes. The woman never gave herself enough credit. Few of us did. "I'm not going to stand here and list off everything you've done for me, but you know. I know you know because I'd do the same for John Earl given half the chance." In an instant, the light-hearted mood died. I began to cry. "I may never have that chance though."

I followed her down the stairs, but my ankle reminded me of its condition, and buckled. I tripped and pushed Gladys forward. The tray flew out of her hands. Time slowed and a few seconds seemed like minutes. The coffee mug remained intact rolling down the carpeted stairs, but the coffee spread a stain like blood. Could be Ruthie or John Earl's...or both.

The plate came to a rattling halt between the balusters, but didn't fall to the wood entry floor below.

The whole scene mirrored my emotions. First, falling into a rut of depression and then straddling the precipice of emotional turmoil. My best friend and son were out of reach, maybe dead, and I was powerless over the situation. At least, when I discovered Paul's affair, I'd found the strength to throw him out despite his pleas to let him stay and promises to be a devoted husband and father.

This was different. Neither Ruthie nor John Earl had done anything or said anything to deserve their fate.

I lay on the stairs, sobbing.

As she had so many times, Gladys pulled me into her nurturing embrace. "Now you listen up, Sue. Both Ruthie and John Earl are going to be fine. You've just got to hold onto your faith."

"Do you really expect me to believe in a God who would allow this to happen, especially to an innocent child?"

Her arms dropped to her side. She took a few steps and retrieved the tray. She stared back up at me. Anger and disappointment had replaced the pride in her eyes. "God doesn't allow these things to happen. The devil is at work here." She gathered the dishes, and continued down the stairs.

A cloud of sullenness hung over me as I dabbed a little make up to conceal the red blotches on my nose and cheeks. I couldn't imagine my life without my son and my best friend. The words to my favorite hymn rang in my head, bouncing around with the leftover ache.

But I didn't have a friend in Jesus at that moment. He'd let me down.

The doorbell rang and I hobbled with all the speed I could back up the stairs and into the bathroom. I sped up what John Earl calls my "getting ready process." *God, I miss my boy. I just want to see that grin with the gaps where his baby teeth once hung. Laugh at one of his grade school jokes about poop or the knock-knock about the orange and the banana.*

I hobbled down the stairs, warning myself not to start crying again. I reached into the front pocket of my capris and pulled out a wad of used tissue just in case.

Bill, The Reverend, and Mama waited in the entry. The scene reminded me of one of those wedding photos, only I wore no bridal gown and the day lacked any happiness. That day would come when I got my son and Ruthie back.

Either he had a remarkable intuition as to my mood, or Gladys had filled him in on the morning's events. He stepped forward and took my hand. That weak, scaredy-cat in me wanted to lean against him, soak up his strength, but I needed to prove to myself I still owned a modicum of independence. I didn't need a man to comfort and support me.

"I thought I'd come by and see how you were feeling. If you're feeling up to it, I thought we'd go down to Sadie's for breakfast."

Food was the last thing on my mind. Even the dry toast was sitting heavy on my tumbling tummy. On the other hand, I couldn't pass up a chance to eek out more gossip from the place. The last time I was there, I got the sense that Cami knew more than she let on.

The Reverend burst my bubble of impending excitement. "Hold on, Sue, I think you should stay here in case the kidnapper tries to get in touch with you about a payment."

He was right. Again.

I looked to Bill, disappointed.

He flashed his quirky, endearing smile and snuck a quick wink. Then he put on his best official stance: shoulders back, chest out, and speaking with depth and authority. "Reverend, we have that covered. We've set it up so that any calls coming in on the landline to this house are automatically rerouted to my cell number."

The Reverend grumbled a low, "Oh, I see," and that was that.

Then I remembered my dead phone. I was about to tell Bill about it when Gladys handed it to me. "I found it in your pocket and thought it might need recharging so I plugged it in last night."

She definitely had my vote for Mother of the Year.

Bill's arm swept the air toward the front door. "Shall we go? I believe Jack and the FBI agents are waiting there for us."

The Reverend shot me a look of disgust and warning, and with no doubt of the meaning behind it. Behave and concentrate all your energy on John Earl.

It was my turn to shock him. To ease his mind, and to thank him for the tenderness he had displayed earlier, I ran to him. I put my hand on his shoulder and boosted myself onto the tips of my toes. Then I did something I haven't done since the day I married Paul. I gave him a kiss on the cheek. "Don't worry. This breakfast meeting is strictly business. I'm only going to find out if the sheriff has discovered anything new."

Lie number…oh hell, I've lost count.

TWENTY-TWO

On any given Sunday morning during the summer, Sadie's was the place to be if you wanted long conversations full of the best gossip, and plates heaped with eggs any style, any breakfast meat your little clogged arteries desired, or a stack of Cami's infamous peach-pecan pancakes. Cami and two other women hustled from table to table, carrying coffee pots and water pitchers.

People stood four deep just inside the door, waiting for a table or a booth, but didn't seem to mind. They knew good food was on its way, followed by as many refills of fresh brewed plain or flavor-of-the-day coffee, steaming hot or iced.

Cami hollered a friendly hello when she heard the tinkle of the bell on the door. She carried four plates of food, one on each forearm and one in each hand. "All ready in the back, Sheriff."

Bill snuck up from behind and put his hand on my shoulder. His whisper came one decibel above silence. "Sue, Cami's cleared that big table in the back for us." He smiled at a few of the patrons he knew. "I want to keep your presence here as low-profile as possible, but if the kidnapper is watching you, I want him to know you're not hiding at Palmer's like a scared rabbit."

He would have to go and say something like that. I'd been trying, unsuccessfully I might add, to forget the fact that someone might be after me, too. If anyone was waiting to nab me, standing in the crowd at Sadie's afforded the perfect opportunity. I didn't dare turn my head. I scanned left, up and down. Then I repeated the same to the right. The motion created a headache, or maybe just rejuvenated the leftover one.

A hand touched my back.

I froze.

I sucked in a breath and held it. Beads of sweat formed on my face, and my hands got clammy. I rubbed them together and touched my cheeks. They burned, and without looking in a mirror, I knew I was beet red.

I could've sworn I screamed, but no sound came forward.

My head whipped around. Pain coursed across my forehead.

No menacing man came forward. No one grabbed my arm, dragged me through the crowd and out the door. Eyes glared and faces stared. Maybe I had screamed. Only when I saw Bill urging me forward through the crowd did I clear my lungs of the fear with a sigh.

That voice, Bill's voice, the one I'd come to rely on for calm and security tickled my ear. He drew me from ridiculous thoughts.

"Sue? They're waiting." His touch grew stronger on my back, and I moved through the crowd excusing myself as I went.

I could feel every eye staring and lips a-flapping. One woman sitting at a table by the window whispered to her friend, "That's her, you know. She's the mother of that lost boy and the missing woman is her best friend."

Carmichael, another man in a uniform, and the two agents from FBI's Missing Persons Bureau waited at a table set for ten in a small, separate dining room. The town's Chief of Police sat at the head of the table, next to a man Bill introduced as Autauga County Sheriff. Agents McCoy and Linton sat in the two chairs on the far side against the wall. Carmichael claimed the spot across from McCoy. I stood next to Bill and across from McCoy and Carmichael.

The ranger was staring, and I thought I recognized the look. It reminded me of John Earl whenever he was keeping a secret.

A hot breeze from a window air conditioner ruffled café curtains. The police chief sweated as he rocked on the metal chair's two back legs until I thought for sure he would topple and crack his head on the wall behind him. What a headline for the newspaper, "Police Chief Death Ruins Breakfast for Unsuspecting Citizens."

Stop it, I thought. Whenever I get nervous or the situation is beyond my control, I get sarcastic.

Bill pulled out the chair. "Sit down, Sue." A cheery grin lifted tanned cheeks. "You remember Bart Harris and agents McCoy and Linton."

I sat as ordered. The feet of the chair scraped the tile with an eerie shriek.

The FBI men fit in well with the locals, with short-sleeved white dress shirts, ties, and dark slacks like they were dressed for church. Their brows glistened with perspiration and wet spots showed on their shirts.

I nodded a simple greeting. "Gentlemen, what have you learned?" I've always wanted to say that, as though I were a part of the official search and rescue team.

A great effort came from McCoy, who appeared to be the younger of the two, as he leaned back, crossed one ankle over the other knee, and smirked. "Man, she doesn't waste any time, does she?"

I leaned on my elbows pressing into the table, but not before looking around for eavesdroppers. Then, I let them have it with both barrels. "My son and my best friend are out there somewhere, suffering who knows what at the hands of some maniac." I jerked my hands off the table and they came to rest in my lap. I couldn't allow anyone to see them shaking. "And you all are just sitting here enjoying breakfast and coffee."

Bill took the chair beside me, turned it so he straddled the back. Under the table and out of sight of the three men, he patted my hand. I yanked my hand away and gave him a sharp look. I didn't need calming down especially from him. I was mad, damn it, and I'd earned the right to be.

He picked at the outer rim of his ear under his hat. "You know that's just not true, Sue. We're doing everything we can to find those two, but every lead so far has come up empty."

His bony elbow rested on the table while McCoy flipped pages in a yellow legal pad. "Lab found no fingerprints on the original letter you received, but at least Ruthie was alive at the time of its writing."

The Autauga County Sheriff chimed in. "Rumor around town is that Naomi Claremont killed Archie because he found out she was having affair. And Mrs. Lester over on Vining Street in Selma says her mailman told her Roy Pennington has found evidence that Archie's claim to that tract of land is bogus. I've got the clerk of courts researching the title on all the land surrounding The Boondocks, but a lot of the data was destroyed in a fire."

Carmichael admitted to being at the bar. "The man Naomi has been seen with is Thomas Allgood, Sue's brother."

Agent Linton chimed in, glaring at me: the bad cop routine. "From what I've been able to gather, and Ms. Backman, perhaps you can fill in some details for us, your brother and father had a falling out several years ago and your brother left home. Until two days ago, you hadn't spoken to him. Is that correct?"

I presented an angry persona, but my soul ached for our lost time as siblings. "What does my brother's relationship with my father have to do with this case?" I wanted to escape, find Thomas, and ask the questions I knew were coming, and get the answers I didn't have. My chest swelled with the pain of those lost years, not knowing anything about my own flesh and blood.

Trembling with rage, I leaned against the back of the chair. A deep breath calmed me a bit. "You have to understand. The Reverend is a wonderful man, but his beliefs refused him patience when Thomas turned his back on the church."

I searched for the words that would best illustrate The Reverend. "My father is the most spiritual man I've ever known. To him, denying one's faith is tantamount to a personal insult. He would not allow Mama or me to see or speak to Thomas after he left home. I was raised to respect my parents and their rules, even if it meant denying Thomas existed. I've seen him more in the past

285

two days than I had in seventeen years. I saw him at The Boondocks last night."

Carmichael rose up off his seat and planted his fingertips on the table. "Lord A-mighty, girl, what were you doing there again? Don't you know how dangerous that was?"

I glanced over at Bill. "So I've been told, but I'm frustrated with the lack of effort to find Ruthie and John Earl. I decided to do a little investigation of my own. I went there hoping to find the man I saw Friday night in the woods." The trembling ceased. With each word, my resolve grew strong. "While I was at the park yesterday, I saw someone rowing to one of the islands. I found Vernon there. He told me he couldn't go back to The Boondocks because Naomi's boyfriend, a mean white man, told him to stay away. Turns out that man is my brother, Thomas."

My emotions were stuck on the Tilt-a-whirl. "I'm still not convinced Vernon is talking about Thomas."

Agent McCoy had remained a quiet observer until that moment. "What did you talk about with your brother last night?"

My shoulder blades met the back of the chair. Frustration overwhelmed me. "He told me repeatedly to leave. He said it wasn't safe, but he wouldn't tell me why" I stared at the agent trying to stop the tears from flowing. "Is he involved in the kidnappings?"

Agent McCoy didn't bother looking up from his notes. "We can't release that information."

TWENTY-THREE

I watched the FBI, Bill and the other men walk, then meet on the sidewalk for a second meeting. I didn't care what they were talking about this time. I had other plans. Talking about seeing Vernon the night before at the park got me to thinking about the will and this rumored land sale. I needed to hear more about it from the horse's, or should I say, mare's mouth.

Cami stopped me on the way out. "What's your hurry? Don't you want to stay for another piece of pecan pie?"

"No time. I laid money on the counter for the two sweet rolls and coffee I'd had during the meeting with law enforcement. "I'm on my way to see Aunt Virginia."

Her black eyes darkened. "Honey, surely you know she died when Twelve Oaks burned to the ground."

I just smiled. "Well, according to Vernon, Roy's been hiding her out at the nursing home all these years. Probably under an assumed name."

She snickered through her nose. "Well, ya'll be careful anyway. Wouldn't want anything to happen to you." She looked around, and then leaned across the counter and whispered, "Specially now that Sheriff Bill has taken such a liking to you." Her left eyelid bounced a wink.

The cell rang. I only answered it after I realized it was in my pocket since it was Mama's phone. "Sue, Jack. Seems the FBI found a discrepancy in the title to the parcel of land around The Boondocks. Why don't you drive out to the station and we can fill you in."

"I'll be there as soon as I can, Jack, but right now, I'm on my way to visit Aunt Virginia."

I didn't allow him to voice his disbelief before I ended the call.

I got directions from Cami to the home. A red brick sign with letters chiseled into stone told me I'd found the place. The round-the-clock senior care facility surprised me with its modern satellite design. The center of the campus consisted of a traditional nursing home for the invalid and elderly. If Aunt Virginia was in there, I was going to find her.

A panel of fifty buttons and residents' names hung on the wall in the entryway. The word adjacent to the zero read "Reception," so I pushed it.

I peeked through the glass door at a petite blonde-haired woman sitting behind an arced reception desk. The buzzer must have startled her, because she jumped, looked at me, rose, and came to open the inner door.

"I'm here to see Mrs. Virginia Pennington."

The name on her tag read Carol, but she didn't look like one to me. She seemed more of a Buffy, you know, the high school cheerleader who began her life as a brunette and slowly transformed into a blonde.

She settled back in her chair before facing me again. "Nobody here by that name."

I stood my ground. "Look, I'm her niece, Sue Backman. My best friend and son are the ones who've been kidnapped over at Pennington Pond. Are there any residents named Virginia?"

"There's one, Virginia Covington, but she won't see you. She hasn't seen anyone but staff and one son since she got here. She's not right in the head."

Ignorant woman. She wouldn't be right in the head either if she'd lost everything, including husband and one son in a house fire. And Roy, how stupid of you. If you really wanted to hide her, why on earth would you use grandmother's maiden name. "I still want to try. It's a matter of life and death that I see her."

"Well, I'll ring her room, but I'm telling you right now, she won't see you." Carol turned away and spoke several words I couldn't hear into the phone.

While she was turned away, I took the opportunity to walk around the desk and hurry down the first hall to my left. I had to ignore my throbbing foot. No time for that now. The doors to each room held slots with the occupant's name typed on sections of note cards. Third door on the right read Covington. I knocked and opened it several inches. "Aunt Virginia?"

A weak voice squeaked magnolia sweetness. "I told Carol and now I'm telling you. I don't want to see anyone."

"Please, Aunt Virginia, I know you don't remember me, but I'm Gladys and Jedidiah's daughter. My son and best friend have been kidnapped and I think you might be able to help."

"My son, Roy, already talked to both sheriffs and the park ranger." The door inched closed.

I put up a hand to stop it and pushed back. "Aunt Virginia, I know about the fire. I'm sorry about Uncle John and Robert, but my seven-year-old son's life may depend on something you know about the ownership of your land, and I'm not going away until we talk."

Silence. Then the door opened and she stood aside. "Fine, come in, but shut that damned door. I don't need all the residents of this place knowing my business."

A silk scarf covered part of her face, but revealed the green eyes of a terrified woman. She returned to the hospital bed, which occupied a good share of the room, and pulled up the sheet to her chin, her arms and hands hidden by the bed linens.

I'd stepped into a freezer at a meat packing plant. The temperature in the room had to be below sixty degrees. The minute I closed the door, this tiny woman could tell I was shivering. Advantage, Virginia. "I'm sorry about the temperature, Sue.

"So you do remember me."

She snapped, "I don't forget my kin."

"And I can't forget mine. My son's name is John Earl." I dug in my purse, pulled out my wallet and stuck out a picture of him, but her hands never moved from under the sheet.

"I'm sorry about the temperature, Sue, but my condition precludes cold."

My curiosity overwhelmed me and I asked the rude question. "What condition, Aunt Virginia? Why the sham of a fake funeral? Why have you been hiding out all these years?"

A laugh came through the cloth, causing it to move like the air conditioning bothering the window curtains with its breeze. "I assumed someone would've told you. You see, your Uncle John had planned a surprise fiftieth birthday party for me at Twelve Oaks." She emitted a sob. "But someone decided to surprise me another way and set fire to the house, while I was out shopping with friends. When we returned, the entire building and several of the outbuildings were engulfed in flames. I couldn't find John, Timothy, or Roy. I lost my head and ran through a wall of fire to look for them."

She unfolded the scarf and flashed her face and neck. Where I presume once had been creamy smooth skin, only rutted pink scar tissue remained.

"I was sent to this God-forsaken place away from the stares and whispers of the outside world."

"How did you survive the fire?"

"When the little dinky fire department arrived, they saw Vernon trying to pull me out." She began to sob. "John never made it out, neither did Robert. Roy claimed he was looking for them. Afterward, a thorough search of the grounds produced John and Robert's remains locked in a room of the cellar." The crying stopped with the same speed with which it came. "I had a nervous breakdown. I made Roy go through the ruse of a funeral, and I pay the staff here well to keep our secret. I don't for the life of me know why I'm telling you all this. A sort of confession I guess." She motioned for me to come closer, so I pulled a wood chair close to the bed. "Can I confess one more thing?"

I nodded almost tingling with anticipation.

"I'm afraid of Roy."

The door opened, and my head reeled around to see who had entered. Roy stood halfway in the doorway, wearing a striped shirt with the sleeves rolled to his elbows, dress slacks, and a quizzical frown.

"Mother, who is this beautiful creature come for a visit?" His accent gave him away. He had never been too far away from Alabama for any length of time. His smile revealed his sense of self-worth, over-rated I surmised.

I offered my hand. "Don't you recognize your cousin, Roy? I'm sure you must know that it's my son and best friend who were kidnapped."

He took my hand in his, holding it a minute longer than propriety allowed. "Sue Allgood, it's nice to see you after all these years. I dare say, you are the first visitor other than me to grace this room for some time, but now I fear the excitement has tired my mother." He was rushing me out and I knew it. He wanted to find out what I wanted.

"Just one more thing." Fishing pole ready, hooked, and baited. "A question for both of you now that you're here too, Roy. Is there any truth to the rumor that the ownership of the land The Boondocks sits on is in question? And that a company is trying to buy it, divide it, and sell it for water-front property for those who can afford it?"

"No question, really." He was quick to answer. "Archie and Naomi created this cock-and-bull story about how our five greats back willed that…her grandmother five greats back some of our land." He stopped before he said the word the three of us knew he meant. "That will never existed, and with the fire at the courthouse, and the fire at Twelve Oaks, there's no way to discover the truth." He glanced at Aunt Virginia.

She sat up and her voice sharpened. "Roy, you have no right to call names, even if implied."

"Sorry, Mother." He returned his gaze to me. "If Naomi thinks there ever was a will she's sorely mistaken, and I intend on getting our land back."

I studied Roy's face, looking for any sign he might be hiding something other than a deep hatred for Naomi's family.

Nothing surfaced.

"So it's not a rumor." I turned to go, but spun around to face Roy. I'm sorry, but I came up with one other question. Do you know how to fly small engine planes?"

"You've been talking to your husband." He straightened hunched shoulders. "I've taken him flying over Pennington Pond many a time." He kissed his mother on the head and told her he was going to speak to the staff about her dinner.

After he left I pulled out a pen and paper, wrote 678-446-7256 on the back of an old receipt, and handed it to Aunt Virginia. "If you think about anything more regarding our earlier conversation, please call me at this number. And don't worry about Roy. I'm going to make sure he doesn't hurt you." I left the room and retreated through the lobby, where Carol stared me down. I admit I enjoyed seeing the shock on her face.

"Aunt Virginia invited me to visit anytime." I was lying of course, but she didn't know it. "And I'd watch that son of hers. Did you know he'd threatened her?"

* * *

Since I'd have to wait until morning to visit the county courthouse for a gander at the deed and the will, if

293

possible, I made a quick stop at the sheriff's office to see if Martha'd heard from Bill, Jack's call long forgotten.

She called a cheery hello from behind the protective glass. "You're ex-husband is a royal pain in the ass."

"You're telling me. Why do you think he's my ex?" We laughed for a minute forgetting the circumstances.

"Listen, I'm really sorry about your little boy. You know Bill's doing everything he can to find him and your friend."

The radio crackled. "You calling for me, Martha?"

"No sheriff, Sue Backman's in the office. We were just discussing her son and friend."

"You tell her to sit her hinny down and wait for me. I'm in route back from a meeting with the FBI and Calvin over in Perry County."

My heart leapt for joy. Could it be the first break-through had finally come? I turned back to Martha "While he's on his way, do you know of any place other than the old courthouse I could look for information about my family's property? You know, deeds and maybe the original will?"

Bill barreled through the door, cowboy boots click-ing. The sound reminded me of a scene from those old westerns when the sheriff flips open the swinging doors on the saloon and strides across the floor to face the bad guy. Guess that meant I was the crook.

"You know as well as I do that the original county courthouse burned down in 1902. Took most those records with it. Barb's still searching through the database."

My heart locked in my throat. "So what do we do now?"

"*We* aren't going to do anything," he said with emphasis on the first word. "My men, Jack, the FBI, and some of the sheriffs from the surrounding counties, along with the ranger from the Talladega National Forest are meeting here shortly."

His hand pressed into my back, and I noticed he stood closer than in any of our prior meetings. "Listen, Sue, I know you're terrified and angry at me for not finding them yet, but I'm telling you now, you must return to your parents and stay there." He opened the door and shooed me out. "Now go back to Lee's and stay put until I call you."

Yeah, like that was going to happen. I needed to be close to John Earl and Ruthie, so I returned to the last place I'd spent time with either of them, the state park, but first I needed protection so I went back to Palmer's, found his old Ruger and stuffed it in my purse.

TWENTY-FOUR

Since Ranger Jack would be meeting with Bill for the duration of the afternoon, I didn't need to hide the car. Sunshine gave the area a peaceful appearance. The revival tent lay rolled and ready for transport back to the church basement. I sank into the warm grass beside it, recalling the bat incident and John Earl's protection speech. Tears returned and I wept openly.

"John Earl, where are you?" The noise threw birds off their perches and wings fluttered all around me.

I ignored lingering pain in my ankle and started down the path to the lake, but partway there, intuition halted my steps. I stood dead still. Leaves and twigs snapped behind me.

"Vernon?"

No response.

A figure crouched behind a five-foot tall azalea.

"Vernon, it's me, Sue. Come out from behind that bush this minute."

No movement. My heart fluttered like bird wings. I clenched and relaxed my fists trying to push the needle in my brain from panic to calm. "Whoever you are, I want you to take me to my son right now."

The figure arose and took off down a path away from me. I followed, but lost him at a fork in the trail. The path to the left circled back around to the road between the church property and the park, the one to the right to the point. I had to admit I was spooked and royally ticked. I'd probably been standing no more than a hundred yards from the kidnapper.

I dropped my phone when it rang, but picked it up on the third ring.

"Sue, it's Virginia. I'm almost certain that copies of John's will and his grandfather's were hidden in a cavity behind a foundation wall in the old house. If the fire didn't destroy them, they may still be there." She struggled for a breath.

Had Roy returned? Was he struggling to get the phone away from her? I wanted to thank her, but she'd already hung up before I got the chance.

Someone was rowing away from the shore just a few hundred yards away from me. I waited and listened, trying to determine direction. Then, with only the movements necessary to propel me toward the shore, I made my way there. An impression of the hull smoothed the sandy clay.

I flipped a boat and rowed toward Vernon's island. I needed to get to the remains of the house and find the copy of the will. The bad ankle turned me into a bit of a klutz. I tripped into the boat and sat down hard on the middle seat. Add sore coccyx to a sprained ankle. I managed to delay the onset of the pain and began rowing until the boat hit shallow water and a sandy shore.

Low branches and scrub trees thrashed at my face, but I just pushed them aside. Getting into the hole was a more difficult task. I scrunched my face into a grimace anticipating the pain of landing, and jumped.

I hadn't thought to bring a flashlight. Filtered natural light supplied little help. I remembered the lantern

I'd seen on my first visit and began feeling around for it. I kicked it against the stone wall, but it still worked.

The floor of what had been the cellar was damp and overgrown with kudzu and more than likely poison ivy, but it'd be worth it if I found the will and perhaps a clue to the kidnapper's identity. I swept the light over every inch of the four walls, only to find eight spiders. I cringed.

Another sweep found a spot on the east wall lighter than the rest. The corner of one brick jutted out, and I pulled it. It came away from the rest with ease. I tried the two nearest it, top and bottom. They both came loose from the wall after considerable persuasion.

I shined the light into the hole I'd created. I couldn't quite see what was stuffed in the back of the cavity, so I stuck my hand in. I touched something hard and, as I explored, I discovered its circumference equal to a soda can, but too long and wedged in too hard to remove from the six inch hole I'd made.

Adrenaline surged, while my fingers made quick work of the remaining bricks. By the time I realized I'd discovered someone's remains, my pulse could have beaten Seattle Slew. The story of Vernon murdering that woman and hiding the body came forth, and the will became the furthest thing from my mind.

"Don't touch that." Vernon was on me before I could take another breath. He yanked me to my feet.

My eyes remained closed. My heart and mind were racing at equal speed. I couldn't escape. Even if I could manage to climb out the hole, he was twice my size and strength. I waited for some sort of life-ending injury, a hammer to the head, or maybe he'd simply strangle me.

Nothing.

"I'm sorry, Sue, you all right?"

I opened my eyes and found him staring at me, but his eyes were filled with fear, not hate.

With a deep breath, the heart rate slowed.

"Who do those bones belong to?" I pointed at the skeleton partially visible in the wall of the foundation.

"That's all that's left of my daddy." He replaced the loose brick with the care of a loving child.

"I'm sorry Vernon." I regained my strength and conviction. "I spoke to Aunt Virginia a while ago. She claims a copy of the will might be down here."

It ain't here." He stood in the middle of the space, the soft-spoken Vernon I'd grown to love. There was a piece of paper once, but Naomi told me it wasn't worth anything. There's writing, but I can't read so I don't know what them words say."

I was so excited I could hardly speak. "Can I see it?"

"I don't think so. Naomi told me to never show it to anyone."

He allowed me to precede him up the ladder and noticed my limp. "You should go back to Mr. Palmer's and put some ice on that ankle. Besides, with Ms. Ruth and John Earl missing, you could be in danger."

What was I supposed to do then? Ask if he was the source of the danger. I watched and waited.

He waited until I was a few yards from shore before he turned back toward the island.

I was about to climb into the boat and follow Vernon's suggestion when I saw him at the Southern tip and stopped.

The distance between the island that held the plantation house foundation and the next nearest was only ten years of shallow water. He jogged through the mud and disappeared into the jungle of low-growing maples and pines. Then I saw him again rowing away toward an island to the east.

I hobbled back into my boat and followed.

I caught up to him in front of a run-down shack on the far side of the island. I heard something coming from what had once been a fancy boat house, probably once of many along the pond that once belonged to the Penningtons, but I was more concerned with finding Vernon. The front door of the cabin was open so I went in.

He was standing in front of a bedside table with a book in his hand. By the crumbling leather and the gold title I recognized it as the Bible. He spun and rushed toward me, hiding the book behind his back. "Thought I told you to go back to Palmer's. It's too dangerous out here."

"Why, Vernon? Why is it dangerous out here? Because Roy's threatened to move you off this land if you don't keep your mouth shut and help him hide his secrets?" I was pulling anything I could out of the air, but it was working. "Is that your family Bible you've got? Is that where Naomi told you to hide the will?"

He backed away and started to dash out the back door, but I was able to move around him and get in his way. Pretty amazing since my ankle was on fire with pain. "Let me see the paper, Vernon. I promise I won't take it."

I was surprised at its newness.

"It's a copy," Vernon stated.

And there it was, the last will and testament of John Royal Pennington I. I opened it with great care and scanned the proper cursive written one hundred fifty-six years ago. "And I do bequeath to my love, Ruby and her husband Abraham Fielding, one-hundred acres, including and adjacent to the pond to be handed down to each male in the next generation."

"Vernon, this is what all the fuss has been about. This proves that you are a Pennington and you are the owner of all this land." I couldn't help myself. I hugged him. "Would you allow me to take this to Sheriff Bill? I think I know why Ruth and John Earl were kidnapped."

"Why?" He held the innocence of a child.

"So I would find this for Roy."

TWENTY-FIVE

I knew Vernon was still in the cabin so footsteps crushing acorns and pine straw told me I wasn't alone, but then I didn't expect to be. A mental debate ensued. I could turn around, get back in the boat, and row away like a frightened little girl, or I could face Cousin Roy, the murderous, kidnapping son of a—

Then I heard it—John Earl frantically calling my name. My aching body filled with momentary joy. He was alive. "John Earl?"

"Mama? Take me home. I want to go home."

I had to sound strong, confident we would come out alive. I crawled down the sandy shore next to the boathouse. "I know, John Earl, so do I, and there's a lot of people out looking for us. They'll be here soon." I wasn't sure who I was trying to convince more.

"No one's coming to look for any of you." Someone else spoke above me. When I looked up, Roy was staring down. That bumbling sheriff doesn't have a clue. You two are going to have to stay down there." He reached down and grabbed the will.

He tried to grab me, but my fist balled, and I cracked him across the face with a right uppercut. While he was down, I took a rock and hit him over the head. He went down hard. I grabbed the paper and shoved it in my back pocket. "I don't think so." I ran through the shallow water along the shore. Red clay had seeped up around my sandals, between my toes and mixed with the sweat pouring from every pore of my skin. My heart stopped for several beats when Paul's face appeared out of the shadows.

"Sue, are you all right? What are you doing out here alone?"

"I wasn't. I knew you'd be here." He took on a look of disbelief like he had no idea what I was referring to. "I followed you out here. I wanted you to know I stopped by the sheriff's office. Martha told me that Vernon confessed to kidnapping Ruth and John Earl. He claims they're out here on one of these islands. I came out to look."

I stomped my foot. "You liar. Vernon is innocent. You and Roy kidnapped Ruthie, probably because she wouldn't go along with your scheme to steal Vernon's land. God knows why you took John Earl. Was it just to scare me into leaving well enough alone?" I was screaming now. "Let me guess, you killed Archie to terrify the poor woman into relinquishing the land, no questions asked."

I heard something and glanced down at the bush beside me. I gasped when I recognized Thomas hiding there.

He held a finger to his lips and shook his head hard from side to side.

"Sue, that's ridiculous. You know I'd never hurt Johnnie."

I reached in my bag and presented him with the barrel of a gun. "Just like you never hurt me?"

He backed up a few steps. Something came out of the bush and tripped Paul, causing him to fall hard on his backside.

Thomas came out of his crouch. He held a gun on Paul. *When did he start carrying a gun?* "Suz, put that thing away before you hurt yourself."

"Like hell I will. How do I know you're not in on this too?"

Paul tried to scramble to his feet but Thomas pushed him back with his foot. The gun moved closer to his head.

"Let him go." Brush rustled as footsteps grew closer. "Enough of this shit. Let's just forget the ruse and get on with it."

TWENTY-SIX

Ruthie stood there, alive and well, pointing a gun at Thomas—and me. "Suz, you're coming with me. Paul, take care of the trash." She shook her head, almost remorseful. "God, how I wish you'd just stayed out of it. Remember we talked about you going home?"

A shot came from the forest. It grazed Paul's left arm. Jack stepped out. Paul spun and shot Jack.

Thomas stepped forward and grabbed the gun away from Paul and tossed it toward me.

I grabbed a clump of Ruthie's hair and placed the barrel of the gun against her temple. "Don't make me shoot you. We used to have such fun together. I'd hate to spoil the memory."

A nanosecond was all it took for Ruthie to reach behind her back, grab my arm, and force the gun from it. She always was stronger and quicker. How I hated her for that.

Thomas grabbed Paul's good arm and put him in a half-Nelson, with one arm around his neck. "Would you shoot him?" Where'd he get the other gun?

"No silly, I wouldn't shoot my partner."

Paul sent an elbow into Thomas' gut. When Thomas tried to rise to his feet, Paul kicked him in the chest. "Don't even try it, Allgood. Ruthie will shoot you. You've been nothing but a thorn in our side since this whole thing started."

I screamed Thomas' name thinking that would be the last I would see of my brother. He'd disappeared into the thicket. Thanks a lot, bro.

Ruthie fired a few shots into the woods. She threw me to the ground, stuck a rag in my mouth and bound my wrists with tape. "I'm sorry it came to this, Suz, but you and that little brat of yours just wouldn't leave well enough alone."

She grabbed me by the arm and dragged me along the path. She walked fast, yanking me along, and I lost my balance several times. When I did, she just pulled me to my feet and kept going.

Every inch of my body hurt. My skin crawled from the reality. My ex-husband and my best friend were in cahoots. She'd faked her own kidnapping and may have shot a deputy to cover her tracks. What was she hiding? I screamed through clenched teeth behind the gag. "Why?"

She kept up her pace as she began to prattle on. "Let's face it; we haven't been friends since college. Always playing the innocent preacher's kid and, at the same time having an affair with one. What a hypocrite."

My thoughts screamed my retort. Is that what this was all about, an elaborate scheme of revenge for not living up to her expectations? Christ, I knew she could be a drama queen, but wasn't that a bit extreme? Just pay the money and get a psychiatrist.

Ruthie kept talking. "Paul, Roy, and I had it all settled 'til Archie reneged on his end. Then you brought on the law and butted your nose in where it didn't belong."

Ruthie opened the door to the boathouse. My toe caught on a loose board in the doorway. I lost my balance and fell, but she kept dragging me. My head hit the planks on the floor, but we never stopped until we got to the back. "Hope you don't fall through." The back end of the shack stuck out ten feet above the murky lake. But drowning me was not her objective. She drew a chain around my wrists and locked it to an iron ring attached to a wall support. She yanked the rag out of my mouth. "Once I secure you here, you can scream all you want. You and that brat of yours are going to die together."

I heard John Earl sobbing in the corner. So much for being the heroine. Then, anger replaced the self-loathing. "Tell me one thing. Why did you kill Archie?"

Ruthie glared at me with a hatred I'd never seen on her face before. "I didn't do it, silly. Paul did." She sounded proud of their actions. "Our original deal was twenty-five percent of the profits of our plan to buy up Pennington Pond and develop it, if he agreed to go along. But then he reneged and we couldn't have that getting in the way."

The only copy of the will was tucked under my shirt in the waistband of my pants, but I wasn't about to tell them that.

With cold calm, she slammed the door, leaving me to scream obscenities at her. Get mad, I told myself. It could be your only means of survival.

* * *

A gunshot shook the shed. I was sure the floor would collapse, and John Earl and I would fall to our deaths.

We screamed.

309

Something splashed in the shallow water below us.

I swung my right leg and kicked the rotting wood, creating a hole in the wall. Bill's name came with a second scream from my mouth, when I saw him floating face down. His shirt puffed with air.

Another shot and we heard someone moaning in agony.

I kicked again and most of the wall gave way.

Ruthie was kneeling beside Paul, weeping. This one got him in the chest.

Thomas was handcuffing Ruthie. He reached in her pocket and removed the handcuff key. "Sit there quietly and I won't shoot you."

Then he yanked a badge from his front pocket. "You're both under arrest for illegal sale of land, the murder of Archie Claremont, Deputy Cody, and the kidnappings of John Earl and Sue Backman." He winked at me. "See, Sue, your black sheep brother did amount to something."

"You're a cop?"

"Special agent with the Department of the Interior. We've been investigating the illegal sale of this land for months." He unlocked the cuffs and pulled me up. Then he repeated the process for John Earl.

My son collapsed against me, hiccupping sobs. "I thought Daddy and Aunt Ruthie were going to kill me. Is daddy dead?"

I pushed his head into my chest and rocked him. "Oh my God, where's Bill?"

We all watched as Thomas ran down the slope, splashed into the water. He yanked Bill up by the back of his head and threw him over his shoulder. "We've got to get him to a hospital. I think he's lost a lot of blood." He laid Bill down on the pine straw, took off his shirt and pressed against Bill's shoulder. "Damn it, Bill, breathe."

I did the only thing I knew; I drew close to Bill, held his hand to my cheek, and prayed until he coughed up a part of the pond. Still only inches away from my face he smiled.

I glared in shock, and then cackled with laughter.

Thomas joined in. "He's gonna be fine."

I hadn't noticed, but Thomas had returned to the spot where Paul had grabbed me and returned with Jack over his shoulder. "He's lost a lot of blood," he told the deputy. "He needs immediate attention."

I remained close to Bill. "Thanks for coming to save us."

I rowed one boat with John Earl sitting behind me pressing his shirt to Bill's wound, while Thomas rowed, seated backward in the other, eyes trained on Paul and Ruth. I stared back at my former best friend, handcuffed to the oar ring. She would never be Ruthie to me again. Watching her fawn over Paul disgusted me to nausea.

Thomas used Bill's radio to call for ambulances to meet us in the parking lot at The Boondocks. A short time later, he called back that Paul hadn't made it.

John Earl didn't shed a tear.

The deputy put Ruthie in the back seat of his car and drove her away.

Marie Warren didn't object when I insisted on riding in the ambulance with John Earl. She tended to Bill in route to the hospital. His blood pressure dropped once during transit, and she radioed back to the EMT with us. When he got through he handed me the radio. "She told me to tell you to talk to him, Sue, give him something to live for."

I grabbed the radio with both hands. "Don't you die on me, Bill Halvorson. You promised to take John Earl and me fishing at your secret spot."

I closed my eyes and wept.

"Why you crying, Mama?"

I cupped his chin in my hand. "The sheriff has become very important to me, and I'm worried. Do you understand?"

Gladys and The Reverend met us at the emergency bay doors. Our reunion was cut short by a passel of medical personal, which unloaded three ambulances. The first carried John Earl and me, the second hauling the body bag carrying Paul's corpse, and the third, Bill.

Again John Earl refused to cry. He had suffered no more than a few scrapes and dehydration. The doc said he wanted to keep him overnight for observation and intravenous fluids.

Mother greeted me with the look, eyes pinched in an angry stare and a smile. She scolded me for going out there alone, and cried, delighted we were all right.

The Reverend hugged me. "I'm just glad you're both all right. You had me pretty worried, young lady." He pushed me to arms length. "And I know you were divorced, but I'm sorry about Paul."

"Thanks, Daddy." It was the first time I'd called him that this visit. "Now, if you two will stay here with John Ear, I'd like to check on Bill." There, I did it; I called him by his given name in front of my parents.

Gladys turned to The Reverend. "I told you she wasn't interested in the park ranger."

John Earl spoke from the bed. "Can we go back to Mr. Palmer's house now? I want to have one of my cookies and show you where I was in the sandbox when Daddy kidnapped me."

I wanted that to be a word he soon forgot. "Tomorrow. Now you need to rest and recuperate." I kissed him on the head and went next door to Bill's room.

* * *

Thomas came around the corner and joined me on uncomfortable vinyl chairs in the waiting room. "Sue, Jack Carmichael died a few minutes ago. He confessed to being part of everything expect shooting Duffy. He said that was Paul.

"So it's true, he, Paul and Ruthie partnered with Roy to scare Naomi into giving up her land and developing it illegally? Too bad they didn't know Vernon was the rightful heir."

He grabbed my hand, I think, because he thought I was going to crumble into a mass of hysterical female parts. "Bill's in surgery."

I placed my other hand on his and looked him in the eye. It was then I noticed how clear his eyes had become. "I'm okay, Thomas, as long as John Earl and Bill are all right.

"Do you want to come with me later while I tell Bill to tell you about Jack?"

I nodded.

"In the meantime, want to go get something to eat?"

I nodded again. I was starving. I craved a slice of Cami's pies, but hospital food would suffice.

Bill was in surgery for a little less than an hour. Two hours in recovery and he was in a room bellowing to be released.

Thomas opened the door and poked his head in. "Okay if we come in?" He tugged my arm and pulled me in the room. "I've got some bad news. Our main suspect didn't make it, and Jack died in the boat on the way in."

I touched Bill's cheek. "I'm sorry; I know you and Jack were close."

Bill reached for my hand. "I'm sorry; I know you loved Paul once. I'm sorry for John Earl too. So young to lose a father."

"I thought I loved Paul a long time ago. I've known he was a scoundrel for a long time. Ruthie is the one who shocked me. I didn't think she could be so evil as to kidnap my son and fake her own abduction."

Thomas spoke from behind me. "At least the pond is safe from someone selling lakefront property to out-of-town buyers."

Bill's expression switched to sad puppy. "And that ex of yours shot my best deputy and my best friend. Most important, I almost lost you."

I heard the door open and close. When I looked around, Thomas was gone. At least this time I knew how to contact him.

Bill motioned for me to move closer. "After I'm sprung from here, I'd like to talk to you."

Words caught in my throat and never made it any farther. I did manage to nod, though.

TWENTY-SEVEN

Sunrise from the lookout on Pennington Pond was a sight compared to no other on earth. As it rose over the distant ridges of the lower Appalachians, its glow spilled out on the water's surface like mercury from an old broken thermometer.

The spooky sounds, scratching limbs and small furry beasts running rampant in the underbrush during those long nights searching for Ruth and John Earl transformed into more familiar daytime noises. Chickadees and sparrows twittered in the trees overhead, while an early morning angler trolled the shallows off a distant island. The gears of a big rig, grinding up a hill on a distant road echoed across the valley.

Bill sat on the bench, staring out at water-sodden trees rising out of the pond. He was nervous and avoided eye contact. "The remains you found in the Twelve Oaks foundation belonged to Grace Camden. According to Vernon's full statement, she came to town looking for her share of the Pennington fortune and Roy killed her. Roy had hidden her body in the foundation and made Vernon swear never to tell a soul or he'd send him away."

"So what's going to happen to Ruth now, Bill?" I was tense, refusing eye contact, afraid I might haul off and kiss him.

"She's been arraigned on charges of faking a kidnapping and accessory to murder and kidnapping."

He touched my chin, forcing me to look at him. "The DA will want you to testify. John Earl, too."

Someone emerged from the forest below and habit caused my heart to race.

"Morning Sheriff, Ms. Sue." Vernon stood at the bottom of the embankment, waving.

I held up one finger, jumped off the wooden structure and slid down the slope. I grabbed him and hugged him as tight as I could. "Thank you. If you hadn't led me out to the island, Paul and Ruthie would have killed us."

He didn't speak, just ducked his head and grinned. "Couldn't let kin die. Just wish Ranger Jack hadn't."

"I know, but you still got Bill to be your friend. And me." I kissed his cheek, then climbed back up the hill. When I reached the outlook, he was already deep in the trees. Bill had assured him he could live out his days on his islands.

We watched four deer run across the same spot where we'd been standing. "I suppose you'll be going back to Atlanta now?"

"My job's there, Bill."

He remained unmoving, staring out at the lake. "I'm not going to run for sheriff again. I've had enough of this life. All that crap was going on right under my nose, and I didn't even see it. Like I said yesterday, I almost lost you because of it."

I stood beside him looking out on the silver surface of the water. "Folks around here are going to lose a good sheriff."

"They'll get used to it. They got used to me." A moan came with his words. He was a man who thought he'd lost everything.

We were skirting the inevitable.

"So, you're thinking about leaving town?"

"Nah; lived here too long. Figure I'll take a job as a crossing guard at the school, or maybe see about applying for the ranger position." He turned his head toward me, just enough to flash a sheepish grin. "There's a little house for sale across from the entrance to the park. Just right for you and John Earl. I still owe you that fishing excursion."

I bounced up on my toes and back down again. "How far would we be from the elementary school?"

"Three miles on the bus. He'd be riding with Martha's grandson, Nate. Those two will get along great, I promise. Maybe John Earl would like to join the scouts. I'll take him fishing anytime." His lips pressed against mine and his tongue forced them open. Too soon, it ended.

"Maybe after we see how it goes, we can talk Martha into sitting for John Earl. Give us a little time alone." A blush appeared under his beard stubble. I never noticed how Bill's eyes changed shades of blue from ocean to periwinkle when he laughed. "I mean for a date...if you're willing."

I wrapped my arms around his waist and kissed him.

As if on cue, my son came running up the path toward us. "Gross." He yelled back up toward Gladys and The Reverend. "I caught 'em kissing, Grandmother."

She just gave him one of her understanding smiles. "That's what people do when they care for each other, John Earl." To prove it, my father, took my mother in his arms and laid a slobbering smooch right on her lips.

John Earl scrunched his face into a sour frown. "Double gross. You're too old to be doing that."

TWENTY-EIGHT

Perfection best described that day the next May. A yellow sun melted onto the pond and all the tiny islands within it were alive with the songs of cardinal, wren, and the occasional crackle of a blue jay. Ancient pecan trees and Georgia pine created excellent back-drops to pink honeysuckle vine and lavender blossoms of the mimosa trees, with their honey-sweet fragrance. Leaf shoots budded from the branches of the giant oaks and maples, as if trying to rid the trees of their gray mossy coats.

My father, The Reverend Jedidiah Allgood leaned in. "Sue, everyone is waiting."

I blinked away the past, only to realize the ensemble was waiting for me to say those words I'd long to utter for months. I gazed into Bill's eyes with tears of joy caught in the corners. Then I cleared my throat and said as clearly as I could, "I do."

Something caught my attention on the shore below.

Even in the warmth of that May afternoon, Vernon wore a long-sleeved denim shirt and overalls, and heavy work boots on his feet. His face was dirty from perspiration and time spent combing the woods for treasures.

"Hey, Vernon whatcha doing down there? Mama and Bill are up here getting married," John Earl called out. "Why don't you come up?"

Gladys stepped up onto the gazebo and grabbed John Earl's arm. "I'm sure Mr. Fielding has more important things to do than attend your mother's wedding. Let's let him go on his way."

Bill stepped closer to the rail. "It's all right, Vernon. You're welcome to join us. We'd have sent you an invitation, but you don't have a registered address."

Vernon climbed the hill on hands and booted feet and soon stood behind Bill. "That's okay, Sheriff Bill. Didn't figure anybody'd want me here."

Bill patted his shoulder. "Well I do."

I took Vernon's hand and gave it a gentle squeeze. "So do I."

John Earl wiggled out of Gladys' grasp and took two steps forward. He stood in front of Vernon. "Me too. You're part of the family."

Made in the USA
Charleston, SC
20 October 2010